NADINE LITTLE

To Tame a Monster

Hunters & Dragons 2

LITTLE PUBLISHING

Cover design by 100 Covers

This book is written in British English.

First edition

ISBN (paperback): 978-1-8380884-7-7
ISBN (hardcover): 978-1-8380884-8-4

*This book was professionally typeset on Reedsy.
Find out more at reedsy.com*

Sign up to my mailing list for a free character sheet and discover the backstories and quirks not included in the novel. Members of my mailing list get other free stuff and exclusive behind-the-scenes material.

Members are always the first to hear about my new books and discounts.

See the back of the book on how to join.

'Beware the darkness of dragons,
Beware the stalker of dreams,
Beware the talons of power and fire,
Beware one who is not what she seems.'
Tui T. Sutherland

'Don't fashion me into a maiden
that needs saving from a dragon.
I am the dragon,
and I will eat you whole.'
Unknown

1

I love my family but sometimes I wish they didn't exist. No grieving father, no feral sisters. No having to be the perfect daughter to protect us all. I wish they knew how much I hate it.

But will they still love me if they find out I'm a fake?

The mascara wand pokes me in the eye and smears black across my lid, streaking my eyeshadow.

"Shit."

My gaze flicks to the mirror and my guilty expression even though I'm alone. No heartbeats.

I shooed the twins away ten minutes ago to pester our sister, Libelle, instead of giggling over my underwear. Their rooms are in the opposite wing of the house so no risk of my improper language being overheard.

The snippets of privacy are all that keep me sane.

I slide the mascara brush into the pot and pluck a wet wipe from the packet, shifting on the padded bench in front of my dressing table. Reapplying my make-up steadies my hands and my heart rate. My guilty look smooths under my icy armour. I examine myself for imperfections. Cornflower-blue eyes stare back at me beneath a shimmer of gold.

Cold eyes, some may say. Cold and scary, befitting my status.

If only they knew.

The last of the sunset fades through the gauzy curtains of my balcony door, my room facing west along the coast, our house perched on its isolated cliff near Yellowcraig in East Lothian. There used to be a holiday park nearby until my family bought up the land and turfed them out. We're more urban than the other Drakul but my mother had a soft spot for Edinburgh, and loved the sea. The cave system below us is also unique.

I fluff my hair until it frames my face and tumbles past my shoulders to tickle my skin. Honey-blonde, just like my mother's. I dyed the tips electric pink so my father wouldn't look sad whenever I walked into a room. Wishing I were someone else.

It's my fault he's sad. My fault my life is a nightmare. My fault.

Quit it, Maddy.

I stand, and straighten my dress. The violet material looks great with my hair, the spaghetti straps leaving my shoulders and back bare. The mermaid cut makes my boyish hips womanly.

Libby inherited the curves and the white-blonde hair, the same as the twins. I may be slim but there's nothing boyish about my tits.

My eyes flick to the mirror.

Breasts. A lady has *breasts*. Or a bosom, if you really want to be proper about it. I remember the many, *many* lectures from my mother and tutors. How to speak and act as befitting the second golden daughter of a powerful Drakul family.

I give myself the finger.

Footsteps skip down the corridor and Libby sweeps into

my room thirty seconds later, her hair pinned up, tendrils escaping to tease her red, fitted dress. She shoulders me away from the mirror and slicks another layer of gloss on her already shiny lips, trailing the sweet, cloying scent of peaches.

"Sodom and Gomorrah are showing our honoured guests to their seats. You ready?"

"I wish you wouldn't call them that."

Libby manages to roll her eyes and pout at herself in the same motion. "Fine. The darling twins are taking the wonderful Kaskbirches to our dining room. Shall we deign to join them, oh fair and glorious Madisyn?"

I swat at her and she dodges with a laugh, capturing my hand and placing it in the crook of her elbow.

"Are you going to be on your best behaviour?" I say as she leads us towards the stairs. "This could be good for you, you know."

"Come on, Maddy. Libelle Kaskbirch, really? Everyone would call me a birch behind my back."

"They already do," I say, and she sticks her tongue out at me.

You'd never tell she's the eldest by five years.

But thank god she is, otherwise Gerome Kaskbirch would be here to petition for me. He may be powerful but he looks like a troll.

Fitting, then, that his family are based in the Scandinavian Mountains. They jetted in from their fiefdom two days ago, staying in our townhouse in Edinburgh for the duration of their visit.

"Anyway, Della Valle is the only name that matters," Libby says. Her glacier-blue eyes dim and she frowns at her shoes.

I know who she's thinking of. Her mate. Murdered and quickly followed by three of his brothers and the matriarch of the Romanov family. We thought they were untouchable. *They* thought they were untouchable. Evelyn Romanov ruled over our global elite as its wicked queen, privileged in both human and Drakul society. Feared by the latter, her sons a chip off the old, sadistic block.

I'm glad they're gone. One of the many secrets I have to hide.

I pat Libby's arm. "Everyone else wants to be a Della Valle."

"Damn right they do."

I raise my brow at her, eliciting another eye roll.

"You don't have to follow every societal nuance to the letter, Maddy," she says. "You can rebel a little."

If only.

The Drakul may be a law unto themselves, hunt humans for sport and maintain power through brutality but I can't let my mask slip. I can't show my disgust at our whole way of life.

The stairs spiral into the caves below the house. Three tunnels branch off, the walls buffed to a shine by an army of Lessers. When we had an army of Lessers—humans bitten by a Drakul to become a half-way hybrid. We follow the flickering candlelight in the largest tunnel, our heels clicking on stone. The corridor widens into a huge room carved by the flow of water, the beautiful, swirling rock witness to years of horror.

Though not tonight. Tonight, we're being civilised. A veneer of etiquette over monstrosity.

The mahogany dining table has been set beside the window looking out on the dark. Nothing to see but our reflections. If I close my eyes, I can imagine the lap of waves beyond the glass.

The twins sit prim at the table beneath my father's watchful gaze, dressed in identical dresses of eggshell-blue. My dad is handsome in a charcoal suit that highlights his grey hair and trimmed beard.

"Daughters, you know the Kaskbirches," he says, rising until we've taken our seats.

The three stocky shapes crowd the other end of our table. I nod politely and spread my napkin on my lap. Libby sits beside Gerome and whispers to him. His broad cheeks flush red. Before I can kick her under the table, dinner is served by normal human servants rather than Lessers.

It's frustrating to have ignorant human staff. Another layer of watching what I say and do. Thankfully, they're only employed for meals and cleaning, and none of them are live-in.

The starter of scallops with hazelnut picada is whisked away as soon as it's eaten. Empty small talk carries us to the main course. The smell of cooked meat wafts from the plate placed in front of me. My gaze darts to Dad while the Kaskbirches fawn over the food. His pale-blue eyes are grave but unflinching. I give a tiny shake of my head. He frowns and indicates the Kaskbirches, already sawing into their meat and smacking their lips. Blood dribbles down Gerome's chin and oozes from the slab left on his plate. My stomach rolls.

I convinced Dad I was allergic. Told him it makes me ill. It does but not because of an intolerance. It's the thought of what it used to be.

A hint of pleading cracks my father's stony expression and I know I have to eat it or we'll appear weak.

The vultures miss nothing.

I pick up my knife and fork, and spear a sliver. My hand hesitates half-way to my mouth without a command from my brain.

It's pork. It's just pork.

Sure it is.

I swallow it whole, not chewing, and take a sip of wine. The smokiness hides the taste.

"Are you unwell, Madisyn dear?" Irena Kaskbirch says, her wide face herded into a moue of sympathy. "You're hardly eating."

Her plate is wiped clean. She pops a last bit of bread soaked in bloody juices into her mouth, her teeth flashing as she chews. I slice off a bigger piece. Swallow.

"I prefer my food alive and wriggling," I say, my smile sharp.

She laughs and tips her drink at me. "Don't we all, dear. Don't we all."

I chop my meat and chase it around my plate, hiding most under a bed of rocket. The ache in my gut lessens when the servant finally takes it away. I gulp my wine and dab my lips on my napkin. Dessert arrives—safe, glorious gateaux—and Irena taps a long nail on her glass.

"Thank you, Jackson dear, that was lovely. I've missed the taste of real meat. Do you know our supply has been tampered with?"

"You mentioned as much when we last spoke."

"Yes, and we all know why," she sniffs. "It's been six months since the Romanovs were destroyed and the surviving runt married the human whore."

Libby opens her mouth to snarl something.

"An abomination," I say in the false voice I hate.

A lie. I live and breathe lies.

Libby gets distracted by Gerome panting in her ear and she settles like a bird with ruffled feathers.

"Quite right, Madisyn dear," Irena says. "We have waited this long to approach out of sensitivity for dear, sweet Libelle but I feel enough time has passed. It's time to consolidate our power."

Dear, sweet Libby has been stringing their son along for weeks. He'll do anything for her while she sends him off unsatisfied. I'm surprised his balls haven't ruptured.

"We would be honoured if Libelle would mate with our son. You are the reigning family since the loss of the Romanovs. Accept us. Lead us, and remove the traitor and his scourge before it's too late."

Dad turns his gaze to Libby. She bats her lashes at him.

"I'm too distraught over my dear, sweet mate. I miss him too much to be the matriarch Gerome deserves." Unshed tears glitter in her eyes.

Gerome seems unfazed by the news but I suspect her rubbing his dick under the table is helping. He struggles to maintain a blank expression, his mouth slack, eyes half-lidded.

My sister, sweetly grieving.

"Of course, dear," Irena says, though anger, quickly smoth-ered, darkens her mud-brown eyes. "What about Madisyn? She would be an acceptable match."

My fingers tense on my wine, and glass tinkles. I relax my hand before the vessel shatters.

Darn Libby. I'd let myself feel safe because as long as she was available, no one would be asking for me. All the males chase after her first, until she gets bored and their lust for power turns to me.

I'll be no one's consolation prize.

My father mated my mother for love and he's still reeling, seven years after her death. He refused to choose another even though it damaged our standing. That's what I want—intense, all-consuming love, not to sacrifice myself to strengthen the sinking foundations of my family. Seems I'll never get what I want.

And whose fault is that?

"You flatter me," I say, another brittle smile masking gritted teeth. "Permit me to discuss your proposal with my father and give you an answer later?"

What does that buy me—days? A week? To refuse would be an insult to the Kaskbirches. They would take their fury to the other families, whispering about our weakness. The others are just salivating for the Della Valles to get what they deserve.

Behind every polite smile is a jagged row of teeth.

Irena frowns. "I realise you were also promised to a Romanov—Dominic, was it, dear?—but he was not yet your mate. Your grief cannot be much."

As in, sorrow for his death is not a valid excuse. I fear nothing is. And sorrow is the last thing I feel for Dominic Romanov.

"Is that discontent I hear, Irena?" my father says in a low, careful tone. "I pray it is not."

Irena's face pales. "No... no, of course not, Jackson. Jackson dear."

"My daughter will consider your proposal. Her answer is final."

"That would be acceptable," Irena splutters.

My father claps his hands, and I jump, my quick reflexes all that stop my wine from slopping onto the tablecloth.

He may have changed since Mum's death, become more reclusive and taken a step back from Drakul politics, but he's still an intimidating force.

"Good," he says. "Let us retire to the parlour."

He herds the Kaskbirches towards the tunnels. The twins skip along after. Gerome turns a whine into a cough when Libby quits massaging his dick.

"I'm going to listen to music in my room with Gerome," Libby calls, and my father waves a hand over his shoulder before disappearing into the tunnel.

Gerome goes from crestfallen to almost coming in his pants. You think he'd learn after the last few times.

Men are stupid.

They run off, giggling, before I can say anything, though my mouth is too dry to speak. The staff clears the dishes in silence. I rest my forehead on the table and force my breathing to slow.

I'll have to mate Gerome. Let his wide mouth kiss me, his thick fingers touch me. Accept his heavy thrusts and moist breath in the dark while he pictures Libby instead of me. Birth his screaming brats. A loveless marriage is a worse prison than this gilded cage.

I suck in air and it swirls with the bile in my stomach.

If I refuse, the other families will talk. They're too scared to challenge my father for now—his reputation precedes him despite his withdrawal since the loss of his mate—but show a hint of soft underbelly and they'll fall over themselves to usurp him. They've grumbled about the lack of a Della Valle matriarch for years. With Dad gone, we'll be slaughtered for our shame. I can't let it happen. I have to protect my family.

I push to my feet and stride from the caves, my mask firmly on. No music filters from Libby's room, only the thud of two heartbeats, one fast, one slow.

I hope she hasn't taken it too far. My sister may be a cock-tease but her love for her mate was genuine and faithful. His death broke something inside her.

The door swings open with a nudge of my open-toed shoe. Violet, to match my dress. Libby is sprawled in a tangle of sheets on the edge of her bed, red material bunched to her waist. Gerome kneels between her legs, his jaw working.

"For goodness' sake, Libby," I sigh. "You could at least lock the door so Dad doesn't see."

She fixes me with a heavy-lidded gaze. "He's snifter-deep into his brandy right now and—*I didn't say stop!*"

Gerome flinches and slides me a glance, his mouth slick and shiny.

"Are you sure—"

"Keep going."

He ducks his head and resumes his ministrations.

Just think, in a few months, it could be me.

I shiver, and not in a good way.

Libby grabs Gerome's ears and grinds his face against her.

"I can't believe you don't like oral," she gasps at me, her back arched.

I regret telling her that little secret. She was drunk. I thought she wouldn't remember.

Gerome appears to be choking.

"You're obviously not doing it right. Gerome's skilled. You can have him once he's done with me." She lets out a long moan. "Which will be in about twenty seconds."

Gerome's fingers tighten on her thighs.

I remember the sensation. My first sexual encounter at sixteen. A cruel, blood-tinged smile.

My shoulder hits the door frame. Libby is too far gone into squirming and moaning to hear my squeak of, "No, thanks!"

Chill air steals the flush from my cheeks. An unforgiving

wind howls off the sea and whips my hair around my face. Frosted grass crunches under my shoes. I pause at the wide terrace on the cliff edge. Waves crash below, and I taste salt. I shimmy out of my dress and underwear, folding them into a weather-worn chest with my shoes on top. Moonlight glows on my bare skin and casts my shadow on the tiles.

This is the only time I can be free.

I plant my foot on the stone balustrade and launch into nothing.

2

I shift before my body loses altitude. The sensation is like being stretched in all directions. It's a swollen feeling. A powerful feeling. It sings in my blood and spills from my mouth in a roar.

I'm told I have the smoothest change anyone has ever seen, often in a voice tinged with envy.

My wings snap out and catch the air. The wind buffets my side but my tail keeps me balanced as I flap hard. My scales shine silver under the moon, though they're a deep, honey-gold. I bare my teeth to the wind and dive for the sea. The shock zips through me, bubbles roiling past my face to tickle my neck and chest. I pedal my talons and leap into the sky, trailing water.

The peace of flight settles into my bones, the anxiety over keeping my family alive fading with each beat of my wings. Out here, there's nothing to worry about but air currents, height and avoiding the rapid pitter-patter of human hearts. I don't have to bow to societal pressure and pretend to be a crueller, colder version of me.

I twist, tucking my wings to my flanks. Wind howls past the ridges on my face and moans through the horns extending from my head. The freezing sea muffles all sound. I snap my jaws on a shoal of mackerel before they scatter in a panicked flash of silvery-blue.

The oily, earthy flesh is better than what I had for dinner.

I fly through the water, weaving around the ropes of lobster pots disappearing into the depths. My lungs ache for oxygen, and I climb into the sky.

There are few fishing vessels out tonight and they won't see me unless I cross in front of the moon, a silhouette gone in a blink. A shape they'll attribute to tired eyes and salt water because monsters aren't real.

I soar and let my thoughts wander.

Julian and Raine Romanov—the surviving runt and his human whore. It's all anyone's talking about even after six months. A Vanatori falling for a Drakul. She killed Lukas— Libby's mate—and his mother, the rest of his brothers dying in a battle with the hunters. Their relationship is wrong, shameful, *sick*.

I think it's sweet. They fell in love, despite who they are, and now they've splintered from our society, building a community of Drakul, Lessers and Vanatori all working together. It's unprecedented.

I wish I could join them.

Sure, and sign the death warrant for my family.

I always thought Julian was cute but I shunned him like the rest. Associating with him angered his mother and no one wanted to be on the wrong side of Evelyn Romanov. I felt sorry for him, though. I never tormented him like his brothers. Like Libby. How lonely he must have been, surrounded by people who hated him. I'm surrounded by people who love me but I hate myself enough for all of us.

'*Why do you fly over the sea?*' Libby says in my head. '*It's so dull.'*

A shape swoops next to me, wing-tip to wing-tip. She grins, flashing rows of wicked teeth.

'It's peaceful,' I say.

'Exactly—dull.'

Libby's dragon form is a larger pale-gold. A whale to my delicate thoroughbred. Even the twins are bigger than me. I suspect it's the lack of a certain meat in my diet. Julian's dragon is tiny, too, and he didn't eat people. At least by choice.

'Did you get bored of torturing Gerome?' I say, gaining height.

Libby matches me, puffing a little. *'He makes it so easy. I was naked in bed, begging for him of course, when mummy and daddy called him away. He almost cried.'*

I circle around her, her heavier body less nimble. She can lumber in a straight line but there's no grace. No finesse.

'You don't have to mate with him, you know,' she says.

My flight dips, and her wings graze my belly. I bank and steady at her side.

'It would be a good match for our family,' I say in a placid voice. *'The Kaskbirches won't accept anything less.'*

She can't hear my screaming inside her head, not unless I want her to.

'Who cares about the Kaskbirches? We're the Della Valles. No other family has four gold daughters. We're finally on top. We can do what we want.'

As much as Libby loved Lukas, she loathed that his family were more powerful than ours, despite their mother being the only gold. Oh, and Hektor, the father. It's easy to forget about him when he spent most of his time cowering in Evelyn's shadow.

He's really come out of his shell or so I hear.

'We still have to lead by example,' I say. 'We insult too many of the families and they'll come for us.'

Libby waves a hand, her talons bronze. 'We can take them. And they won't if we make them as afraid of us as they were of Evelyn Romanov.'

'Evelyn was a sadist.'

Libby chuffs a laugh, her breath puffing white. 'Then I'll follow her example.'

'You're not the matriarch, Libby. Dad has to marry someone else or give his blessing and step aside.'

'Says who? We're the most powerful now. We make the rules.'

I liked it when the Romanovs were in charge. Not their methods or their brutality but that they were under more scrutiny than us, though that scrutiny was well-hidden since everyone was petrified of Evelyn Romanov's wrath. With her gone, everyone else hungers to lead and that means fighting a constant battle against the back-stabbing and undermining by the lower families. There were less whispers and sneers when we were second-most powerful.

Sometimes, I struggle to get out of bed, crushed beneath the weight of their expectations. Their thirst for failure and blood.

I fly faster until my muscles burn and Libby whines for me to slow down.

'Sod and Gom want to go dancing,' she says, her chest heaving. 'You in?'

I huff a burst of flame at her. 'That's not an improvement on the names.'

Her tongue lolls her amusement at my scolding. She never listens. I wish I had her carefree attitude. Or her savagery. With Libby as the matriarch, especially the way she's been acting since Lukas's death, she would be a younger version of Evelyn Romanov. Our family would be safe.

But I couldn't live with it. I barely survived Evelyn's wicked reign. I can't do that again. I have to maintain the facade while steering us towards a less bloodthirsty future without anyone noticing.

It's exhausting.

'Race you back,' Libby says, deaf to my inner turmoil, her larger wings powering her into a slow loop.

I silence my thoughts and stoop into a dive.

I win by miles.

3

Lights swirl through the fog, colouring the faces of humans in various states of drunkenness. The Edinburgh nightclub is thick with the sweetness of alcohol and the musk of sweat. Heavy bass thuds in my chest and replaces my heart. I lose myself to the beat.

Libby dances like she wants to have sex with everyone in the place and, knowing my sister, it's not far from the truth. The twins follow her lead, gyrating in their miniskirts and cropped tops, all long limbs and creamy skin.

"Let's get a drink," Libby purrs in my ear. "All these hot stares are making me thirsty."

Hungry eyes track us to the bar.

Libby has rebuffed every advance so I'm not exactly sure what she's looking for. Maybe she just wants a girls' night.

Nah. My sister will be screwing one of these guys before dawn.

"What do you want?" she says.

"Lemonade and blackcurrant."

She rolls her eyes. "Why do I have a teetotaller for a sister? That's so dull."

Getting drunk is too risky. What if I did something foolish?

Libby orders G&Ts for her and the twins, plus shots. I sip

my fruity bubbles and watch them. The twins pour themselves onto stools and giggle at everything. A puddle of beer seems particularly hilarious. Libby leans back and props her elbows on the bar, scanning the crowd. Her dress is black this time. Skin tight. It barely covers her bum. I'm a little more demure in a skirt and knee-high boots. My turquoise top hugs my boobs.

Maybe Libby won't be the only one screwing someone tonight.

Excitement fizzes in my belly, and I excuse myself to go to the bathroom. Fix my make-up, fluff my hair. The corridor to the toilets is narrow but brightly lit. I collide with a figure turning the corner from the dance floor. He stumbles back a step while I barely wobble on my four-inch heels.

Humans. They're so delicate.

"Sorry," the male says. "Are you all right?"

His hands are raised as if I'm in danger of falling but no human has ever bowled me off my feet. Dark, grey eyes stare into mine instead of scanning the merchandise like every other male. My boots put me perfectly level with his face. His tousled black hair is styled into a flick, the tips dyed metallic green and violet, gleaming under the lights like a magpie's wing.

"Nice hair," I say.

My heart flips at his slow smile.

Wow, dimples. Cute.

"Yours, too," he says.

I angle myself so he can squeeze past. His shirt is the same colour as his eyes, his shoulders not too broad. Narrow hips and long legs in dark jeans. A silver feather dangles from his left ear and brushes the collar of his leather jacket.

Very cute.

He tosses me another smile and a, "Have a good night," on his way to the bathroom.

Man, what a great bum.

I rejoin my sisters with a smile of my own.

Human males are so much simpler than Drakul males. Harmless, almost, since they can't overpower me. There's no risk of being hurt and the itch gets scratched to everyone's satisfaction. I've never slept with a male of my own kind. Not even a Lesser. When the urge needs to be sated, I go to the cinema or a bar or a restaurant in town. It doesn't take long before a guy looks at me and smiles and I let him take me home.

One night only. Safer for everyone that way.

"Oh, yes, he'll do perfectly," Libby says, shoving away from the bar.

I follow her gaze to the man I bumped into. He pushes through the writhing people to the other side of the room and a stubby, stern-faced guy standing alone.

Drat. With Libby's attentions, I may as well be invisible.

"Come on," she says. "It's time we made another Lesser."

My mouth drops open. "Wait, what?"

Eady and Dory squeal and scamper past me. I gape for a second then dart after Libby, tugging on her arm.

"We don't need another Lesser."

"Course we do. All ours fled to Julian and Raine Romanov, bleating about acts of cruelty." She dodges a pillar and a furiously snogging couple.

"Well, if you hadn't treated them like slaves, maybe they would have stuck around."

She waves her hand. "I have other plans for this one."

"Such as?"

She hops up a short step and pauses a table-length away from the man and his friend, their backs to us.

He definitely has a great bum.

"Such as sending him into the Romanov compound as a spy. He can have a sob story about how we were all mean to him and they'll accept him, no question." Her face hardens into a mask scarier than my own. "They have a lot to pay for."

"Libby, this is a bad idea—"

"Wait here," she says, and struts towards the men.

"I hope she lets us play with him," Eady giggles.

"I volunteer to bite," Dory says.

"You two are too young," I say in my stern, older-sister voice. They pout. "We're seventeen."

"Exactly."

Libby taps the man on the shoulder and he turns to face her. They talk but the music is too loud even for me to hear what they say. Libby flips her hair and thrusts out her breasts. The man smiles and my heart flops into my stomach. His scowly friend scowls harder. Libby laughs, briefly touching the man's arm. Textbook flirtation skills. She sashays back to us and the humour fades.

"His name is Kai and he has a girlfriend," she says. "The ugly guy with him is his girlfriend's brother."

"That's a shame. Why don't we head home—"

"Oh, no, this isn't over," she says. "I just need to wait for the perfect moment."

So much for a relaxing night of dancing, maybe a little anonymous sex to sweeten the deal. When Libby gets an idea in her head, all I can do is tag along and make sure nobody bleeds out.

Libby's perfect moment comes when the grumpy friend heads for the bathroom, leaving Kai unprotected.

Libby grins at me. "Show time."

I try to grab her but she's like a wisp of fog. Way more graceful in her human form than her dragon. She taps Kai on the shoulder again. I edge closer. The twins crowd in. Kai's smile stays friendly. Libby stares up into his face as if hypnotised.

The poor guy has no chance.

His pleasant expression smooths to blank incomprehension. His dark eyes glaze. Libby plucks his drink from his limp fingers before the glass falls. She tucks herself into his side, her hand on his chest.

Powerful Drakul get nifty tricks. I can stop others from shifting or force them back into human form. I did it once to a rival when she was flying. She was going to challenge Eady for some fabricated insult.

I still hear her screams. The crunch of bone when she hit the ground.

Libby tangles her fingers in Kai's hair and yanks his head down to claim his mouth. His hand flaps at her arm, his struggles weak. She attempts to lick his oesophagus while dry-humping his hip.

"What the fuck are you doing?" shouts a voice.

The scowly friend storms towards them, blind to my little cluster with the twins. Libby ducks to the side, the thrill of battle glowing in her face but the guy shoves Kai, who reels as if drunk. He bounces off the railing circling the dance floor.

"I knew you weren't good enough for her," the friend yells, and swings a punch.

His fist connects with Kai's jaw and spins him around. Kai

falls in a tangle of limbs, blinking at the ceiling. The man barrels through the onlookers and disappears into the crowd. Libby peels a dazed Kai off the sticky floor. I support his other shoulder, though she could easily carry him herself, and we steer him towards the door, the twins skipping behind.

"Was that really necessary?" I say.

"No, but it was fun. And this way, maybe fewer people will start looking for him."

We tumble into the cold night, Kai silent between us, his legs stuttering where we aim them. I guide us to my car parked across the street. My Ford Mustang rears at the curb, the paint as grey as Kai's eyes.

I'm always designated driver but then my sisters also drive ridiculous, two-seater convertibles. I love my American muscle car.

That was one advantage of the Romanovs living in Nevada before they relocated to Scotland, apart from having them further from us. I got to experience the delights of the country on our many visits. Scotland used to be our turf until the rise of the Vanatori and the turmoil of the 20th century made things unstable in Europe. The old families disdained America as too vulgar, despite its wilderness and Evelyn's fascination with it. They prefer a culture with more class, basing their territories in the Alps or the Carpathians or the Black Forest. But Scotland is a prime location for a second, third or fourth home if you want a remote and inaccessible estate, with ownership hidden behind layers of shell companies.

It's getting crowded.

Eady and Dory drag Kai into the backseat between them, Libby hopping in the front. The engine rumbles to life, the vibrations shivering through my bum. I head down George

Street then onto Queen Street and London Road. The giggling increases from the back and I glance over my shoulder.

"Eadrea, Doria," I snap, "don't make me pull this car over."

The giggling continues but they stop molesting Kai, zipping his jeans instead of trying to peek inside his boxer shorts.

How am I going to control my three rabid sisters while keeping an innocent stranger relatively unscathed?

I sigh and press the accelerator pedal.

It's going to be a long night.

4

Kai is even cuter in the flicker of candlelight. It flits shadows across his face and sparkles off the quartz in the walls of the chamber. He sways in the centre of the cave, his gaze unfocused. A waterfall tinkles down the stone behind him and disappears into the floor, flowing deeper underground. Libby stalks around him, trailing her fingers over his chest, his arms, as if he's a beautiful sculpture rather than flesh and bone.

Sorry, Kai. You picked the wrong night to go clubbing.

I control my heart rate, though my sisters would attribute the rapid beat to the excitement. Eady and Dory's hearts are racing. Libby's is stone-cold steady.

"It's not too late," I say. "We could take him back to Edinburgh. He lives near The Meadows, according to his driver's licence. He'll wake up and not remember a thing."

Libby stops in front of Kai. "This is too good an opportunity to pass up. If we can infiltrate Julian and Raine's little love-in and burn it to the ground, no one will question our rule. You'll get to fight off way more eligible men than Gerome slab-faced Kaskbirch."

"Let me worry about Gerome."

She levels a smirk my way. "Oh, I'm not worried."

She snaps her fingers in Kai's face. He blinks. Personality rushes into his slate eyes.

"What…?" He shakes his head, his earring flashing silver. "What the hell is this? Where am I?"

He looks at me over Libby's head, and frowns.

"You—"

Libby pokes him in the chest. "Remember me?"

He rubs his temple as if he has a headache. Eady and Dory twitter near the only exit into a dark tunnel.

"You were at the Lulu Bar." He glances around the cave, lingering on me for a beat. "Did you drug me? That is messed up."

"It's about to get messier," Libby says with a cruel smile.

"Yeah, I don't think so," Kai says.

Stormy eyes fix on me and I want to scream, *"Stop staring! I'm doing my best."*

Humans are not top of the food chain. *We* are. That's just a fact. Does the cow plead with the slaughterhouse worker before the bolt enters its skull?

Probably.

Kai spins on his heel and strides for the tunnel. Eady and Dory slide into his path, forming a delicate barrier of giggles and legs.

"I don't know what game you're playing but please get out of the way." A hint of frustration trickles into his voice.

I have to hand it to him—he's taking it well so far. But then, human males are rarely threatened by females.

Poor, ignorant Kai.

"Fine," he growls when Eady and Dory refuse to move.

He reaches for Dory. She spins in what is likely a blur to his human eyes and wraps her arms around his waist from behind. She plants her feet and tosses him across the room. He hits the stone with a thud, rolling a couple of metres to end on his face. He shoves to his hands and knees. Blood oozes from his knuckles.

"What the hell are you," he pants, "a freaking ninja?"

Eady and Dory dissolve into laughter.

Libby gives him a pitying smile. "Oh, we're so much better than that. But you're right—we're taking advantage. How about we give you a chance? Eady?"

Eady manages to stop giggling, her pale-blue eyes all a-sparkle. She closes her hand into a fist and the candle flames snuff out. Kai's breath catches in his throat. The sound tugs at my gut and tingles between my legs.

A prey noise.

Kai's eyes widen, darting around but his world is pure blackness, while mine is etched in grey. What must it be like to be blind in the dark?

"If you manage to get to the exit, we'll let you go," Libby says.

He jumps. "You're all psychotic."

"Oh, you have no idea."

He may have some idea.

He stands slowly, one arm stretched out. He takes a step. Another. Libby catches his hand and throws him over her shoulder.

"Would you fucking stop that!" he yells.

His voice echoes. My sisters laugh. He holds his breath and crab-walks towards me. I move out of his path but Libby gestures at me. I nudge him with my foot. He slaps a hand on the ground and swipes at me with the other, though I'm no longer there. His heart rate is fast now. It matches his breathing.

"Just let me go," he says quietly.

Eady and Dory shove him between them when he regains his feet. Eady yanks his jacket off, driving him to his knees. She snuggles into the leather.

"He smells like coconut," she says.

"Who the hell are you?" he whispers.

Libby nods to Eady and she flicks her arm, her hand lost in the longer sleeve of Kai's jacket. Flames leap upwards from the candles, bathing the cave in golden light. Kai flinches, huddled on the ground, a smear of dirt on his cheek. His hair flops into his eyes.

"This is how I like my men," Libby says. "Sexy, dishevelled and afraid."

Kai's gaze finds mine but I give him nothing.

"Now for the fun part," Libby continues. "I'm going to make you a Lesser."

He swallows. "A what?"

"I have a brilliant idea," she says to me, ignoring him. "I'll bite off his leg. Instant sob story for the runt and his murdering whore."

Oh, crap. My sister has always had a cruel streak and it only got worse when she mated Lukas Romanov, tormentor of the weak. I hoped it would fade after his death, returning to occasional meanness rather than all-out lunacy.

Should I get Dad? He could put a halt to this. But what if he doesn't? What if he watches, pride on his face? I used to go to him for everything but now I'm ashamed to. And it's probably too late. I'll return with him and Kai will already be minus a leg.

"Libby," I say in my best placating voice, "that would likely kill—"

"And he can't run away. Win-win." She turns on Kai with a grin. "Which leg would you like to keep?"

"Stay the hell away from me."

He scrambles backwards until his spine hits the wall. Water spills over his head and soaks half of his shirt, sticking it to his chest. He yelps, and jerks sideways.

"Then I'll decide." Libby's voice drops to a depth that vibrates in my stomach.

The weight of her change shivers in the cramped confines of the cave. Kai must feel something as his face pales, his eyes huge and dilated. The tips of his hair are the only colour left.

"I'll do it," I snarl, and barge past Libby.

My clothes rip and flutter to the ground. Golden scales flow over my skin. My talons scrape on rock. Wings burst from my shoulder blades and stroke the air. Kai gapes in horror.

"This is a dream, right?" he says almost hopefully. "I'm dreaming."

Dory punches him in the jaw on the maroon mark where his friend hit him earlier. He slumps onto his side and I strike while he's dazed.

Maybe he won't remember.

He screams when I open my mouth. His arm flies up as if that will protect him. I bite his forearm as gently as I can. Teeth slide into flesh. His blood tastes glorious yet awful. I lick him and force myself away, crouching on my haunches.

He cradles his arm to his chest, his ribs heaving, and whispers, "What-the-fuck, what-the-fuck, what-the-fuck."

His heels push at the floor but there's nowhere to go unless he merges with the wall. His shirt sleeve is tattered and bloody. His eyes bounce around without focusing on anything. And definitely not on me.

Libby pouts. "That's not quite what I was picturing but it'll do. If you wanted to make him, why didn't you say so?"

I shrug.

"Well, hurry up and change back."

I shift to human. Kai shivers in a ball and appears not to notice my nakedness.

He must be in shock.

Eady throws me his jacket and I shrug it on, zipping it closed, the leather warm against my skin. He does smell of coconuts.

My skirt is the only piece I can salvage, torn down the hem. I tie it around my waist like a sarong, flashing a lot of thigh. Kai makes no comment but I don't hold it against him. He's had a rough night.

Though it could have been worse.

"Is he ready yet?" Libby says, peering at the shivering Kai.

His lips are blue, his eyes still darting around. He really needs a blanket and a hot chocolate, not what I'm about to do next.

"I don't know," I say, tamping down the guilt. "I've never done this before."

"You should feel different. Heavy."

I step closer to Kai without thinking. His gaze leaps to me and he shoves harder against the floor. I stop before he hurts himself.

"I feel... something," I say slowly. "A pressure. Heat. Buzzing."

"Try it then. See what happens."

I don't want to. Apparently, the first change for Lessers is agonising but if I don't control it, it'll come on him anyway and could kill him. It may still kill him.

I should never have let this get so far.

I hold a hand out. Kai shakes his head, his damp hair whipping his eyes.

"Don't touch me," he says. *"Please* don't touch me."

I really hate myself sometimes.

My fingers sink into that invisible pressure, and tug.

5

The pressure bursts with an audible pop. Kai shrieks and launches off the wall, stumbling two steps before he falls to his hands and knees, his spine bowed. His fingernails claw at the floor. A shudder runs through him. There's the wet rip of flesh, the softer rend of cloth. Buttons click on stone, and his shirt bunches to his neck. Golden wings unfold from his shoulders. A perfect, miniature replica of mine. They flick out and splatter the wall red. Kai collapses, semi-conscious and shivering, slick with blood.

God help me, I like it. The same lust—can I shag it *and* eat it?—glows in the faces of my sisters.

"Oh, this is even better," Libby says. "It makes sense for a defective Lesser to run away. They're worthless. You were right, Maddy—biting off his leg was too much."

He's not defective, not really, but the prized Lessers morph talons or teeth. The rarest spit fire. The useless forms grow wings or tails or random scaly patches.

I drag my gaze from Kai. The taste of his blood fills my mouth. The urge for more buzzes in my teeth.

"We could eat him and make another," Eady says, her breasts heaving with her rapid breaths.

Dory tip-toes closer. "But after we play with him a little."

31

"Oh, yes, we are definitely playing with him." Libby's smile is crueller than any I can fake. "I want to fuck him while he's confused and in pain and slippery with his own blood."

"Libby—"

Her head whips towards me, her pupils dilated. There's nothing human in her face.

"—I get to go first," I say in a rush. "He's *my* Lesser."

Her mouth splits in a grin. "Can I watch?"

"Absolutely not." I match her grin, though my jaw aches.

"We're after Maddy," Eady and Dory chorus, clapping their hands.

"Fat chance, Sodom and Gomorrah. *I'm* after Maddy."

I cross to Kai while they bicker happily, Libby explaining how they need to try and keep him alive. No more blood loss. Bruises are okay. Biting with human teeth only.

Have we always been this monstrous? I thought I had it under control.

Kai seems oblivious to my approach. The shivering tapers to the occasional shudder but I'm not sure that's a good sign. His back looks like chewed meat, and he whines on every exhalation. I slip my hand under his uninjured arm.

"Come on, Kai," I whisper. "You need to stand up."

He groans. I pull gently. His hand flaps at nothing. A spasm jerks him up enough for me to place his arm across my shoulders and get him on his feet. He sags against my side, his head bowed. His new wings flop warm and wet but his skin is icy. I aim for the tunnel, and his feet start to shuffle.

"Where are you going?" Libby says.

"I want him in my bed."

"You'll get blood on your sheets."

"I usually do."

32

My sisters whoop. Kai winces at the noise.

"Human males have a problem getting it up when they're not in the mood," Libby says, her voice bright with glee. "You might have to sit on his face."

Their laughter echoes in the tunnel. I pick up my pace, holding most of Kai's weight with one hand clamped around his hip, the other keeping his arm on my shoulders.

What's so weird about not enjoying oral? Who wants someone down there, peering at your intimates? It puts you in a way more vulnerable position than just sex.

I take Kai out the nearest exit into the gardens, the path shorter than weaving through the caves into the house. Dawn blushes the horizon over the sea. The stars wink out. Kai's breath shudders in a white cloud. His legs kick.

"No," he mumbles. "Please, stop. Please, no."

Each soft plea punches me in the gut.

"It's okay," I say in a soothing voice. "You're okay."

Oh, sure. He's just peachy. God, I hate myself.

Kai's toes drag in the frosted grass. A shape drops from the sky in front of us, the landing thudding through my bare feet. Kai raises his head and a jolt runs through his body, pulling a horrible, pained whimper from his mouth. The gold dragon's nostrils flare, scenting blood and fear.

"Hi, Dad," I say, and Kai faints.

'Good morning, Daughter. Are you well?'

I shrug the shoulder supporting a limp Kai. "I made a Lesser. He only has wings, though."

'I can dispose of him for you.'

No flicker of emotion twists my face.

"Thanks. I'll see if he can fly first."

'So few of them do. Such a waste.'

My father bunches his legs and leaps skyward in a blast of wind and heat. The leather flapping fades as he disappears over the house. I bump Kai into a fireman's lift, my shoulder nocked in his stomach. One wing slaps across my head like a limp dishrag.

In my room, I lower him onto my bed—the first man ever to have the privilege—and arrange him on his front. His shallow breaths brush my grey, silk sheets, his tousled hair sticking to his forehead and cheeks in emerald- and violet-tipped spikes.

The slow trip of his heart worries me.

I sprint to the kitchen and return in record time, trailing the scent of turmeric, ginger and garlic, with the pleasant undertone of coconut. Kai hasn't moved. His bloodied shirt parts under my scissors and I toss the remains on the floor. I smooth my heated poultice on the abused tissue of his shoulder blades, carefully spreading his wings.

They're beautiful. Shimmering gold. Neat, small scales. Delicate membrane. A spike juts from the wrist of each. A good fighting weapon, though likely to gouge his eye out if he panics.

I wrap a bandage around his bitten forearm, the wound already scabbed. It's too early to tell if he'll inherit my rapid healing. The transformative wound always heals fast, due to my saliva, though he'll have the scars forever.

The Lesser mark never fades.

My fingers knead heat into the clammy muscles of his back and follow the cleft of his spine. His jeans sit low on his slim hips.

Oh wow. He has dimples down here, too.

My fingertips tingle, aching to stroke them. I balance a hot water bottle on the firm curves of his bum instead and

34

shift position to spread a blanket over him. A raven tattoo decorates his ribs on his left side, its wings arching backwards, the heavy beak pointed towards his stomach, the feet aiming for his hip bone. I trace the intricate feathers captured in black. I curl my hand into a fist to stop from exploring all his fascinating lines and hollows.

I'm no better than the twins trying to get a glimpse of his penis. The poor guy has been tormented. And he has a girlfriend. Mustn't forget the girlfriend.

I drag my reclining chair opposite the bed, and change into leggings and my favourite Iron Maiden t-shirt. Comfort clothes. I'd never wear these in front of anyone else, not even my sisters. The only acceptable pyjamas for a Della Valle are silk. Cashmere at a push.

I curl into the soft cushions, draping Kai's leather jacket over me. The blanket rises and falls as he breathes, humped over his wings, the top of his head unmoving. His heart steadies to a more natural rhythm. My eyelids droop.

Maybe I'll make him that hot chocolate when he wakes up.

6

Dominic Romanov is kissing me!

He must hear the flutter of my heart as all my teenage fantasies come true. And I thought visiting the Romanovs to barter me and my sisters would be demeaning.

Dominic presses me harder into the wall of the first-floor corridor, his hands buried in my hair.

He's so strong, so *bulky*. I'm unused to being weaker, even against a male. It's exciting and scary at the same time. How do human females stand it?

Dominic's tongue swirls around my mouth, our lips slick and slurping together. My first kiss.

It's wetter than I imagined.

"Fuck, Maddy," he says, pulling away with a pop. "You get me so goddamn hot."

His curses send a delicious thrill through me. Dominic Romanov finds me desirable!

He's cute with his flop of chestnut hair and wide, amber eyes. He looks like his younger brother, though he'd hate the comparison. His face is harsher, leaner, than Julian's. More intense. As a bronze Drakul, he's a better match.

He tugs me off the wall, our lips slamming together and mashing on my teeth. His arms crush me to his broad chest, my feet lifted off the floor. He spins with me in his grip and fumbles at something, the kiss unrelenting and leaving me breathless. A door opens. He stumbles a few steps. I try to see but his hand on the back of my head holds me in place. His heavy body pins me to a bed.

I'm in Dominic Romanov's room!

I probably shouldn't be in his room.

His hand slides up my bare leg in a rush of goosebumps. My heart slaps against my ribs. His pulse is loud but slow and steady. Heat spreads where his weight lies between my legs, pushing my thighs apart. His fingers sneak under my skirt.

I grab his hand. "Wait, Dominic. What if my mum and dad—"

"Why wait? We're practically promised to each other."

He nibbles my neck and my muscles dissolve.

Something that feels this good can't be bad.

His hand twitches, and I press harder.

"And *if* we're mated, then you can take my virginity."

"That's years away, Maddy," he growls. "You've already got me all worked up with your short skirt and your little panting noises. I know you want it."

I wriggle out from under him and sit on the edge of his bed, my knees pressed together. He huffs a breath and slithers to the floor at my feet.

"We can still kiss," I say hopefully.

"I thought you were a woman, not a child."

I flinch. "I'm not a child. I'm sixteen."

"Prove it. Show me you want to be with me."

"I do want to be with you but… I'm not ready, Dominic."

"Your sister wouldn't say no," he says in a cold voice.

Why does Libby have to screw every male with a pulse?

Can't I have one thing that's just mine?

Tears prick my eyes. I firm my wobbling lip and stand with all the dignity I can muster. Dominic grabs my ankles and flips me onto my back.

"What are you doing?" I yelp.

"You said we could kiss." His mouth twists in a sneer. "You didn't say where."

He yanks my legs apart. I struggle to sit up but he shoves my knees high.

He's too powerful. Older than me. I can't escape.

Goosebumps, so different to the ones before, pebble my skin.

"Dominic, stop it," I say, my voice thick with tears.

"White cotton panties," he says, and tuts. "How juvenile."

Material jerks on my hip and he rips my underwear off. A sick, awful feeling rolls through my stomach. I try to close my legs, hide myself, but his fingers bruise the inside of my thighs. He bends his head, hot breath scalding my private place.

"Dominic, no—"

Something warm and wet rams into that private place. Teeth slice delicate petals of flesh. Dominic thrusts himself away before I can scream.

"I may not get your virginity but I made you bleed first," he says and grins, his lips smeared red.

* * *

I jerk awake to a heartbeat that's not mine, the rapid thud drumming in my ears.

Has an animal got in my room? Or Dominic…

Not Dominic. That was seven years ago and he's dead. A

38

week after it happened, my mother was dead, too.

I fight the soft cushions of my chair, and scrape a tangle of pink and blonde from my face. The leather jacket folds into my lap. The heartbeat skips then gallops harder. A tense shape mounds the covers on my bed. Stormy eyes stare through bars of black hair.

Kai.

I swing my feet to the carpet. Kai scrambles off the bed, the blanket trailing and caught on his wings. Cloth-wrapped poultices scatter to the floor. He yanks on the door to the balcony but it's locked, weak sunlight glowing through the gossamer curtains. I stand and raise my hands but he still lunges to the side as if I'm going to strike him. His wings flop all over the place. His eyes widen at the flash of gold and he spins as if he can get a better look at his extra appendages. He grabs the edge of one wing, and pulls, eliciting a cry.

Pain, disgust, both? How does it feel to have something alien sprouting from his back?

He retreats so fast, his bum hits my cabinet and slams it into the wall.

"This isn't real," he says. "This *can't* be real."

His wings flail hard enough to create a draft. I wince at the spines slashing the air, a whisper from tearing his cheeks.

"Stop," I say, and wince some more.

I take a step, and he backpedals. The heavy cabinet thumps the wall then thuds into place, nudging Kai closer to me. He backs up. Thump-thud. Thump-thud.

"That's it, Maddy," Libby shouts through the door, "give him a good ride."

How long has she been listening? I must have been too distracted to hear her approach.

"Go away, Libby," I say, acting breathless. "You're putting me off."

Her laughter shivers through the wood. Kai seems about to climb on top of the cabinet, his eyes rolling white and darting between me and the door.

"Don't be greedy and wear him out. You've had him for hours. It's my turn."

"You can have what's left of him tonight," I say in the bright, cruel voice I hate.

Kai launches for the balcony as if he can smash through the glass and keep going in a rain of glittering shards. I tackle him half-way, and twist in mid-air. My shoulder slams the carpet and absorbs the blow, my vision obscured by golden scales.

"Just make sure there *is* something left," Libby chuckles, her voice and heartbeat fading.

Kai elbows me in the cheekbone. My grip loosens at the blast of stars and pain. He scrabbles for the balcony. I catch his arm and spin him towards the bed. He bounces off the mattress, his skin dewy with sweat, and wraps his hands around the bedpost, his knuckles mottled. He bounds across the bed for the door. I intercept. We wrestle between the door and the balcony until we're both flushed, and it takes a lot to make a Drakul sweat. He drops to his hands and knees, his ribs heaving.

"What—the hell—are you?" he growls between pants. "What—have you—done to me?"

"I'm not going to hurt you," I say.

He glares at me, his wings quivering, the white of the bandage pristine on his forearm.

"Anymore," I clarify, guilt twisting my stomach.

Surely, I could have stopped this way back at the club instead

40

of forcing the Lesser curse on him? It's a violation. A rape.

And I know what that's like.

I slump on my chair. Kai sits hard and leans on the side of the bed, trapping a wing between his arm and the mattress. He shudders, and I speak before he spirals into another panic attack.

"Look, I can't let you leave until you learn how to control your wings. The quicker you do that, the quicker you can go."

"What sick game are you playing, lady? How do I even have *wings*? What the fuck are you?"

"I'm not playing, and my name is Madisyn. You have wings because I made you a Lesser. I'm a Drakul."

He shakes his head, his earring dancing. "Like Dracula—a goddamn vampire? You turned into a dinosaur."

"Are you blind?" I snap then shut my mouth.

The poor guy has had a traumatic night. I'll forgive him the insult this once.

"Fine—Godzilla or Cthulhu of whatever the hell you are."

"I'm not—" I suck in a breath and ease it out. Another. How is he riling me so easily? "Do you want to leave or not?"

"No, I'd love to stay here and chat with you, *Madisyn*," he says. "Why don't you bite my other arm while you're at it?"

I turn a snarl into a cough. "Well, you might have to stay if you don't concentrate. You have to hide your wings."

"With what? I don't think a shirt is going to cut it."

I snort a laugh. He scowls at me with eyes the heavy grey of a winter storm.

"As if you're going to let me leave," he says, his voice low. "Is this part of the torture? Pretend to help me escape then finish me off when you've destroyed my body *and* my mind?"

"I'm trying to help you," I say calmly. Through my teeth. "If you can control your wings, I'll let you go."

"Like I can believe anything you say. You've kidnapped me, assaulted me, turned me into… into…" He bats at the air, his gaze fixed anywhere but on the wings quivering from his shoulder blades. "And those other fucking monsters want to *rape me*."

I pick an imaginary piece of lint off my leggings. "Then the sooner you control your wings, the sooner you can get away. I can only hold them off for so long."

Fear flashes in his eyes, quickly smothered beneath a glower.

"Fine, I'll bite"—he winces, a palm soothing the bandage on his forearm—"how do I get rid of them?"

"You have to draw them inside yourself. Imagine sucking them back into your body."

"Oh, well, sure, when you say it like that, it explains everything."

"Would you just try?"

He crosses his arms over his bare chest and frowns at his lap. His wings flutter. He hunches his shoulders but nothing happens apart from the tantalising bunch of his abdominal muscles.

What is his girlfriend going to think of the new appendages? If he masters his control, she may never know about them. Though his next orgasm could be an interesting experience for them both.

"You have to feel your wings as part of your body," I say, ignoring my blush, and standing up. "Here, let me show—"

Kai scuttles backwards, wedging himself between the cabinet and the bed.

"Don't touch me," he says in a rush almost as fast as his heartbeat.

I swallow the sudden lump in my throat.

Are my hands shaking? My hands can-*not* be shaking.

"I was trying to help—"

"I don't need help from a monster wearing some woman's skin."

The barb slices deep, and I want to argue. I'm not a monster. I want to be nice, soft, sweet. I want to have human friends. I want a relationship with a man that's more meaningful than a power grab or a one-night stand. But I have to pretend and sometimes I get lost in the pretence.

What if I forget who the real me is? I'll become as cold and cruel as the mask I wear until I shatter, nothing inside me but ash. Funny, that's also what we become when we die.

"This is my own skin, thank you very much," I sniff.

Out of indignity, not because he's upset me.

I lower myself into the chair while he tries to mould himself into the furniture.

"Curl your hand into a fist," I say, my voice steady. "Remember the feeling. Now, do it with your wings."

He glowers at me for a dozen more of his heartbeats. I raise my chin instead of wilting.

Madisyn Della Valle does not wilt. She eats grumpy human boys for breakfast.

My stomach rolls. I calm it with a hand but force myself to stop under Kai's judgemental gaze. He warily scoots out from his alcove. His wings stroke the air and curl around his shoulders like a cloak. He shudders and they jerk backwards, slapping together. I resist telling him they're pretty, not repulsive.

"It's like drawing them in," I say instead. "Imagine you're telescoping them inside yourself."

His breath huffs out. "I don't know what you're talking about, you goddamn psycho."

My face hardens into its familiar mask. Kai's eyes widen and he slides back into his nook, his knees to his chest. I will myself to relax, though it's strange, letting him see glimpses of my normal reactions rather than the ones expected of me. It's freeing, even if he is calling me names and cowering every time I breathe in his direction. Most Lessers cower around me.

Another thing I hate.

"You're stressed," I say in a cool tone. "It's difficult to manipulate your Lesser ability when you're stressed. That's something you'll have to be aware of when you get the hang of it. Strong emotions work both ways—stopping the change or bringing it on."

Kay stays rigid in his alcove.

"You mean if I get angry, the wings will appear? People will see I'm a freak?"

"You're not—"

"*Why did you do this to me?!*"

I jump at his shout.

"I was trying to—"

"For the love of god, if you say you were helping me, I'll…" He hugs himself tighter into a ball and mutters, "You're a dragon so there must be slayers. I'll find a freaking dragon slayer."

They call themselves Vanatori—hunters in Romanian—but I choose not to tell him that.

I need to comfort this prickly, fatigued and scared human until he relaxes enough to master his wings. I could force the change on him, like I can with anyone in dragon form, but he

44

needs to learn if he ever wants his life back. Something tells me that's not going to happen in the next hour.

A long night followed by a long day. Fantastic.

7

Kai huddles in his alcove and scowls at me.

What do humans talk about? The men I sleep with are more interested in getting my clothes off than intelligent conversation and I don't hang around after for cosy chats or cuddles.

"I like your tattoo," I say. "Does it mean anything?"

Kai's eyes narrow, and I worry he won't answer. He'll just sit and glare at me, wings out, until we die of starvation. Or my sisters get bored, barge inside and drag him away.

"Loss and bad luck," he says, reluctance etched in his face and in the tension in his muscles.

"Oh. Yours?"

He renews his withering stare.

I try again. "How long have you had it?"

"Since I was eighteen."

He sighs as if talking to me is tedious. Well, I'm not having fun, either.

"And that was…?"

"Five years ago."

I give him an encouraging smile. "You're the same age as me."

His deadpan expression tells me he is unenthused by this.

My smile cracks a little. "Did it hurt?"

This is more exhausting than wrestling him on the carpet.

He frowns at his scuffed boots, matched by his jeans from when my sisters tossed him around. I should probably get him a shirt rather than forcing him to remain half-naked, though I find myself strangely reluctant.

"It was the most painful thing I've ever felt." He raises his head and spears me with his gaze. "Until recently."

Darn it. There's the guilt again.

I scramble for another topic.

"So the guy you were with at the club is your girlfriend's brother?"

His arms tighten around his knees. "Did you kidnap him, too? Turn him into... *this?* What did you call it, a Lesser? What the fuck is that?"

Good idea, Madisyn. Remind him of last night. Surefire way to get him to relax.

"You're a hybrid. Parts of you can take dragon form while the rest of you stays human. And your friend left you at the club."

"Why would he do that?"

"He, um, saw you kissing my sister."

Kai's eyes spark. "I did *not* kiss that crazy bitch."

"You may have been unaware at the time."

He fists his hands in his hair, mussing it worse. The black and violet and emerald look great with his dark irises.

"Are you kidding me?" He pats his pockets. "Where's my phone? I need to call her."

"Who?"

Another frosty look. "My girlfriend. I need to see her. That's if you're not lying and will actually let me go."

"I'm not lying. But how are you going to explain those?" I say, and circle my hand at him.

He bares his teeth. "This is how you and your twisted sisters get your jollies? You pick a guy and ruin his life? Make him a monster, like you?"

"I'm trying to save—"

"Fuck you," he says, and I flinch.

I hug myself. My lip threatens to wobble and I tell it not to be ridiculous. This isn't the first time I've faced anger or resentment. Usually, it's with an audience. Cruel Maddy takes charge and they back off before I have to force their submission. The occasions where I had to prove I was more powerful still haunt me.

But with no witnesses, no one to judge if I'm behaving as a proper gold Drakul female should, the real Madisyn can do what she wants. Maybe Kai will be less grumpy if I feed him.

I stretch for the phone on my dressing table. Kai twitches, wariness carved into his body. If he gets any tenser, he'll break something.

A servant answers in the kitchen. I order a full cooked breakfast, a pot of coffee, porridge with honey and a bowl of fruit. Kai watches me as if I've asked for knives, whips and acid. We sit in silence until a heartbeat approaches. Cutlery clinks when they set the tray outside my door as instructed. I wait for the pad of their footsteps to disappear, open the door and retrieve the tray before Kai can attempt another escape. I claim the porridge and fruit and nudge the rest towards him.

The coffee smells heavenly but there's only one cup and Kai deserves it more than me.

I sit cross-legged on my chair and devour my food. Kai creeps slowly out of his hiding place like a reluctant hermit crab. He hooks a finger on the tray and drags it to his alcove, his eyes never leaving mine. As if I might bite him.

But I've already done that.

He examines a piece of bacon and takes a cautious nibble.

"I wouldn't have pegged you as an Iron Maiden fan," he says.

He initiated the conversation! The food is working!

"Why not?" I say.

He smirks. "Pink-haired girls aren't their usual audience. Though I guess the vampire-monster part fits with heavy metal."

"Are you deliberately being insulting? I'm a *shapeshifter,* not a dinosaur or a vampire. Drakul is derived from the Latin word for dragon."

He swallows the rest of the bacon and licks the grease from his fingers.

Oh my. His tongue is pierced. The sight of the silver ball tingles into my stomach. Or I ate my breakfast too fast. That makes more sense.

"And yet you're going to let me go, though I know what you are. I could talk. Show people my wings. Is that what you want?" He picks up the plate and shovels bacon, egg and sausages into his mouth as if it might be his last meal.

"Oh, believe me," I huff, "none of this is what I want. I never get to do what I want."

He stops chewing. I duck my head and focus on spearing a final chunk of melon.

I've said too much. This stupid talk is supposed to get him relaxed, not me. Though he seems at his most comfortable when he's being snide and derogatory.

"Why did you do this to me?" he says. It has less venom but a quiet despair that's worse.

"Would you rather I let my sister bite off your leg?"

He flinches, trying to disguise it by pouring himself a cup of coffee. I drool at the smell. He takes a long sip and cradles the mug, steam curling past his chin.

"So your dad is... like you. Is your mum?"

"My mother is dead."

He pauses in the act of taking another drink. Something stirs in his grey eyes but it's gone before I can read it.

"Oh." He puts the cup down half-finished. "Sorry."

I shrug one shoulder. "It was seven years ago."

"How did she die?"

"Car accident," I say.

A lorry braked on the motorway. Massive head injuries even she couldn't heal. Her attention wasn't on the road. It was on me.

Stop it, Maddy.

Her death and my father's refusal to mate another was blood in the water to the circling sharks, jealous of the Della Valle name. Dad promised me to Dominic Romanov since it was what Mum wanted. Our wedding was supposed to be last autumn. An event I had dreaded for six long years. Hiding my joy at his death was the best acting I've ever done.

"Are there more like you?" Kai says. "More mons—more dragon shapeshifters? More hybrids like me?"

I stack my bowls on the dressing table. "Try your wings again."

"How many?"

I give him my best blank face, and he makes a disgusted noise.

"Fine. I don't care. Just prove you're not a liar and let me out of here."

"*Wings,*" I say.

The scowl returns to his face but his wings arch above his shoulders, beautiful and golden. A delicate shiver runs through them.

"Dammit," Kai snarls, and pounds the carpet with his fist. "Can't we cut the stupid things off?"

I open my mouth. Giggling filters from down the corridor. Kai doesn't seem to hear them until nails scratch on the wood.

"Come on, Maddy," Dory wheedles. "You're taking *ages.*"

Kai shudders and retreats into his alcove, gripping a fork for a weapon.

"It's not fair if you wear him out before we can play with him," Eady says.

How did I ever think I could control my sisters? I can't control anything.

"You'll get him when I'm good and finished." I swallow bile but my voice doesn't change. "He's worth the wait."

They skip away while I wrestle with my self-disgust, lest it show on my face. I avoid looking at Kai.

"You're all sick, you know that?" he whispers.

"I won't let them touch you," I say, and force myself to meet his gaze. "*I* haven't touched you."

He raises a disagreeing eyebrow.

"Stopping you from running away doesn't count," I say.

"Oh, well, as long as it doesn't *count.*"

I pinch the bridge of my nose, a headache brewing. "Why don't we try silent contemplation?"

"Fine," he snaps.

"*Fine.*"

Man, I really need a coffee.

8

It takes until early afternoon for Kai's wings to retract into his human form. He drank all the coffee so the jitteriness, combined with his resentment, probably didn't help. He doesn't notice the change at first, intent on carving something into my bed frame with his fork. No doubt it's uncomplimentary.

"Kai," I say softly.

His shoulders hunch but he ignores me, as he has for the last two hours.

"Kai, look behind you."

He heaves an irritated sigh and glances over his shoulder. The fork slips from his fingers, the tines bent. He bows his head and a flop of hair hides his face, though not the shudder that ripples through him.

"Thank god. Thank god, thank god," he mutters, and shoves to his feet, his eyes sparking a challenge. "I want to go *now*."

I stand slowly to mirror him. "Not until you've done it a few times. Morph them again."

"No." His lip curls. "They're gone and they're never coming back."

"Kai, I've told you it doesn't work like that."

"Get out of my way, Madisyn."

He growls my name but it's the first time he's said it without derision. It sounds nice.

"Do it a couple more times, and I will."

His hands fist and his gaze drops to the fork as if he's thinking about carving something derogatory into me next. Tension sings up his arms to the somewhat distracting curve of his shoulders. His wings slither free and his eyes widen, a different kind of shiver running through him.

"It feels good the second time and all the times after," I say.

"Goddamn you," he whispers.

"Again," I say in my steely voice, no hint of compassion. It's cramped in my stomach with all the other emotions I have to hide.

If I weren't a Drakul, I'd have ulcers by now.

Air whistles in Kai's nostrils. He really has the best scowl. I wonder if he practises in the mirror, like I do.

His wings fold behind his shoulders and disappear. Reappear. Once, twice. He cocks his eyebrow.

Another of his great many expressions that scream, *"Fuck you."*

He cuts an intense figure with his black hair, furious eyes and broad shoulders, the wicked beak of the raven visible on his ribs. It's somewhat ruined by the rapid thud of his pulse in the hollow of his throat.

I want to lick it.

I yank my cupboard open and toss him a too-large-on-me, black t-shirt. He wrinkles his nose at the image of Eddie in chains and surrounded by lightning.

Powerslave. My favourite Iron Maiden song, and apt, given the situation. We're both slaves now.

Kai seems unamused by my wit or he doesn't get the reference. His lips thin into a pale, distrustful line.

I remember how he smiled at me in the club. Before. Will I ever see his dimples again? His cheek dimples, of course. Not his butt dimples.

He drops my t-shirt and rubs his fingers on his jeans as if he's touched something nasty.

"I'd rather you just gave me back my jacket," he says, "or are you taking that from me, too?"

Whoops. How did I forget about his jacket? I never forget the details. They can save your life.

I scoop up the buttery leather and hold it out. Kai snatches the jacket and shrugs it on, zipping it as high as it'll go.

"You have to follow me and do exactly what I tell you," I say, ignoring a stupid bleat of sadness, "otherwise you'll get caught."

"Am I not already caught?"

"Not by the worst of us," I say through my teeth.

Who cares about his dumb dimples? He can go glower at someone else. I want my room back. And some damn coffee.

I open the door and wave for him. He follows after peeking around the frame to check both ways, angling his body away from me whenever he can. There's no one anywhere near us but I guess it's still too early to tell if he'll get the quick healing *and* the super hearing. Or only the wings.

I lead him on a zig-zag route to avoid the heartbeats of the servants cleaning the rooms or cooking in the kitchen. My sisters should be in their bedrooms, my father in his study or the lounge. I give them all a wide berth lest someone question why a maid's heart is racing and not with the happy trip of exercise but the hard thud of fear. Kai's teeth grind together, his antagonism increasing with every twist and turn.

He's good at masking his panic with frustration.

Now, imagine having to do that while also controlling your heartbeat and breathing in front of creatures who know exactly what each hitch and stutter and rapid little flutter means. When you can hide nothing.

The swing door into the glass-fronted garage squeaks, and I freeze. Kai bumps into my back. He leaps away as if scalded, his heart loud enough to pound in my stomach. Winter sunlight dulls the brilliant white of the space. On the far side, the boot lid of my Mustang pops open at the press of the fob in my hand.

"Get in," I say.

Kai's leather jacket creaks when his shoulders hunch. "No freaking way."

"Do you want to leave or not? If anyone catches you out here, it's all over."

His earring quivers his displeasure but he swings his leg over the edge of the boot and curls inside. He crosses his arms, his fingers clamped in his armpits. I rest my hand on the lid.

"You can't tell anyone what happened," I say. "Nothing about dragons or your wings. You have to keep them hidden. What you are—what I am—must be kept secret."

"Will you kill me if I talk?"

"Not me," I say sadly. "But one of us will."

A Lesser owned by the Romanovs fled to the police and blabbed about monsters, slavery and abuse. She morphed her teeth into sharp points. The officers were shocked, apart from one. An hour later, a terrible fire burned the station to the ground, killing everyone inside, including, people assumed, the Lesser.

That would have been kinder.

She was dragged to Evelyn Romanov's underground lair.

She lasted eight hours. Have you ever listened to someone scream for eight hours? There was little left bar red meat and the fractured white of bone.

I shake my head to clear the awful images. "I have to make sure the coast is clear but stay in the boot and be silent. There's too much security for you to escape without my help. When the engine stops, don't make a sound until I pop the lid. Then you can run."

"How do I know this isn't the finale of your torture game?" Kai says.

"I've kept you safe for hours, haven't I? Taught you mastery of your wings. Kept my sisters at bay. Guess you'll have to trust me."

He snorts. "Trust you?"

I start to lower the lid. Something flickers across his face and dissolves his frown to a solemn expression.

"Maybe this'll be the worst thing you do to me," he says softly.

The lid clunks shut.

9

I sprint to my room and tug on a pink cashmere jumper, leaving one arm flailing out, and my APO jeans, unbuttoned. The rear is studded with gold and platinum, the front fastened by a diamond. They probably cost more than Kai's car.

If he has a car. He has a driver's licence, at least.

I fly down the corridor to my sisters' rooms, the untied laces of my golden Jimmy Choo wedge trainers flapping behind me. The door slams into the wall.

"He escaped," I gasp at Libby. "I closed my eyes for a second."

She's already sitting up in bed, the magazine she was reading abandoned on the duvet. Eady and Dory thunder into the room while I'm threading my arm into my remaining sleeve.

"That's not possible!" Eady says, and stamps her foot. "How did he get past the gate, the cameras?"

"Maybe he can fly."

"Then let's chase the little birdie." Libby swings her legs out of bed. "Can you feel where he is?"

"I think so," I say. "Or I have indigestion."

Libby laughs, and wrinkles her nose. "I always hated that part. Who wants to be so connected to a Lesser that you ache to be near them? Though it does make screwing them interesting."

I'm too distracted to admonish Libby for her language. Now that I'm no longer next to Kai, his presence tugs deep in my stomach, like an extra pulse. For the rest of his life, no matter where he is, I'll find him. If he dies, I'll know and be able to go to where it happened.

Not telling him he's my pet on a leash is the worst thing I've done to him. I told him the basics but didn't want to antagonise him more. I probably should have warned him that Lessers also crave the touch of their masters. That one works both ways. If I never see him again, I'll always have an empty, unfulfilled longing. And so will he. A longing to be with the person who hurt him.

I squat to tie my laces and hide my face from my sisters.

"He's managed to get quite far," I say, my voice steady. "He must be going for the train station."

Libby makes shooing motions. "Get the car ready. We'll put our shoes on."

"It's fine, I'll wait. It's not like he can hide."

Libby and the twins pull on a variety of designer boots then we troop towards the garage.

"I can't believe I fell asleep and let him get away," I say, loud and annoyed.

My heart beats harder. Will they hear his? Will this all be over before I can start the car? I should have taken Libby's suggestion and run ahead.

Eady's sharp elbow pokes me in the ribs. "He's not supposed to tire *you* out, Maddy."

"He may be human, or used to be human, but he has good stamina." I bark a laugh and it grates in my ears. "You know, once he got over his initial reluctance."

"So what exactly did you do to him?" Libby slides me a

smirk. "Or, more importantly, what did he do to you?"

I push into the garage. Kai's pulse skips and thrums like the freaking tell-tale heart from within the Mustang's boot. A frisson of panic zips down my spine.

A brittle smile crackles across my mouth. "I took your advice and sat on his face."

Their whoops of glee carry us into the car. The vehicle rocks with the slam of the doors. I ram the key into the ignition.

"As for the rest," I say, my voice too forced, "you'll have to find out for yourselves."

The engine roars, drowning Eady and Dory's giggling. I crank the volume on the audio player and blast *Run to the Hills* from the speakers. The garage door opens at the prod of a button and I gun out onto the long, sloping driveway.

"Put something else on, Maddy!" Dory bellows from the backseat.

"We're on a hunt." My Mustang swoops into the trees hiding us from the main road. "I am not listening to the *Frozen* soundtrack or any blooming K-pop."

Libby, the K-pop fan, sticks her tongue out at me. The twins pout. I ignore them and sing along to the lyrics.

The front gate slides open and I power into the gap without slowing, weaving through a maze of tracks to the A198. Rain spits onto my windscreen, the day grey and damp. I zoom into the drizzle to North Berwick train station and park next to the platform where any extra heartbeats will be confused by the people waiting for trains. I pop my door before the engine rumbles to silence.

"Come on, he's close," I say.

My sisters tumble after me, chattering with excitement. I pace to the other end of the car park. Frown. Look both ways.

A young family loads themselves into a battered Volvo. The fan belt screeches.

"Is he not here?" Libby joins me beside the bare bones of cherry trees and a scraggly hedge next to the entrance.

"I've never done this before. I can't quite get a fix on him."

"Strange. I never had a problem finding a Lesser." Libby grins at me. "Maybe you didn't bite him hard enough."

I search between the cars, and the Volvo finally leaves, the fan belt bemoaning the chill.

I turn and look across the car park to the station buildings. "Wait. He's heading north, towards the beach. He must have seen us."

Libby jogs ahead, Eady and Dory skipping behind her. The lust of a good hunt shines in their eyes and bared teeth. They clatter up the metal stairs to the bridge across the railway line. I press the boot release button on my key fob, my sensitive hearing able to pick up the clunk of the lid. I run after my sisters and don't look back.

Goodbye, Kai.

I wish I could've said sorry.

10

For the next two hours, I lead my sisters on a wild Lesser chase, keeping them away from the train station. The lust of the hunt dims in their eyes as we trot up and down residential streets, a steady drizzle dampening our clothes.

None of us brought jackets. Our body temperature runs hot in our human form so it's easy to forget.

Wet sand clumps on our shoes. The beach stretches empty on either side, framed by grey clouds and frothing sea. Marram grass scores Eady's leg, her tiny shorts somewhat incongruous when we're around humans bundled in their winter coats. She hisses, and a burst of flame consumes the blade to black ash.

"This is lame," she says, stretching out the last word. "We should have found him by now."

Blood beads in a line on her shin, scabbing immediately. In an hour, there will be no trace.

Libby shakes a piece of seaweed from her white fur boot. "Can you tell where he is yet?"

The pulse of Kai is fainter. Distant. It tugs from the direction of Edinburgh so I imagine he's back home near The Meadows, his perception of the world altered forever. Will his girlfriend accept whatever justification he uses for kissing a stranger and staying out all night? I hope for both their sakes he doesn't tell the truth.

"I can't get a fix on him," I huff, burying my hands in my sodden hair for good measure. "He must be defective. I suppose the wings were a clue."

"What was the address on his driver's licence?" Libby says as we trudge up from the beach.

Streetlights flicker on, bronzing the swirling drizzle. Cars hush by and kick up spray.

"It was near The Meadows, that's all I remember."

"Let's drive around. See if you pick up anything."

North Berwick train station looks abandoned in the dark, puddles shining under the security lights. The boot of my car is shut. No heartbeats but mine and my sisters'.

The drive into the centre of Edinburgh takes thirty minutes of whizzing past other vehicles in a spume of water, my engine snarling its dominance. I suppose I should be more careful but my Mustang loves to gallop. And it's the only time in my life I can be reckless.

Kai's presence calls to me from a top-floor flat opposite Summerhall—previously a veterinary school, now a vibrant cultural centre. I follow the tree-lined Melville Drive that skirts The Meadows, ignoring the longing to park the car and knock on the door for a glimpse of stormy eyes and green-and purple-tinted hair.

It's just a side effect of making a Lesser. It's not because I actually miss him. I'll control it and ignore it like everything else.

"Any luck?" Libby says.

I shake my head and turn into Bruntsfield, zig-zagging east through Marchmont.

"Maybe he's topped himself," Dory sniggers. "Humans are weak."

"He isn't so human anymore," I say softly.

Is he alone in his flat? Tomorrow is Monday. Maybe he's getting ready for work, desperate to act normal and pretend everything else was an alcohol-induced nightmare. I picture him, topless and standing in front of a mirror, examining the unblemished spread of his shoulders. I ache to run my hands up his smooth back, my thumb brushing the intricate raven tattoo on his ribs, climbing higher until his control shatters and his wings spill out, my fingers cupping the bases as intimately as another piece of his anatomy, my mouth claiming his—

"Maddy? The light's green."

I jump at Libby's voice.

Jeez, where did that come from? I never thought the skin hunger for a Lesser would be quite so *hungry*.

"Sorry," I say, calming my heart rate, "I was concentrating. Trying to find him."

I ease my foot down on the pedal and head right past Kai's flat, accelerating until the throbbing in my lower belly fades a little.

"Anyway, Maddy would have felt it if he died." Libby looks at me, headlights from another car sweeping across her face. "It's like falling."

Dory butts in before I can reply.

"Clearly, there's something wrong with the connection."

"He could be dead," I say.

Eady kicks my seat. "This isn't fair!"

"We should make more," Dory says, "and Eady and I get to go first."

Eady claps her hands. "Yes! A second night of dancing and debauchery."

Oh, god, no. I can't take another human staring at me like I'm a monster. Other Drakul and Lessers—fine, I'm used to it. But human males only ever looked at me with the hot, predatory gaze of someone wondering what I'm like in bed. Far preferable to fear and revulsion.

"It's too soon to return to the club," I say in a mild voice.

"So let's pick a different one."

My hands tighten on the wheel. "This is a mess I'd rather not repeat. How do you think Dad would react to our carelessness?"

He didn't seem overly concerned by me making a new Lesser this morning but my sisters don't need to know that.

There are twin sounds of slumping and sighing from the back seat.

"You're such a goody two-shoes sometimes, Maddy," Libby says with some heat, her arms crossed.

"We should have run it by him."

She smirks. "Oh, I plan on running many things by him. Things we should've done months ago."

Oh, crap. When Libby starts planning, my stomach starts cramping. And someone always gets hurt.

We pass our townhouse on East Preston Street, the Kaskbirches ensconced inside, enjoying our hospitality. With a shudder, I take Holyrood Park Road onto Duddingston Low Road, Arthur's Seat hulking next to us and swathed in low cloud. My wipers smear greasy drizzle across the windscreen.

Eady's palms slap the glass. "There are deer on the hill."

Libby grins and wiggles her eyebrows at me.

"Fresh meat," she says.

She leaps from the car, the twins scrambling behind. I blow out a frustrated breath and coax the Mustang up the kerb onto mown grass.

We're in the middle of freaking Edinburgh and they want to change. Okay, so it's unlikely anyone's on Arthur's Seat in the cold, dark and wet but we're not invisible.

I park far enough from the lights on the road so no human eyes should be able to see. I gather my sisters' discarded clothes and dump them in the boot, folding mine next to them. A subtle hint of coconut teases my nose but I tell myself I'm imagining it.

Kai was more sweat and angst than anything so pleasant at the end.

After stashing my keys in a magnetic box attached to the chassis, I sprint up the hill, the wind caressing rain-slick skin. Two legs become four and my talons furrow the grass, my wings tucked to my sides. The thrill of the chase, the shift, fizzes in my veins. The scent of blood fills my nostrils and I swoop past Eady and Dory, their slim muzzles buried in hot, spurting flesh. A leg twitches, still trying to run. Libby snuffles at an area of gorse.

'*One went in there,*' she says. '*I hear it shaking.*'

Her chest puffs as she readies her flame sacs, water sizzling in the sudden heat. I clamp my claws on her snout.

'*No fire. Too obvious.*'

I dive over the gorse, my growl vibrating into the bushes. A deer bolts for higher ground, its flank striped by bloody lines. Libby coughs her triumph and lumbers in pursuit. I drop onto the terrified animal and sink my teeth into its neck. Warm copper floods my mouth. Froth coats the deer's muzzle, its ribs heaving. Its legs thrash but I bite harder, cutting off its air. Its struggles weaken, though its heart is still hammering when Libby arrives and swallows a leg in one gulp.

I hope the poor thing isn't aware enough.

Its heart stops, black eyes rolling white. Libby slices a talon down its abdomen and spills its guts onto the grass. Her happy slurping drowns out the wet rip of muscle as I feast on neck and shoulder, the rich meat sliding down easy. I snap the ribs and gobble the heart before Libby hoovers it up. We leave little behind bar scraps of hide and bone, the rain washing away the blood.

I clean my snout and claws, bounding over the gorse before shifting to human. Libby thumps next to me, her change slower. More popping joints and groans. Crimson coats her face and sticks her hair to her cheeks. We collect the twins and walk back to the car, four naked girls covered in various daubs of flesh and innards.

Nothing some clothes and moist wipes can't handle.

I blast Iron Maiden on the journey home, though no one tries to talk. Killing gets us all introspective. Or sleepy.

I bid my sisters goodnight and close my bedroom door, slumping against it. Exhaustion weighs my limbs and shutters my eyes.

A servant has tidied the room, removing the breakfast tray and scattered poultices. The sheets on my bed are crisp and tucked tight into the mattress, though I bet Kai's scent lingers on the material.

The staff are too frightened of my family to question the bloodied shirt. They think we're some kind of mafia, which is safer for them to believe than the truth.

I stumble across the carpet and tuck myself into Kai's nook between the cabinet and the bed. My fingers trace the series of angry lines sliced into the frame by his fork. I concentrate on the roughness, the scrape of splinters. My heart speeds but I don't let the words come into focus.

Not yet.

I suck in a breath. Once, twice. I'm sure I've been called whatever insult it is. Why should I care?

The message swirls, and my laugh stutters out. Carved into the wood in precise letters is 'Here be dragons.'

11

The caves beneath our house offer a space where we can stretch our wings and roar and play without the worry of some human witnessing what they shouldn't, and dying for it. It's tough being a dragon in the age of camera phones, CCTV and night-vision technology.

Our ancestors had it easy.

My claws spark on stone, reflecting in the quartz crystals seamed through the walls. I spit a fireball at Libby. She snorts and shakes her head, thundering after me, her tongue lolling out the corner of her mouth. I bounce from wall to wall and quickly lose her in the maze of tunnels, Eady and Dory chuffing their laughter and giving away their position. Libby's heavy tread fades in that direction.

I spring into the huge cavern where we entertain guests and torture the unfortunate. The dining table has been packed away, the tunnel from the kitchen barred to keep any servants from interrupting us. I spread my wings and circle the dim space, the exercise warming my muscles and lightening my heart.

I can't stop thinking about Kai. It's starting to bug me. My self-control is all I have for protection. I can't be distracted by some pretty, wounded boy. Out of sight, out of mind helps me stay sane.

I flap harder, a golden whirlwind doing laps of the room. My heart pounds. Air rasps between my teeth.

I dreamed of him last night. The flash of his dimples. The bewitching smell of coconut, so sweetly erotic. I chained him on his knees between the posts of my bed but the heat in his eyes—the grey of smouldering ash—said he didn't mind. He was naked and another part of his body said he *really* didn't mind. I licked the dimples on his lower back. Chains rattled. I nibbled his sexy bum and he growled my name—Madisyn, not Maddy.

Friends and family call me Maddy. He can be the first to call me Madisyn without hate or fear. To purr my full name like no one else has.

The dream swirled, as dreams do, and I was in his arms, kissing him, his fists buried in my hair, his mouth hot, demanding. His tongue found mine and the hard stroke of his piercing throbbed through my entire body.

How would it feel rubbed on other places, surrounded by the slick heat of his tongue? Lower places. Vulnerable places…

I gasped awake, wet and aching, the echo of his name fading in the room.

Stupid, uncontrollable dreams.

I skid to a halt and press my snout to the one-way glass at the far end of the room, my talons splayed on either side of my head, wings arched. The sea is as dark as the day, smashing itself against the base of the cliffs in plumes of white.

What is Kai doing now? Is someone taking care of him?

He has a girlfriend, moron. I bet she's a lot kinder and cuddlier than you.

I rap my forehead on the window, my horns clunking against

the glass. My heavy sigh sends fog in a wide arc.

"Daughter," my father says behind me.

He never used to be this formal. Before my mother died, he was playful. Affectionate. He was strict in teaching us how to be proper, formidable, unbreakable, but there was always games and laughter afterwards. Now, he's distanced himself not just from me but the rest of our society as well. He's a passive threat instead of a dangerous force, though he can still be riled into action.

How long do we have until another family sniffs out this weakness?

He's wearing a white silk shirt tucked into jeans, his feet bare. Casual clothes for wheeling and dealing from his home office to keep us all in shoes and cars. I cock my head to show I'm listening.

"Gerome Kaskbirch has come calling," he says.

My stomach lurches. But even in my dragon form, I wear my mask of ice.

A clatter of wings announces Libby's arrival. She trots into the room and nudges Dad with her muzzle. He places a hand on her head but keeps his gaze on me.

'Send the troll packing,' Libby says, her wicked teeth bared in a grin. *'Or do what I did. You'll get a few orgasms since he's gullible enough.'*

Dad's face remains placid since she's only directing her thoughts to me.

"Kaskbirch is a good match," Dad says.

Libby snorts. *'If you like squat men who are squat all over.'*

"Leave us, Libelle. Unless you want to reconsider?"

'No thank you, Father,' she says sweetly and adds for my benefit only, *'It'd be like fucking a mushroom.'*

She trundles into the tunnel and the click of her claws fades. Dad pats the air as if her big head is still beneath his hand.

"Shift, Daughter. I'd like to see your face."

I slide into my human form and stand naked before my father.

Normal humans are weird about nudity. It makes them feel vulnerable and embarrassed. They would hate to be exposed in front of family, as if it's shameful. But there's comfort in the touch of skin, the bond of who we are. Plus, if I didn't get naked a lot, I'd ruin more clothes. Libby and the twins don't care as much but I dislike waste.

"Gerome is a good match," I say, my voice carefully bland. "His family are next in line after ours. Their holdings are vast."

Dad stands beside me at the window, the roil of the sea reflected in his pale-blue eyes. He smells of wood and lavender—his aftershave, Drakkar Noir.

"Is this match what you want?" he says.

I swallow my own snort and follow his gaze beyond the glass.

"It's not about what I want," I say, and scream inside. "Aligning with the Kaskbirches would be… prudent."

The corner of his mouth twitches. "You always were more pragmatic than your sister. Older than her in wisdom, if not in years."

"All I want is to keep us safe."

"That is a burden that should not fall to you. But, after your mother…" He places a palm on the glass and bows his head. "Sometimes I wish…"

We breathe, the pounding of the surf as quiet as our steady hearts.

Sometimes, I wish, too.

Tell him, Maddy. Tell him the truth.

What if he blames me as much as I blame myself? We've grown apart and that's another weight on my conscience. Is it too late? I want to return to the relationship we had before, where I could tell him anything. He'd listen with patience and respond with shrewdness, not the short, stilted interactions we have these days. There's so much I need to tell him. So much I need to apologise for. He could lift me from this suffocating reality I find myself trapped in.

I open my mouth to spill everything and beg his forgiveness.

Dad straightens and snaps his cuffs into place. "Irena will be pleased but do not let her rush you into mating. I hear autumn is a lovely time for a wedding."

He squeezes my shoulder and strides from the cave, leaving a hint of citrus and fir.

"Gerome is waiting for you in the conservatory," he says, his voice drifting from the tunnel. "I'll call Irena with the good news."

I lean my forehead on the cold glass.

And autumn used to be my favourite season. Now, it's just another thing to dread.

12

Gerome struggles to stand when I enter the conservatory, his wide buttocks stuck in the soft cushions of the sofa. Fabric rustles and his stubby legs pinwheel before he manages to hoist himself upright.

This—*this*—is the son of the second most powerful Drakul family in the world? I wish he'd crawl back to his Scandinavian cave and leave me alone.

I've pulled on a daisy-print dress rather than the Iron Maiden t-shirt I wanted. *Bring your Daughter to the Slaughter.* Funny in an edge of madness kind of way.

Gerome's muddy eyes drop to my cleavage and stay there while he thrusts a flower bouquet in my direction. The suffocating scent of lilies assaults my nose.

"Hi, Maddy," he says to my tits.

I accept the flowers and drag my nails along his hand, drawing welts. His startled gaze jerks upwards.

"It's rude to stare, Gerome," I say, and give him cold, deadly eyes.

Sometimes, I don't have to pretend.

He gulps and snatches his hand back. I place the lilies on the coffee table, their odour drowning the sweet, subtle smell of the sunflowers lining the windows, each pot a cheerful colour.

Sunflowers were my mother's favourite.

Gerome smooths his fingers down his black suit. I'm sure it cost a few thousand pounds but even it can't flatter his square figure. He's a brick with legs and a boulder for a head.

Kai would look great in black. Dangerous. It'd bring out the vibrant tips of his hair.

"Mummy says you and I should be mated in the spring." Gerome plops his unsexy bum back on the couch.

Oh, god. I always knew he was a mummy's boy but no man should use that term beyond the age of fifteen. He's twenty-five.

I hide my shudder of revulsion by sitting gracefully on the other end of the sofa, my legs crossed before his greedy little eyes can try to peek.

"Your mother seems very certain of my decision."

Unfortunately, the smug cow is half-right.

Gerome smirks. "She says the other families will talk if you refuse."

A servant enters with a tray of oolong, giving me a chance to control my anger. He pours golden liquid into two delicate china cups, and melts from the room. I sip the grassy tea and fantasise about melting Gerome's slab of a face.

It wouldn't make him look any worse.

Bushy brows, not quite meeting in the middle, accentuate his bulging forehead and sunken eyes. His nose is a squashed blob, his lips wide and flat. He has the prominent jaw of a caveman and possibly the same dental hygiene.

Not like Kai. He's all cheekbones and dark eyes and dimples, his lips full and curved. Kissable. Broad shoulders narrowing to slim hips. Long legs. The tongue piercing I can't get out of my head.

Gerome shifts on the seat, his throat bobbing, and I realise I've been glaring at him in silence.

Stupid Kai, distracting me again. I need to keep Gerome happy so he doesn't go whining to his mummy.

"The other families will always talk," I say, and swallow another mouthful of tea. "I thought you'd be more upset for not getting to mate Libby."

An ugly flush blooms in Gerome's cheeks and blotches the flesh under his chin. It's too short to call a neck. He slides closer, not quite touching. I breathe through my mouth instead of inhaling his overpowering floral scent.

He smells like his mother.

"I know exactly what your tease of a sister was doing." He curls a strand of my hair around his thick finger. "You can make it up to me. You wouldn't want your future mate to be unsatisfied, would you?"

I guess he's not so stupid after all.

He tugs on my hair and leans in, his wide lips puckering. My stomach threatens to give him more than he bargained for. I turn my face and he leaves a smear of saliva on my cheek, cooled by his huff of annoyance.

"Don't make me tell Mummy," he says with a petulant scowl.

I grab his jaw and squeeze until he whimpers.

"You seem to have forgotten who I am," I growl, and he tries to shrink away. "I am a Della Valle. The day you threaten me will be the day I crush your skull to powder. Do you understand?"

He nods, his eyes wide. He pulls against my grip and I press harder, his bones creaking beneath my fingers.

"I am not finished, Gerome," I say in a low voice. "You will get your wedding but not until autumn. We barely know each other since you've been panting after my sister like a dog in heat. And you will not touch me again until we are married."

He shivers under my hand. I release him and he launches towards the other end of the couch, hugging the arm rest as if it can protect him. I stand, and he flinches. I squash an uncomfortable flash of Kai, cringing whenever I moved.

But Kai would never blackmail a woman to have sex with him.

Male Drakul are all the same. Though Gerome may be easier to handle than Dominic. I just wish I didn't have to handle him at all.

"Thanks for stopping by," I say, my words as fake as my smile. "Why don't you take me out to dinner this Friday? We can get to know each other better."

His head bobs so fast, it's in danger of rolling off his shoulders. He scrabbles to his feet and hustles for the door.

"And Gerome?"

He turns, reluctance carved into his blocky frame.

"Be careful what you tell Mummy," I say.

* * *

I toss the dress on the carpet and fling myself onto the bed in my underwear, bouncing a little with the force of it. I glare up at the canopy of my four-poster.

The weasel. The snivelling, mummy's-boy *weasel*.

I probably shouldn't have been so blunt with him but I can't start our relationship from a position of weakness. And he deserved it. As if I'm going to let him paw at me so he doesn't tattle to Mummy.

God, I don't want him to touch me at all. Autumn is still

too soon. He may be a black Drakul, second in importance after gold, but he's a flying elephant and just as graceful. He'll squash me by accident.

I've seen my share of mating flights. Sex in dragon form is a battle. Brutal and exhausting. The male tries to dominate the female and the female resists, forcing him to prove he's worthy. And I'd have to prove I'm stronger. Much stronger. Capitulating too quickly would be shameful and cast doubt on my family.

Libby's mating flight with Lukas lasted six hours and both of them were scratched and broken at the end, though I suspect she enjoyed it. But I like a little less teeth and blood with my sex.

My hand finds the rough letters carved into the side of my bed.

Kai would be good. Confident but gentle. Skilled enough to tease until I sobbed his name. He'd hold me, his wings curling around us both, caressing my arms, my back. No violence.

Though that's all he knows from me.

My hand continues to trace the slash of words. My other hand slips across my flat stomach and into my pants. I widen my legs. Material stretches across my hips. My heart kicks nicely.

I close my eyes and picture Kai's face when we bumped into each other in the Lulu Bar. The easy flash of dimples. Warm, grey eyes and striking hair.

My finger grazes my clitoris, and I gasp. Tingles shoot outward and clench in my belly. I circle the hot nub, and a heavy throbbing starts low. I stroke the slick cleft between my labia, purring in my throat, and slide a finger inside, where it's scalding and wet and tight.

It's Kai's hand, Kai's finger inside me.

I squirm on the bed, my heels digging into the mattress. My hips move and my hand works faster. I'm biting my lip. My body pulses.

Close. So close.

I plunge my finger deep and the orgasm rushes through me in a thick, pulsing wave. My cries spill into the empty room. Mini-climaxes quiver as I lazily curl my finger, stroking the soft, sensitive place inside me. Languid, I roll onto my front and paint the letters with the slickness from my own body.

"Goodnight, Kai," I whisper.

13

Dinner is a less grand affair when we have no guests, though the view is just as nice as the one from the cave. The dining room of the house looks out over the wide terrace and the sea. Frost rimes the grass and sparkles in the pinprick of stars. Humans would see nothing but black and their own blurry reflections in the glass.

I slice into my steak and chew another bite.

Cow meat. I can eat cow meat.

Dizziness rolls in my head and plunges to my stomach as if to make me a liar. My fork clatters on my plate.

Something's wrong with Kai.

"Daughter, are you well?"

My gaze darts up to my father's concerned expression.

"I, um..." I clear my throat.

I need an excuse. Anything. I have to leave! Panic sinks claws into my gut and scrambles upwards.

"I forgot I told Gerome I'd meet him for a drink," I say, my voice steady but a tad high. "I'm going to be late."

Libby's mouth twists but she hides it behind a delicate dab of her napkin when Dad glances at her. The twins are too intent on tearing into their steaks to care, the little savages.

My chair screeches on the floor. "May I go?"

"Certainly, Daughter. Irena was delighted with the news of your courting, though she tried to insist on a spring wedding."

Of course she did, the heifer.

I ball my napkin onto the plate, my food half-eaten, and hustle for the door, my sandals slapping on polished wood.

"Don't do anything I wouldn't do," Libby sings. I manage a smirk over my shoulder but her attention has focused on Dad. "I actually wanted to talk to you about the Kaskbirches. They come to our territory demanding mates; we should demand a show of loyalty."

I pause in the hall, my feet pointed towards the garage, my upper body twisted to face the dining room and Libby's sweet, reasonable voice.

Oh, god... I can't leave her to plant ideas in Dad's head. Unchecked, my sister will start wars and burn kingdoms.

Hurry-hurry-run, *hurry!* Kai needs me.

But he's not family, despite the connection we share. I've met him once. I can fantasise all I like. He's just some cute stranger unlucky enough to catch my sister's eye. He could be a jerk in real life.

Yet he's in pain because of me.

"What do you have in mind, Libelle?" Dad says, amused.

I picture him, elbows on the table, hands clasped, interest dancing in his blue eyes while I wring my hands in the hall. My heart thuds and nausea pulses to my stomach.

Family first. I have to protect them from themselves. I gave Kai the best chance I could.

"It's time we show the doubters who the Della Valles really are," Libby says.

Wooziness fizzes to white in my vision and I grab the banister at the foot of the main stairs.

Kai is dying.

So he dies! Humans die all the time, Lessers more so. It'll be unpleasant then it'll be over. It's for the best. He's a distraction I can't afford. The indecision is his fault. I'm never indecisive. I do what must be done, no matter how hard it is or how sick it makes me.

I pivot towards the dining room. I'll say Gerome cancelled. I'll sit, finish my dinner and head off whatever crazy plan Libby is concocting before more people suffer. The death of one avoids the misery of many.

I hiss a stream of curses even Libby would be shocked by. In one blink, I'm out of the hall. The corridor blurs beneath my sprinting feet.

No doubt I'll regret it but I can't let Kai die alone. What hold does this stupid human have over me?

The swing door creaks. Bright lights dazzle my eyes as they blaze on automatically. My Mustang welcomes me with a growl and I roar out of the garage before the door has fully opened. My tyres spin on icy roads. The journey into Edinburgh is a haze, my knuckles white on the wheel. A pale face stares back at me from the rear-view mirror, their cheekbones sharp enough to pinch skin.

I abandon the car on a single yellow line on Sciennes and run for a stained, cream door sandwiched between a Best-One shop and something called Considerit. The lock is broken and the door slams into the wall in my haste, rebounding and shutting behind me as I sweep through, already breathless. I bound up the stairs, bombarded by the multitude of different scents—curry, old urine, fresh paint. Two doors face me on the third-floor landing, the tug of Kai strong behind the one marked 6F. I brace my shoulder next to the jamb and apply increasing pressure. Wood splinters. The door catches on a security chain. One shove and the plate detaches from the wall. I wedge the door shut.

A narrow hall. Dark. One slow heartbeat and my own, tripping along. A door slashed with red. I push it open.

The dizziness is stronger now, swirling in my belly and tipping the floor under my feet. Beneath that is the contentment of being close to my Lesser. I long to touch him. Does Kai feel the same?

He lies propped up in a double bed, the navy sheets bunched at his feet. A lamp casts soft, yellow light on the wall. Sweat glistens on his bare chest and shines on the curve of his muscles. The raven on his side glares at me from one baleful, black orb. Kai's ribs barely move. His glazed eyes are half-lidded. He swigs from a bottle clutched in his hand, and amber liquid sloshes against the glass. Whisky and cinnamon mix with his subtle coconut scent.

"Come to watch me die, *Madisyn?*" he says, a drop of alcohol spilling from the corner of his mouth. He licks at it but misses, his tongue piercing catching on his top lip. "Or should I call you Syn because you're the reason I'm in hell?"

An empty pill packet sits on his bedside cabinet next to a dog-eared copy of *One Hundred Years of Solitude.* Kai watches me lazily and without flinching as I round the bed and read the label. Oxycodone. His name on the prescription.

What pain does he need it for?

"How many did you take?" I say, my voice controlled and empty while panic throbs in my temples.

One side of his mouth quirks. The flash of a dimple sends an ache to my gut.

"Enough," he says.

82

I yank my mobile from my pocket. My hands are shaking. Impossible.

I dial 9. Again—

"What are you doing?"

I press the final 9. "Calling an ambulance."

"You do and they'll see this."

He frowns, his face squinted in exaggerated concentration. His hair flops over his forehead and sticks to his cheeks, dipped in purple and green. One wing jerks free, the claw slashing his pillow. Feathers puff out. The other wing follows after a couple of seconds.

I'm surprised they haven't manifested already in his drugged and drunken state. A fluke, or he has excellent control.

The edges of his wings curl gently open and closed.

God, he looks so beautiful, the gold a lovely contrast against his pale skin, black hair and grey, vengeful eyes.

I force his wings away. His gaze widens then narrows, dark with anger.

"You think you can do that all night without anyone seeing?" he growls. "You take me to the hospital and I show everyone what you've done. What you are."

His wings flare in defiance. I sigh, and tuck the phone back in my pocket. Kai smirks, and goes to take another swig of whisky. I swipe the bottle from his hand and gulp it myself. Cinnamon burns my tongue, blooming heat in my belly. Kai's unbuttoned jeans sit low on his hips, sparking a similar kind of heat. I drink another measure and slam the bottle on his chest of drawers, well out of reach.

"Then we do this the hard way," I say.

I grab his arm and yank him off the bed. Hot skin collides with mine. I drag him towards the door I'm hoping leads to an en-suite, otherwise his walk-in cupboard is about to get messy. His arm flails and I stumble, my back and skull hitting the door frame and rattling my teeth.

He's stronger. If he weren't addled by booze and drugs, I might have a problem.

His bare feet paddle on faux-marble linoleum. I get a better grip, forcing his arm up behind him and propelling him forward.

"What're you doing, you—"

I swipe his legs. He drops to his knees, and I wrestle his head over the toilet bowl. He slaps at me with one wing. Hair blinds my eyes. I jam my fingers in his cheeks, forcing his mouth open. He struggles harder, alternating between trying to shove off the toilet and batting at me. It takes everything I have to hold him in position. My index finger slides into his mouth, my other hand keeping him from biting down. Furious breath scorches my skin. He lunges for my wrists. My finger caresses slick muscle and the hard ball of his piercing.

He gargles what may be, "No!" then I reach the back of his throat.

Wet tissues constrict against my finger. His ribs clench, and he gags. Scalding fluid rushes into his mouth. I pull away and slump against the shower cubicle, heart and lungs working hard. Kai vomits into the toilet. One heave follows another until he collapses, hugging the bowl, his head on his arms. The sharp stench of bile stings my nose, underlain by sweet cinnamon. My stomach churns in sympathy.

"I hate you," Kai groans.

"I know," I say.

I whip a towel from the rail beside the sink and hand it to him. It takes him two tries to pluck it from my hold. He scrubs his face. I haul myself upright and splash water into a plastic cup. Kai rinses his mouth, spitting into the toilet and gulping the rest. Capsules float in a scum of chunks, most partly digested.

Hopefully his Lesser metabolism can heal whatever damage he's done to his brain and liver.

"You ruined my life," he mumbles, and spits. "Why do you care if I die?"

"Oh, fuck you," I say, surprising myself. "Everything I did was to keep you alive and you're going to waste it with suicide?"

"Again—why do you care?"

"Again—fuck you."

A dangerous little thrill shivers through me. It shouldn't feel this good to curse. Kai is a bad influence.

"You swear a lot, for a monster." His voice echoes in the toilet bowl.

I swallow a third, "Fuck you," and say mildly, "Well I can't swear in front of anyone else. It's not proper."

"It's not proper to swear but it's okay to kidnap people and bite off limbs?"

"I don't make the rules."

"Maybe you should."

He flops over the toilet, one hand limp and trailing on the linoleum, his eyes closed. His breathing is still too slow and laboured. I coax him back to bed before he drowns in his puke, and tuck him in, banishing his wings so he doesn't shred the covers. He touches my cheek, and I freeze. He frowns, swimming up from semi-unconsciousness. His hand fists and he hugs it to his torso.

"How do you know where I live?"

"Your driver's licence," I say, my voice even.

"How did you know to come?"

I cross to the chest of drawers for another swig of his cinnamon-spiced whisky, and lean my bum on the cabinet.

"Where's your girlfriend?"

He snorts. "What girlfriend?"

"Does she live here?"

His eyes glitter. "Nobody lives here anymore."

I swallow more whisky to hide from his expression. The warm glow spreads from my gut to my chest and wobbles into my head.

What would happen if I kept drinking, Kai sobering to find me passed out on his carpet? Having never been drunk, it wouldn't take much. Probably best not to test him.

I leave the bottle on the chest of drawers, and perch on the bed. There's no chair and I'm tired. Kai appears to be fighting his coma, unwilling to submit.

"It's been three days," he mutters, "how has this healed?"

He shows me his arm, branded forever by the scar of my teeth. I stroke the white tissue, and he sighs. I fold my hands carefully in my lap.

"Think of it as a perk," I say. "You might heal all wounds that fast."

"Great," he mutters. "No girlfriend, no job, no friends but at least I heal good."

"I'm—"

Don't you *dare* say you're his friend.

"How did you lose your job?" I say instead.

His teeth flash in a snarl. "*I* didn't lose my job. Your bitch sister lost me my job."

I shift on the bed. The headboard creaks. Kai's eyes dart

beneath his closed lids as if he's dreaming. His chest is still. I count the seconds. His heart thuds. Slow, slower. He sucks in a loud breath, and I jump.

"What else have you lost?" I whisper in the hushed room.

His head lolls on his pillow.

He blinks at me. "What?"

"Why do you have a tattoo for loss and bad luck? What did you lose?"

"Who, not what," he says after a pause.

"Who did you lose?"

Why am I questioning him while he's barely aware? It doesn't matter what his background is. After tonight, I'll never see him. I *can't* see him. Unless he tries to kill himself again.

"My foster parents," he finally says, his words slurred.

"And your real parents?"

He jerks as if electrocuted, bouncing us both on the mattress.

"Fuck them. I wish they were dead and not just in prison."

"Why?" I say softly.

He lifts his head and spears me with stormy grey.

"Leave me alone, Syn."

I cuddle my knees to my chest. Kai sags on the bed as if his burst of clarity has exhausted him. His muscles relax, though his body twitches. Still resisting the inexorable pull of unconsciousness.

"Just sleep, Kai," I say in a soothing tone. "You'll feel better in the morning."

"I don't want to sleep." Panic flits across his face. He grabs my arm. "What if I die?"

"You're not going to die."

"I don't want to die," he says, his gaze far away, his fingers blanching my arm. "The pills. Stupid. Drank too much."

"It'll be okay. You threw most of them up."

"What am I going to do?" He tosses his head from side to side. "I can't go back on the streets. I *can't*."

He lived on the streets?

I open my mouth and shut it again.

Leave him alone, Syn.

I brush my fingers across his forehead, and he stills. His racing heart slows. I stroke his hair and he nuzzles my hand. I bite my lip on a sudden well of ridiculous emotion.

"Sleep, Kai," I say huskily.

"Why do you care?" he whispers.

I wish I knew.

14

Kai slips into sleep and I stay beside him, listening to him breathe. In case he stops.

Darn it, why do I have to care? My life would be so much easier if I were the heartless bitch I pretended to be.

I wriggle to get comfortable, and stretch my legs out. Sleep calls to me, whispering how good it will feel to shut my eyes. To snuggle in the warmth and coconut scent of Kai. But I doubt he'd be too happy waking up next to me. He probably won't remember much of our conversation, only that I stormed into his flat, dragged him from his bed and stuck my finger down his throat.

He whimpers and turns onto his side. His arm slides around my waist, his hand cupping my hip. The movement tugs the sheet loose. My fingers hover over the raven on his ribs, aching to trace the lines. I curl my hand into a fist like Kai did earlier.

No. I will not touch him when he can't consent. I've done enough.

I ease out of bed and look down at him. Ten minutes pass. Twenty? His chest rises and falls. I follow the curve of each muscle with my eyes if not my fingers. His face is relaxed in sleep, his earring lying in the hollow of his jaw. The feather twitches gently on his pulse. I force myself away when I reach for him again, my fingers itching to caress a perfect cheekbone and the smile lines at the corner of his mouth.

'Whore' is scrawled on his door in paint, the anger of the author evident in each slash of red. Drips streak the white and splatter the floor.

His girlfriend or her brother? Seems more a male thing. A woman would rip all his clothes and toss them in the street, though the locks on his bedroom door may have prevented that—a deadbolt and two sliding bolts. So why didn't he lock himself in to die? Not that it would have stopped me.

I prowl through the rest of the flat. The second bedroom further down the hall is empty except for dust balls and a torn poster of the rock band Paramore. The air holds a hint of Lynx body spray.

So Kai doesn't live with his girlfriend. Ex-girlfriend. There were no feminine products scattered throughout his en-suite to indicate she's a regular feature. Was his flatmate the brother? That would explain the insult.

Another bathroom opens off the hall, not even the toilet paper left behind. The final door leads to a square living room with two windows facing Summerhall across the street. The pattern of dust on the carpet suggests there used to be a couch and maybe a TV stand. An archway gives access to the kitchen, the linoleum scuffed from years of tenants. All the cupboards and drawers have been ransacked, not a single piece of cutlery left behind. The larger appliances remain—fridge but no food, washing machine but no detergent.

Is this what Kai returned to on Sunday? One shock after another and no one there to offer comfort. How quickly the friend and girlfriend abandoned him. Her brother must have gutted the flat in the hours it took Kai to escape home.

Allowing no explanation.

Kai could have been date-raped for all the guy knew. If the guy had watched Kai instead of punching him, he would have seen Kai wasn't kissing Libby back but struggling as best he could in his hypnotised state. If the guy had paid attention and not jumped to conclusions, none of this would have happened. I wouldn't have had to hurt another person to save them.

Anger curdles in my gut.

And sometime between yesterday and today, Kai lost his job. But how was that Libby's fault? Unless he also worked with the brother.

Christ. Bad luck, indeed.

I peek in on Kai, who hasn't moved, his tempting, sexy shape curled beneath the covers.

Sexy shape? For goodness' sake, Madisyn, get a hold of yourself.

No. For *fuck's* sake. Fuck is my new favourite word. For now and only ever in my head when I'm back with my family.

I slip from the flat and leap down the stairs, hustling to the Best-One convenience store on the corner. Open until 10pm. How convenient. I load a basket with margarine, bread, jam, peanut butter, a bottle of cola, canned coffee, snacks and some fruit, tossing in a packet of paper plates and plastic cutlery. Back in the flat, I leave the dried food on the bunker and put the perishables in the fridge.

Kai continues to breathe and sleep. I lie next to him and stare at a crack in the ceiling. Each exhale brushes my cheek with the faint sharpness of vomit but I can't blame him.

He's had another hard night.

I turn my head and memorise his face for when *I* have a hard night.

His hair is tousled all over the place and flopping across his forehead. Black lashes fan against his cheekbones. He has a tiny scar on his eyebrow I've never noticed before, and his nose has a slight bump as if it's been broken. Tiny imperfections that only make him more perfect.

I snort, and roll to my feet. I tell myself not to but can't resist snooping.

His leather jacket hangs on the back of his bedroom door, supple under my fingertips. The chest of drawers is stuffed with books instead of clothes. A mix of genres from literary to science fiction and even a smattering of romance. Black t-shirts stitched with a white 'W' hang in his cupboard next to a couple of shirts, various coloured t-shirts, a green hoodie that would look great with his hair, and one pair of dress trousers. The shelves are taken up by jeans, socks and tight little boxers that give me a hot flush. His bedside cabinet contains a notepad and pencil, condoms and mints. Under his bed is a simple wooden box but I curl my fingers to keep from reaching for it.

Let the man have some secrets, you nosy boot.

In the bathroom, I flush the vomit away and splash water on my face, running my fingers through my dishevelled hair. My eyeliner has smudged so I look like a goth.

The mirrored medicine cabinet reveals male grooming products and aspirin. Another box of condoms—lucky guy— but no more oxycodone. A single toothbrush and a tube of toothpaste rest on the sink. A bottle of coconut bodywash hangs in the shower, and I rub a little on my hands.

I fill the cup with more water and put it on Kai's bedside cabinet alongside a couple of aspirin. I drink a can of chilled coffee, and pace around his room for the next few hours, counting his breaths. The caffeine wears off and I lie next to him. I text Libby, setting my phone alarm for 5am.

There's no way I can stay awake until then without drinking all the coffee and Kai needs it more than me.

I doze. Kai wriggles closer and tucks his chin into my shoulder, an arm and leg thrown across me. I try to ignore the lump in my throat but a tear escapes to dampen my temple.

So this is what it's like to cuddle a boy.

* * *

My pocket vibrates and I snap to awareness. Kai breathes deep and steady against the nape of my neck, his body curled around my back, his arm over my side. His hand lies loose on my breast. I enjoy the closeness for a few minutes, blinking sleep from gritty eyes.

The lamp is still on, the world dark beyond the curtains. A lorry rumbles by on the road below.

I imagine being Kai's girlfriend. Waking him with teasing kisses to the half of his face not buried in the pillow. His mouth curving, one eye opening, sleepy and grey, darkening as the kisses become urgent. He'll roll and pin me, his lips hungry on mine. The sweep of his tongue and the hard bud of his piercing sending delicious tingles between my legs. The scrape of a drawer, the rip of a condom packet. The hollow ache satisfied as he slides inside me.

Morning sex. Is it as wonderful as I'm picturing or more an uncoordinated fumble and bad breath panted in your face? I guess I'll find out in a few months with Gerome the troll, whose only sexual finesse is to come in a sock rather than all over his bedsheets.

I swipe at another traitorous tear and ease out of Kai's arms, slipping into my sandals. He makes a little whimpering noise, and I almost climb right back into bed.

The Lesser connection is confusing my hormones and I'm due my period, so that probably doesn't help. It's also been a few months for me, sex-wise. I'm lonely and Kai happens to be the first cute male I've seen in a while. It will pass once he's out of my life, little left of him but a vague tug in my stomach and I'm pretty sure I can ignore that.

I leave a wad of cash on his bedside cabinet, though it doesn't sit well with the screaming red expletive on his door. Services paid for. I rip a sheet from the notepad and scribble directions since no official address exists. My final words to Kai are 'Go to Julian and Raine Romanov. They have answers, and sanctuary.'

I wish I could go. Show him the way and stay with him. Get him to forgive me.

But Julian, Raine and their band of refugees would see me dead before I set one foot inside their compound. It is a place of healing.

And I bring only pain.

15

My dinner date with Gerome is cancelled. I should be excited about avoiding his grabby hands and having time to curl up in bed and watch a weepy movie—happy ever after, girl gets boy, love conquers all—but there's a different event to attend. All plotted while I was saving Kai's life.

I knew I would regret it.

My breath puffs white in the air, joining the exhalations of the three other Drakul on our lawn. Low and heavy clouds darken the sky, spitting the occasional snow flurry. Our naked bodies glow in the absence of light. Gerome sneaks glances at Libby and me and, when my father's attention is elsewhere, the twins. A shameful lack of propriety and control. Gerome catches my glare and his gaze drops to his feet.

Hairy, like his back. Yuck.

My mind conjures Kai, smooth skin everywhere—okay, maybe not everywhere—but I squash it down.

"Ready, Irena?" Dad says.

He's in good shape for a man in his fifties. Trim, no spare flesh to cause an unsightly bulge.

"Of course, Jackson dear," Irena says.

The years have not been so kind to the Kaskbirch matriarch, though her arse has always been as wide as a bus. The rest of her sags and rolls, her figure more rounded than her blocky husband and son.

Dad smiles a sharp smile. "Then, per your request, follow as I lead to remove the traitor and his scourge."

Apparently, Irena wasn't as enthused about Libby's loyalty test as she was with me marrying her troll of a son. When she mentioned getting rid of the remaining Romanovs, she no doubt meant for someone else to do it while she sat on her bum.

And I sent Kai to the Romanov compound. He's going to think I did it so I could include him in the slaughter. I've only delayed his death, not saved his life.

I shift into my dragon form before my expression can betray me, shaking the clear liquid of the change from my wings. Popping and groaning fill the terrace, quiet under the soughing of the wind. Snow peppers my flank and sticks without melting. My body temperature will remain cool until I ready my flame sacs, and I only plan on doing that for show.

I hope to kill as few people as possible tonight.

Six gold dragons chuff and paw at the grass, myself included as the smallest. It's an impressive display of power, along with the black dragons of Gerome and his father.

Nothing I said convinced Dad to delay his assault on the Romanov's territory. Stellar job by Libby there. I had to pretend I agreed as retribution for Dominic's death—my poor, sweet betrothed—while acting as the voice of reason for why we should wait for reinforcements. Dad called the other families but they all had an excuse: too far to travel, another engagement, blah blah blah. I suspect they're praying for a Della Valle death or two, allowing them to swoop into the void.

Dad launches skyward and we follow in a loose V formation, soon engulfed by the clouds. The air tastes of frost. Eady and Dory babble happily in my head, excited by the impending bloodbath, until Dad silences them with a word. Nausea sits in my stomach like a stone.

I can't even lie and tell myself Kai's not there. I know he's there. I feel him, closer and closer with each wingbeat.

Just his luck to get caught in the middle of a war.

I blink ice from my eyes. It crackles on my scales and falls in a tinkling rain to be captured by the wind.

It's a beautiful night for flying. No risk of detection. The whole sky ours, the world below tiny and ephemeral, shivering in the grip of winter. We are living stealth bombers, bringing fire and destruction.

'*Now,*' Dad says.

We drop as a unit, wings tucked to flanks. Orange blobs mark the streets of Peebles, the nearest village. Trees and hills cloak the Romanov compound in a swathe of forest, gaps showing snippets of grass and driveway, though the area is marked as a dangerous quarry on maps and appears blurry on satellite pictures. Once home to the terrifying Evelyn Romanov, now sanctuary to the Drakul, Lessers and Vanatori striving for a different way of life. A way not dictated by bloodlust and strength but peace and community.

Naive, perhaps, but I respect their courage.

We zoom over the treetops, the bare branches clattering in our wake and interspersed by fragrant pine. My chest burns as my flame sacs fill. We firebomb the front of the sprawling mansion. Windows shatter. My fireball splutters on the roof, the tiles flame retardant. Kai is in a room near the back, protected.

So far.

'Come and meet your death, Julian, traitor to the Romanov name!' Libby shrieks.

Eady and Dory roar but Dad shushes them. We bank over the house. A gun turret erupts on the roof and I have a second to think *that's new* before bullets patter into Irena. She wails and hits the tiles, cartwheeling over the peak to thud on the stone patio below.

'Mummy!' Gerome squeals.

He dives for his stricken mother, trailed closely by his father. My clawed foot swipes at the turret and it clatters on the roof, crashing next to Irena. People spill from the house and the entrance to the huge underground chamber where Evelyn Romanov liked to torture her friends, enemies and youngest son.

Oh, god, Kai is on the move.

Dad looses a wall of flame at the people converging on Irena. I wince but they scatter, singed. Gerome and his father support Irena between them, their wings flapping hard and hoisting her into the air. Crimson liquid dribbles down her hide, and she groans.

Dragon's-bane stings like a bitch and the Vanatori put it in everything. Awful little plant. I imagine the wounds themselves are also somewhat distracting.

'We must get her to safety,' Robert Kaskbirch says.

'Then you will return,' Dad replies.

Robert nods stiffly. He and his son carry Irena into the clouds, and dread curls in my stomach.

They're not coming back.

Drakul launch into the sky, all jewel-coloured and weak. I scan while I dodge but see no sign of Julian Romanov. He's easy to spot with his sleek, grey body and rainbow wings, so different from everyone else.

His mother despised his dragon form but I think it's pretty. When questioned, I said it was shameful and revolting.

I stay close to my family but steer them and the defending Drakul away from Kai. The night fills with teeth and claws and growls. I tackle a sapphire dragon slashing at Libby from behind, and slice a talon through the membrane of her wing.

'Rot in hell, Madisyn Della Valle,' Caysie says as she spirals towards the ground like a leaf from a branch.

Gunfire rattles, and Eady bleats in surprise. Before I can intervene, she turns the shooter into a flaming torch. The human screams and weaves through the trees, blazing orange. I lose sight of them but the horrible screams remain. Another figure aims at Eady. I swoop low and fast, flicking my tail and tumbling them backwards. A crossbow bolt whooshes an inch past my neck. I kick the ground and launch higher. Eady licks at a gash on her shoulder in an ungainly ball of wings and limbs. Libby continues to taunt the absent Julian, slashes bleeding on her flank. Saliva foams between her bared teeth, her eyes wild.

'Hit the house again,' Dad says, closing his jaws on the throat of an emerald Drakul. He shakes his head. Bone snaps and the dragon dissolves to ash that swirls in the wind.

We reform our V, Libby and me behind Dad on either side.

'There are more than I expected,' I say.

'I, too, had not realised they had gained such support.'

'We should turn back.'

'Soon,' he says.

We aim for the house. The other Drakul retreat. I fly over Kai, hidden by the trees.

What is he thinking? Does he know it's me? Why are the other dragons not harrying us?

I fly faster, drawing level with Dad. My eyes search the ground, the trees, the house. Something glitters. Delicate silver wire expands, like a mouth opening to swallow Dad.

I slam my shoulder into him. Despite my smaller size, the force nudges him to the side and he struggles to right himself. His wing slaps at Libby. I glimpse my sister's scowl.

Then I'm engulfed by searing, shrieking agony.

16

I thrash against the pain wrapped around me but it's everywhere, scalding my skin and drawing roars from my mouth. My wings are tangled in it.

A freaking dragon's-bane net.

Air whistles as I fall and I can't do a thing about it. I howl my agony to the indifferent, swirling clouds. Branches crunch and break my descent. I thud onto frozen ground, and my breath huffs out. The net loosens. The pain is too much. My dragon form melts but the searing, burning—*oh*-fuck-*it-hurts*—stay to torment me. I crawl, my palms and knees striped by fire, and reach the soothing wetness of grass. I collapse on my front, shivering and unable to hold in the whimpers. Blisters pop on my back as my skin tightens.

Dragon's-bane—a tiny, innocuous plant that brings the most powerful Drakul to their knees. Or their tits, given my current position. I wish I had Julian's tolerance, even if it is another sign of his weakness. I want to shove a bushel of dragon's-bane up the nose of anyone who's ever congratulated me on my sensitivity.

Dad calls for me but I can't answer in my human form.

'*Maddy,*' Libby says, though her voice sounds far away. '*Maddy, we'll come back for you.*'

Come back for me? Where the hell are they going?

Eady and Dory wail a lament.

'Be strong, Daughter. I love you,' Dad says.

And they're gone.

Other voices babble in my head, congratulating themselves on their victory, their thoughts broadcasting to every Drakul in their excitement. But they fade, too.

Footsteps thunder beneath my cheek pressed to the ground. Branches snap. People murmur. I tell myself to get up but my back is flayed, my skin raw and weeping. The pain is manageable now I'm no longer in contact with the dragon's-bane but I'm not up for running.

Oh, crap. Kai is close. Almost on me.

Maybe I can run after all.

I shove up on my hands. Red welts slash my arms, thighs and chest. My bare chest.

Naked and vulnerable and surrounded by enemies. I don't want Kai to see me like this.

I wobble to my feet. Torches sweep the vegetation and a group emerges from the trees. Anger and hatred twist their faces. I recognise a few—Lessers and Drakul I've hurt trying to help. Kai pushes to the front of the crowd, his light directed at the ground. He has a woollen hat pulled low against the cold so only the dyed tips of his hair stick out to frame his face. His eyes mirror the snow-laden clouds. His leather jacket is definitely not warm enough for a human, though he's wearing fingerless gloves. His jeans are wet at the knees.

Stop staring at him and run, fool.

I pivot on the ball of my foot and throw myself between the trunks. Pine cones and needles spear my soles. A branch whips my cheek in a stinging line.

I need a few minutes to recover before I can shift again. Ten, maybe twenty. A traumatic change from dragon to human uses a lot of energy and now my body is healing, I'm using even more. I suppose I can lead everyone on a merry chase round and around the inside of the fence surrounding the Romanov compound.

I leap a mossy hunk of deadwood. A weight tackles me in mid-air and drives the breath from my body in a whoosh. I lose a few seconds to the pain in my back. The sky swirls. Swaying branches make me dizzy. I blink and Kai is straddling me, pinning my arms above my head. I struggle against his hands but he leans closer, more weight on my wrists.

Fast and strong. Now, that's just unfair. Lessers should be our minions not our masters. Libby never had this problem with any of hers.

Kai stares at me in silence, his expression unreadable. Carefully empty. He doesn't look at my boobs. Not once. And I thought men would look at boobs even if they were stuck to a pile of dog shit.

Does he think I came to kill him? Does he still hate me?

Or course he hates you.

"Kai." My voice breaks on his name. I lick my lips and try again. "Kai, I'm—"

Flaming agony engulfs my ankle. My 'sorry' dissolves into a shriek. Kai's weight disappears. Voices shout. I jackknife to a sitting position, my teeth gritted on another hellish wail. The offending manacle is removed. The woman holding it in gloved hands sneers at me. She's the sapphire dragon I stopped from attacking Libby—Caysie Vanderbelt.

"She's making a fuss because she doesn't want to be chained," she says, flicking her brown hair over her shoulder impatiently.

"It doesn't hurt that much."

"Look at her ankle," Kai says, directing his torch though she doesn't need it.

Blisters circle bright-red skin. I hug one leg to my chest to hide my shaking hands. A sharp stone digs into my buttock.

Caysie sniffs, her hazel eyes hot. "So what? Let it burn her skin off. She wouldn't show us mercy."

I bite my lip instead of screaming, "What I did to you, any of you, *was* mercy."

My icy mask is firmly on and I give them nothing but disdain. Now that the dragon's-bane isn't burning me, of course.

"Caysie, you know Julian and Raine won't let you torture her," an unfamiliar man says, an accent rounding out his serious words.

He holds a crossbow loose at his side, though the muscles in his arm bunch with the effort. The torch mounted on the top highlights a circle of dirt and pine needles. A Vanatori, I think. Tall, dark and American.

"She needs to be chained or she'll shift and escape," Caysie says with a scowl.

She's never liked me, even before I hurt her. It's not my fault she's insecure about her plain features and shapeless figure. Though, even if she'd got over her jealousy, we could never have been friends. A powerful family cannot associate with the weak.

"What if we wrap the metal so it doesn't touch her?" Kai says.

I feign interest in my fingers clamped to my leg to hide the flash of gratitude. My hair slides across to mask me further.

"That'll work," the hunter says.

Caysie huffs. She keeps flicking glances at Kai but his focus is on me. Someone in the crowd passes bandages forward and the manacle is covered, the chain snaking to an honest-to-god ball. Caysie glowers harder and hesitates before clicking the manacle around my uninjured ankle.

She definitely wanted to snap it right on my blisters.

I tense but there's no pain.

Good. I've had about enough of dragon's-bane tonight.

"Stand up," Caysie growls.

I wait until her fists clench then climb to my feet. Her brother, Cameron, appears at her shoulder, holding a pair of bandaged handcuffs connected by a long chain. Shorter brown hair, same hazel eyes.

He glares as hotly as his sister. "Hold out your wrists."

"Wait." Kai clamps his torch between his knees and shrugs out of his leather jacket, offering it to me. "Here."

Caysie looks like she's been slapped but her hurt expression quickly slides into another sneer.

"You know wanting to please her is a side effect of her making you a Lesser, right? That happiness you get when she's around is just another way for her to manipulate you." Caysie directs her sneer at me. "And she doesn't feel the cold."

"She's naked."

"So? She loves being naked. Everyone's attention on her."

Hardly. I'd rather be in my pyjamas, in bed, fingering Kai's carving. And maybe something else.

I smile at Caysie and say nothing. Her jaw bunches, her eyes narrowed to slits. Kai shivers, still holding his jacket.

"Put it back on, Kai," I say. "Caysie's right."

Instead of being smug, Caysie frowns even more. I raise my arms, head high, back straight. Showcasing my best assets. Caysie seems to have swallowed something unpleasant.

Cameron fastens the cuffs around my wrists and darts away as if I'll bite him, though not before he has a peek at my tits. A woman approaches with a wrapped collar attached to a long pole—Ailish. Another fan of mine.

Dad made her a Lesser, and a servant. Libby loved to taunt her.

"Is that necessary?" Kai says, huddled in his jacket.

"Don't let the skinny bint fool you." Ailish settles the collar at my throat and snaps it closed. "She's as devious as a rattlesnake."

"I missed you, too, Ailish," I say.

She spits at my feet but the wind curls a glob onto her burn-scarred cheek. She swipes at it, and tugs on the pole.

"Get moving."

I take a couple of careful steps to avoid touching uncovered chain with my bare foot until the ball rolls behind me. I hold my arms wide and slightly away from my body to keep the handcuff chain taught. Ailish jerks the collar, and I stumble. She smirks at me over her broad, swimmer's shoulder. A lock of ginger hair falls across her face, shaved short underneath. I give her a pleasant smile as hollow as my stomach.

It's nice to know Julian and Raine aren't into torture but there are other ways to ruin me. Or they could just kill me. On the bright side, I won't have to marry Gerome Kaskbirch.

I lose sight of Kai. It takes a lot of concentration to drag the ball, and place my feet. The manacle chafes despite the bandages. Torchlights bob between the trunks. My captors lead me through the trees to the entrance of the underground chamber. Wide, uneven stairs spiral down.

I have so many awful memories of this place, though I'm sure Julian has more.

Ailish yanks the collar. I give her my iciest look, and she turns her head but not quick enough to hide a flash of fear.

Our procession starts down the stairs. I manage two steps then the ball clunks on stone and rolls past me—*clonk, clonk, clonk*—sliding the bare chain over my foot. I gasp, and bend my leg until the weight spins the chain away. Ailish keeps going without looking back.

I wobble on one foot. "Ailish, wait—"

The collar tightens on the nape of my neck. I topple, and the pole punches me in the throat before it whips out of Ailish's grip. I collide with her broad shoulders and push off without thinking. She tumbles down the stairs. The thwack of her soft body on stone cuts off her yell. She disappears around the first bend while I overbalance and sit hard on my bum.

The Drakul have faster reflexes than Lessers. Usually.

Silence greets Ailish's vanishing act. It quickly grows oppressive, weighted by the furious stares of everyone behind me.

"You did that deliberately, you vengeful cow," Caysie hisses.

She shoves past me and a trickle of people follow, all throwing me a nasty look. Their footsteps fade.

"She should have waited," I say.

God, I sound callous. But it's what they expect. I can't melt now and show the liquid core of the real Madisyn Della Valle. If word got back to the powerful families, they'd think I was a sympathiser and use it as further evidence for why Dad should be removed.

Cameron scoops up the pole but hesitates, his fingers barely touching the handle. His gaze darts from me to where the steps turn out of sight. Angry, exhaled breath heats my neck.

"If you don't want the same thing to happen, remove the

ball and chain," I say.

Cameron shakes his head, his hair slapping back and forth.

"Then drag me," I say, "because I'm not moving."

His face flushes dull crimson. The mumbles at my back suggest tossing me down the stairs would suit them just fine. Unless I crack my head open or break my neck, I'll heal.

Ailish might not.

"For Christ's sake, I'll carry it," Kai says.

He appears on my step and picks up the ball, straightening the chain. I stand slowly. He keeps his gaze fixed in front. Our procession restarts.

I tell myself I don't have a lump in my throat from Kai refusing to look at me. It doesn't matter what he thinks. I'm protecting myself and my family, like I've always done.

Even if it makes me miserable.

We meet a group coming up the stairs carrying Ailish on a makeshift stretcher. A bloodstained bandage covers her head, her eyes closed. The paleness of her skin highlights a scattering of freckles across her nose. Caysie, holding the front of the stretcher, renews her scowl.

"If she dies, I'll…"

I raise one eyebrow.

I've practised this look in the mirror. Perfect, haughty contempt that shrivels any defiance.

Caysie's gaze zips away.

"One day you'll get what you deserve, Madisyn Della Valle," she mumbles, and hoofs the wounded Ailish up the stairs.

If only she knew how much I punish myself.

Finally, we reach the bottom. A huge cavern supported by pillars on either side extends into the distance. It was lit by flickering candle flame that heightened the terror of anyone dragged down there but now a warm, electric glow casts from the ceiling. Fairy lights twinkle around each pillar. The Romanovs used the space to change and fly when it was daylight but they'd struggle to do any flying today. Partitions fill the gaps around the pillars and the wall, leaving a central, communal aisle. A swatch of coloured fabric covers the entrance of each room, some tied back to give glimpses of bunk-beds and cabinets. Some of the cubicles on the right contain bathrooms, showers and cooking facilities. The air smells of smoke and incense and sweat.

It's like a hippie commune.

The murmur of people slowly fades as their attention focuses on me. It appears most of the Lessers stayed during the attack rather than get in the way of the Vanatori and Drakul who are better suited for a fight.

Does Kai live down here?

Cameron jiggles the pole. I walk instead of testing if he's brave enough to jerk me into motion. Footsteps echo in the silence. My name shivers through the clumps of people we approach. I keep my head high when it turns to insults and some very uncomplimentary language.

It seems the lower classes of Drakul society have no problem with swearing. How fucking uncouth.

Cameron leads me almost to the far end of the cavern where Evelyn's dais remains but her throne and the dragon statues have been removed. Kai carries my ball without comment.

The scraping would have been horrendous in the whispering quiet.

The Vanatori male who admonished Caysie's lust for my pain jogs ahead to open a barred door recessed into the wall, the stink of dragon's-bane obvious in the metal. The narrow cell has a simple, fold-down bed panel fixed to the wall with chains, and a silver bowl on the floor beneath it. Cameron fastens the end of the pole to a loop in the wall. He twists the cylinder and it breaks in half, the pieces held together by wire, giving me more manoeuvrability. Kai drops the ball, and leaves, still not looking at me.

Nope, not upset about that.

Cameron hustles after him, practically sliding around the walls to avoid coming anywhere near me.

I wiggle my foot. "You could at least remove the ball and chain. It's not like I'm going anywhere."

"Better safe than sorry," he squeaks, clanging the door shut.

"Then what about a pair of socks?" I shout to his departing back.

My welcoming committee disbands after more stock insults, leaving me with a tiny slice of the cavern through the bars of the door. There are no rooms obstructing the view in front of my cell so I can see all the way across to a toilet block on the other side. The patrons take the time to sneer before they head in for a piss.

No sign of the famous Julian or his soulmate, Raine. Part of me is relieved. It's hard to be viewed as scum by the people you secretly admire and wish were your friends, especially when they're right—I am scum.

What in the hell are they going to do to me?

17

The Drakul don't sweat easily so I plonk my bare buttocks on the hard plastic sheet of the bed panel without fear of leaving a bum print. It's not exactly comfortable since I can't lower my arms or I'll burn myself on the handcuffs. The bed sits high, my feet dangling a couple of inches off the ground, enough to keep the chain attached to the ball away from delicate skin.

Trying to sleep is going to be a bitch.

Footsteps approach through the general cacophony of heartbeats and conversation, most of it muttering my name in vain. I sigh and slide carefully to my feet.

The male shadowing my doorway looks the same as when I saw him last—same flop of chestnut hair, same striking eyes, one green, one amber—but also different. Confident. Comfortable in his own body. No flinching around the eyes, expecting every movement to bring a slap.

Julian Romanov, last surviving son of Evelyn Romanov. I still have a bit of a girl crush on him.

"Hello, Maddy," he says, tucking a cloth bundle under his arm and opening the door.

Libby would have an apoplexy if she heard him call me that. Short names are for friends, family and lovers. Full names are for enemies, the weak and when Dad is mad at us.

I quirk my mouth. "Jules. I love what you've done with the place."

He stands close to me with an easy smile, and it's cute but Kai's is cuter. Those dimples.

Julian ignores my nudity, his eyes on my face. He's in grabbing distance but I doubt I can wrestle him for the keys and unlock my many chains before someone responds to the kerfuffle.

And I don't want to.

He places the bundle on my bed, and removes the cuffs from my wrists and the manacle from my ankle. No gloves since his dragon's-bane tolerance is pretty high.

"I didn't have much choice with clothes," he says, straightening from his vulnerable, crouched position. "No one wanted to volunteer. This was the best I could do."

I finger the scraps of material. "I'm not surprised someone wanted rid of these."

He grins. I've never seen him grin. It sparkles in his eyes and brightens his face, making me a little breathless.

I hurriedly pull on the clothes. The top is beige and shapeless enough to step into since the collar is in the way. Even my superior assets fail to appeal, lost beneath the bulge, my arms bare. The harem pants are lime green, miles wide and end above my ankle. The socks are men's athletic socks, one black, one white.

It's not a great ensemble but that's probably the idea. Someone will be sniggering about it in their little cubicle.

The humour fades from Julian's face.

"You were cold and dismissive but never cruel to me," he says. "Why?"

Crap. I guess when everyone else hurts you, you take note

of the ones who don't.

I'm saved from answering—or being cold and dismissive—by the slap of boots on stone and the rapid thud of a heartbeat.

"Is this her?" pants a female voice. "Is this Libelle Della Valle?"

A tiny whirlwind blasts into the cell, an explosion of dirty-blonde hair falling past her shoulders. Intelligent green eyes complement her elfin face and sweep me head to toe. She's dressed in black leather, the hilt of a sword sticking over her shoulder. Julian slings an arm around her and she cuddles into his side.

"This is Madisyn—her younger sister," he says.

Raine looks up at him with an expression of adoration, seeming to forget my presence. A lick of jealousy heats my stomach.

No one's ever looked at me like that.

My parents were the same. Always touching. My dad watched my mother as if she was the most wonderful thing in the world. That's what I want—love and awe, not hate and blood. Or indifference and unsatisfactory humping in an empty marriage.

Raine blinks and her sharp gaze refocuses on me.

"Your sister's mouth has a date with my fist," she says.

A smile tugs at my lips. "She probably deserves it."

Drat. I like her. I knew I would. Small but strong. Says, "To hell with it," to convention and does what she wants to be happy.

"Did you hurt him?" she says softly, a protective glint in her eye.

I glance at Julian. He gives me his blank face, perfected, like mine was, in a society where the wrong expression could lead to punishment.

"Nothing punch-worthy." I keep my gaze on Julian. "They'll come for me."

"I know," he says, though not like he's worried about it. "But I have a plan that'll buy us some time."

"What's going to happen to me?"

He cocks his head. "That's up to you."

With that cryptic comment, they exit my cell. I track their departure by the people who call to them. Excited, angry, sad. Two people died during our assault—the dragon Dad killed and the hunter Eady set on fire. Several voices advocate for my swift execution. Julian answers them all with understanding but his message is firm—I'm not to be harmed.

Why not? My family participated in his torture, Libby worst of all. We represent a rotten hierarchy based on brutality, strength and fear.

I perch on the edge of my bed, scratching carefully under the collar around my neck.

I appreciate Julian's lack of bloodlust but he can't be around every second. What happens when he's not watching? Poor Madisyn has an accident.

I fiddle with the wide spread of my harem pants. Gosh, they're ugly.

My initial trepidation from being captured has faded. Now, I'm just... curious. How does everyone live here? What are Julian and Raine actually like beyond the traitor and abomination rubbish I have to spout? Julian suffered twenty-six years of abuse, trying and failing to be the son Evelyn Romanov wanted before he stood up for himself. Maybe in three more years, I'll have enough courage to change something. To find my own slice of happiness.

If I'm not executed by lynch mob.

"People really hate you, don't they?" a voice says outside my cell.

My stupid little heart flutters and I take a deep breath to mask it, forgetting Kai only has human hearing. Or maybe that's another delayed ability, like his increased strength and speed. Though the two times I've been with him he was traumatised or drugged so they may not have shown.

The cell is small enough, I can reach the door despite the pole attached to the wall. I don't touch the bars, craning my head until I glimpse scuffed trainers and the hem of jeans to the right of the entrance.

"I didn't know we were going to attack," I say. "I wouldn't have sent you here otherwise."

"Why do you care what happens to me?"

I listen to him breathe and count the steady thud of his heart.

"You can't hide behind silence forever, Syn."

I cross my arms, though he can't see. "Yes, I can."

"What else are you hiding?"

More silence.

He snorts. "Well, you were right—Julian gave me answers. Shame I didn't like them."

"Any one in particular?" I say in my mildest voice.

"Let's see—you always knowing where I am; the fact I want to touch you; being so *content* when you're close, like a goddamn dog. *Fuck.*" He sighs. "Why do the wings have to have freaking spikes? They ruin all my clothes. I almost lost a bloody eye."

I swallow past a lump in my throat. "You swear a lot."

He makes a strangled noise, half-chuckle, half-growl. I slide down the wall next to the door, knees tucked to my chin. The collar throttles me but I picture Kai on the other side. We'd be back to back in this position, without the wall in between.

"I'm sorry," I whisper, so quietly he may not hear me.

It's for the best. Admitting fault is too much already. A weakness. The guy gets under my skin despite my trusty ice maiden armour.

"Why?" he says.

I bite my lip to keep the words in but they roll through my brain: because I never wanted to hurt you. Because I wish our meeting in the club could've developed into something pleasant, though your girlfriend would have ruined that little fantasy. Because...

Kai sighs again. Shoes scrape. Cloth whispers on stone.

"Goodbye, Syn," he says.

And he leaves me alone.

18

I soon discover the purpose of the silver bowl under my bed when my reasonable requests to use the bathroom go ignored. I tuck myself into the wall beside the door, and squat. My pee makes a pleasant ringing when it strikes metal. Having nothing to wipe with, I jiggle as best I can and toe the bowl close to the door, careful not to spill. A couple of Lessers wandering past look at the contents and sneer at me. I stare back until their gazes drop.

Let the humiliations begin.

What are my family doing—lying awake, fraught with worry? Planning my liberation? How many will they kill to rescue me? I'm sick of people always having to die.

My mind quiets to match the hush of the cavern, heartbeats settling, the muffled coughs and tossing almost comforting. The main lights have been switched off, the fairy lights on the pillars offering a soothing glow. Someone moans, quickly smothered. In fact, there are a few rhythmic noises punctuating the peace. Sex to celebrate victory and loss.

Kai isn't one of the moaners, thank god. He's back in the house above ground.

Does he moan? Man, there's nothing sexier than a guy's pleasure sounds when he's lost to sensation. At the mercy of my touch. Vulnerable and quivering for release, each groan pooling heat in my belly—

Darn it. I've got myself all worked up but there's no way I'm letting everyone listen to me masturbate.

I roll onto my side, my back to the door. Wonky initials are scratched into the stone near my nose—SC, DW & NR were here.

Well, MDV is here, too.

Sleep teases me. My muscles relax. Something slams on metal and I snap awake but no one lurks at the door, their shuffles of approach and retreat masked by the accumulated noise of people in one space. The echoes confuse it further. It happens every time I'm on the verge of dropping into gentle unconsciousness. Someone bangs on the bars or hisses an expletive then scuttles away. It's like they've made a schedule. I count the hours by them.

Needless to say, I'm not a happy bunny come morning. My eyes sting, my body sluggish and heavy. Hunger claws at my stomach, my mouth dry.

A skinny boy appears outside my cell holding a ceramic bowl. He unlocks a barred panel in the centre of the door and slides it open.

One of our Lessers. Libby made him. She loved to screw him because he cried during the act, though he was always hard for her.

Sometimes, I despair at my sister.

The boy spits a chunky glob into my porridge and sets it on the edge of the open panel.

"Breakfast befitting a Della Valle," he says, and pivots on his heel.

One bound gets me to the door and I Frisbee the bowl at his

departing figure. The sticky mixture splatters on his lower back and non-existent bum. The ceramic shatters on the stone floor. The red burn on my arm is worth it for his startled expression.

My smile is cold and cruel and painful. "I'll tell Libby you said hi."

His face pales and he appears ten years old. Tears glisten in his eyes as he hustles away. Guilt punches into my stomach.

Sometimes, I despair at myself.

If only he knew the number of times I waylaid my sister from humping him, he wouldn't be spitting in my porridge. Just the thought of keeping Libby distracted from her own sadism exhausts me even more. Maybe I should think of my captivity as a vacation. No family to manage, no Gerome to placate.

Did Irena survive her wounds? If she dies, the wedding is off. No matriarch and no gold means the Kaskbirches slide way down the power scale. The next eligible bachelor to ruin my life would be the son of the Barreras. He's easier on the eye but he eats people's pets.

Caysie is my next visitor, twirling the bandaged handcuffs around her finger. She sniffs at the mess on the floor and delicately steps around it.

"Put your hands through the gap." Her frown smooths into a mocking smile. "Oh, isn't that just bad luck for you?"

I glance down at myself. Spots of blood seep through my harem pants.

Brilliant. So the stomach cramps weren't just hunger.

"Spare a girl some tampons?" I say.

Caysie bares her teeth. "You're a monster, not a girl. It's time for you to bleed."

Well, d'uh. I have my period.

I paste on my haughty, fazed-by-nothing face and stick my arms through the slot in the door, avoiding the metal. Outrage curdles in my stomach with the bile. Caysie claps the handcuffs on my wrists and opens the cell. She leads me across the cavern. My full bladder complains.

Will I piss myself to top off my disgrace?

"Ailish will recover," Caysie says without turning around, "though I'm sure you don't care. She has a concussion."

I ease out a breath. The last thing I want is another death on my conscience but I stay mute. Caysie won't believe me if I say something nice and I've had my fill of cruelty for the morning.

I need coffee.

Caysie walks into the closest bathroom, and my bladder twitches. She kicks a pile of cleaning supplies to the side of the door, her smug smile back in place.

"Scrub all the toilets and showers," she says. "They better sparkle or I'll make you keep doing it until your nails fall off."

She slides past me and cups my arm. I hiss and jerk away. A delicate, white-veined leaf nestles in the palm of her hand. A triangular welt rises on my bicep.

"We all have one," she grins, "in case you have plans to make a fuss. Let's see how you like being a slave."

The door slams behind her. I ignore the various sprays and bottles, and hustle into the nearest cubicle. My sigh of relief is almost a groan. Wiping is a balance between holding the chain of my cuffs taut with one hand and dabbing myself with the other. I clean blood from my legs but it's just going to get worse.

I have no underwear and can hardly waddle around with a

ball of tissues stuffed between my thighs.

I wash my hands, splashing palmfuls of cold water on my face. My reflection in the mirror stares at me with tired eyes and tangled hair. The pink dye clashes with my horrendous trousers. I slurp from the tap and wash myself quickly. Red-stained water swirls down the plughole, and I feel refreshed for a second, until more blood dribbles out to itch on my thighs and stain my trousers. My stomach and legs ache.

Today is not going to be fun.

For the next few hours, I scrub sinks, toilets and showers. I polish mirrors and mop the floors.

It must have cost a fortune to get this place plumbed.

My knees hurt, my hands wrinkled and pink from the cleaning fluids. My nose is numbed to the stink of bleach. Lessers, Vanatori and a few Drakul come and go. Each one tries to touch me with a dragon's-bane leaf and most succeed, stippling my arms red. Caysie shoves my lunch sandwich down her pants before giving it to me. I toss it in the bin when she leaves and hope she gets a yeast infection.

Kai stays in the house.

I tell myself I'm relieved. If I didn't want him to see me naked and surrounded by enemies, I definitely don't want him to see me in the world's ugliest clothes patterned by lovely brown and red splashes of period blood.

By dinner, I'm woozy with hunger, though I've been able to drink as much as I want from the taps. I'm on my screaming knees, scrubbing what I pray is my last toilet. I blow lank hair from my eyes and work the foamy brush under the rim.

Boots clomp on tile. Two people.

I stretch my sore back and brace my hands on the sparkling ceramic to help me stand. Bodies cram into my cubicle.

Fingers clamp my biceps, pressing the cursed leaves to tender skin. My scream turns to bubbles when they shove my face in the toilet. Hard hands pin my head, the sting of the dragon's-bane muted by my hair. I struggle but my bound hands slide on squeaky-clean tile.

I can picture my tombstone now: here lies Madisyn Della Valle, drowned in a toilet bowl. The bitch deserved it.

I choke on water, and thank god it's fresh and not the unflushed present that was waiting for me when I stepped into the cubicle. If I'm going to die in a toilet, at least it's clean.

I heave upwards and ram my elbow back at crotch level, one side then the other, moving my linked arms together. Twin grunts echo in the small space. My attackers curse and stumble away. The door creaks and slams. I collapse on the floor in a shivering, spluttering heap, and curl around the toilet.

It reminds me of Kai when I made him throw up but I was trying to save him, not drown him.

A puddle of toilet water forms under my head. I cough the last of it from my lungs, and sit up. My sack of a top is soaked and sticking to me. Water dribbles from the ends of my hair, the rest plastered to my cheeks.

I'm done. I want to go back in my cell where it's safe.

I leave everything where I dropped it and shoulder out of the bathroom. A crowd of angry people greets me at the door.

Oh, *come on.*

19

This is the problem with acting so well—everyone believes I'm as cruel as I pretend. They group together to share war stories. And form my lynch mob.

I scan the sea of twisted faces. Hatred glitters in eyes, every expression severe and unforgiving, though there's a lot of satisfaction at my dishevelled state. My fear is slow to form beneath my exhaustion and weakness.

"You don't even deserve to clean our toilets," Caysie snarls from the fore.

It's hard to focus with hunger gnawing at my belly and wobbling my legs but I manage a half-smile.

"I'm happy for you to take over."

Are the men who tried to murder me in the crowd? None of them seem to be cradling their balls so I can't be sure.

Caysie glowers.

She's going to have some serious frown lines by the time she's thirty.

"You deserve to die for everything you've done," she says.

Kai squeezes to the front. "What did she do to you?"

Crap. When did he get here? I lost track of him while I was inhaling toilet water.

His eyes widen when he takes me in. I scrape my wet hair

back and cock one leg, hiding the streaked crotch and inner hems in the wide folds of material. Dried blood itches on my thighs.

Their plan has worked perfectly—I've never felt so ugly.

Kai controls his features and turns to Caysie, who was taking advantage of his distraction to ogle him. His face is as blank as mine but his heart beats hard. Caysie plants her hands on her hips, valiantly arching her back to give a hint of curve to her flat chest.

"She hurt me," she says in a breathy little voice.

"How?"

She quits batting her eyelashes at him, and scowls. "She whipped me."

Kai glances at me. My mask stays on, though it's starting to pinch. My stomach sinks to my toes.

A session of 'what did Maddy do?' is not going to paint me in a flattering light.

"She *volunteered*," Caysie sneers. "I screamed and begged her to stop but she didn't care. She's a sociopath."

I struggled to hold on to my mask that day. The awful crack of the whip in my hand churned my stomach. Blood streaked the floor and splashed my cheeks. When I was done, Caysie moaning and shivering, slumped against the dragon statue next to Evelyn Romanov's throne, Evelyn congratulated me. She said I reminded her of her youth. I threw up as soon as I was alone. My face in the bathroom mirror terrified me—cold, blood-splattered, my eyes as empty as my stomach.

One day, the mask isn't going to come off and I'll be the monster for real.

"What would've happened if she hadn't volunteered?" Kai says.

"Evelyn Romanov would have carried out my punishment."

"Why were you being punished?"

"I dared to talk to Julian like he was a human being." Caysie crosses her arms and glares at me as if getting caught was also my fault. "A hundred lashes just for that."

"Did you get a hundred lashes?"

"It's kinda hard to count when you're shrieking. It felt like a hundred."

Eleven. I whipped her eleven times and she slipped into shock. I couldn't risk more but Evelyn seemed satisfied with the show.

Evelyn would have whipped her to death.

Kai attempts to catch my eye. I stare over the lovely line of his shoulder encased in his leather jacket, my gaze unfocused to blur the hostile figures beyond.

"Who else has Sy—Madisyn hurt?" Kai turns to the crowd.

Hands shoot to the ceiling.

Oh, man. Has it really been that many?

A Lesser female muscles forward, towering over Kai. "She nearly killed my creator—my best friend—with her bare hands."

Kai motions for her to continue.

"He asked her sister, Libelle"—she spits the name—"to be his mate after she led him on for months, pretending she was sweet and innocent and would be forced to mate Lukas Romanov if no one else asked. He would do anything for her so he asked. He's a ruby. She went bleating to her father about the insult."

Leading men on is Libby's signature move. She gets multiple orgasms and they hardly ever notice the deception.

"Libelle demanded a fight to the death. Ryan refused to hit

her. In front of a jeering crowd, Libelle battered him. He never struck her once, not even when he was bleeding from his nose, his mouth, barely on his feet. Madisyn"—another spit—"ran into the arena and shouted, 'This isn't a fight! Hit me if you won't touch her, you coward.' So he swung at her. And she punched him to the ground."

I smacked him harder than I meant to. But I needed him to fall. The impact blazed in my knuckles and thudded all the way up my arm. I steered Libby away, pandering to the crowd until they swept us off in a jubilant wave, completely forgetting about the man curled on the ground.

Didn't get sick about that one, though I hated myself. Hated the cheers of the spectators and the pride on their faces.

I could really do without this trip down memory lane. My arms are tired, my bones hurt and my breasts ache from no bra support. Oh, and the period cramps.

"Did he die?" Kai says above the murmurs of disgust.

"No, but he's still scared to leave his house and it was six years ago."

More stories spill as quickly as the blood they're filled with. A Della Valle Lesser snapped after weeks of poor treatment, and slapped Libby. The female knew, even before the sound faded, that she'd made a colossal mistake. I shouldered Libby aside—her feral expression chilling me—and dragged the woman to Dad's room.

She was as pretty as her name—Braelynn. Beautiful mahogany hair to her waist. I shaved it all off, nicking her scalp so the dribbles of blood made it look good. I left her sobbing, Libby's fury cooled by her delight at the ruin of something lovely.

The Lesser's hair has grown to jaw-level now. Shorter but

still beautiful.

Another story involving Evelyn Romanov, and me volunteering to carry out the punishment. Libby accused me of being a suck-up. She'd wanted to do it, which forced me to act even when I swore never to volunteer again. I did not want to be admired by Evelyn Romanov. She invited people she admired to watch her torture the less fortunate.

On and on, my acts of cruelty are listed to damn me. Kai asks questions and prompts when the speaker gets overwhelmed with sadness or hate. Each tale weighs on my shoulders, reigniting the guilt and angst and loathing. For Drakul society. For myself most of all.

My heart is steady but my whole body quivers. My icy armour has evaporated in the heat of combined scorn so each barb pierces deep. I struggle to keep my mask in place.

I wanted friends, *ached* for friends, beyond immediate family and the powerful who applauded my savage behaviour. Pretending I'm not lonely is just another way of deluding myself.

"Why are you so interested, Kai?" Caysie says.

My head jerks up, bowed almost to my chest. Cowed and weak.

Keep it together, Madisyn.

"You can't possibly think she's acting out of some twisted altruism," Caysie continues, her lip curled past her nostril. "Controlling how much we suffered. That's bullcrap. She was eager to hurt us because she's a psychopath like the rest of her family."

The crowd mutters their agreement and drifts away, seeming to forget their reason for gathering in the first place. Caysie joins them after a dismissive sniff and a, "Put the bitch in her cell."

Kai's considering look threatens to undo me. I pray he doesn't probe for answers because I don't have the energy to lie.

I shuffle towards him.

"Are you bleeding?" he says, his gaze below my waist.

Ah, *tits*.

I clamp my lips together but a wave of impotent fury clenches my fists and squeezes my throat, tears springing to my eyes.

"I started my period and they wouldn't give me anything." My voice breaks, completely raw.

"What happened to your arms? And why are you wet?"

Say *nothing!* I'm not going to whine to Kai as if I'm the victim here. Manipulate him to protect me out of some misplaced honour. Or maybe he'll laugh and say I deserve it. In my current fragile state, I couldn't bear it.

He spins on his heel and stalks towards my cell. I trail after him, blind to the rest of the room as I focus on not letting a single tear spill over. Pressure builds in my throat and chest until I can't breathe. I float into my prison, and the door clangs.

I guess Kai doesn't have a key to unlock my cuffs. Or he doesn't want to.

"Kai," I say, though it's closer to a sob.

But he's gone.

20

Without the pole and collar restricting my movement, I tuck myself into the corner next to the door where no one can see me and let the tears flow, silent and hot. My chest hitches. It hurts to hold the sobs in. I hug my legs, my awful clothes protecting me from the handcuff chain, and rest my forehead on my knees. I cry harder at the mustiness of old blood and the stink of distress wafting from my skin. The smell of stale pee drifts from the silver bowl.

I guess I was supposed to empty it myself, though wasn't given the chance.

A fresh burst of tears soaks my thighs. I allow myself ten minutes of wallowing then swipe angrily at my cheeks, and flop on the bed.

Enough. One day minus the trappings of comfort and I'm blubbering. How spoilt am I?

Everyone seems to be interested in dinner and socialising rather than me for the moment. Maybe I can grab a nap before my food arrives, garnished by snot and pubic hair. My stinging eyes close. I float in a half-way place. Am I calling Kai's name or is he calling my name?

"*Syn,*" he hisses.

I twitch awake and rub my bleary eyes. Kai drops a plastic

bag and a paper sack through the bars of my door. A glorious scent floods saliva into my mouth. My stomach rumbles loud enough to echo.

Is that… hamburger?

I roll off the bed and onto my knees, tearing at the paper sack with the bright yellow arches on the side. I practically eat through the box to reach the soft bun and juicy meat.

God, I love pickles.

The burger disappears in three bites. Sauce slicks my lips and fingers. It's the best thing I've ever tasted.

"That's not how rich girls eat," Kai says from the doorway.

Crap. I forgot he was there.

I lick my fingers with exaggerated nonchalance. "I skipped breakfast and lunch."

"Skipped or wasn't given?"

"Oh, it was given, just not in a condition I wanted to swallow."

So much for not whining. I cram my stupid mouth with a handful of fries, and hold the cardboard packet out to Kai. Something flashes across his face, too quick to decipher, but he reaches through the bars, takes a fry and nibbles it.

Even that is cute.

I stuff more chips in my mouth to distract myself. My belly stretches happily once I've reached the grease- and salt-smeared bottom of the packet. I investigate the second, bulging bag. My gaze snaps to Kai.

I try to fight it, mask up, pretend, but a tear glides down my cheek before I can stop it. Kai bows his head, a flop of hair hiding his eyes. He turns and slides down the wall to sit on his bum, only his arm visible through the door. I bite my knuckle until the risk of a weeping fit has passed. I dump the contents of the bag on my bed, and strip off the ugly harem pants and men's socks without hesitation, my arse to the wind. The bag contains tampons and sanitary pads, Kai not knowing what I prefer and taking the precautionary route. I rip open the box of tampons and insert one, not caring who's watching.

Unless it's Kai.

A peek confirms he's not.

Moist wipes scrub the blood from my legs, leaving a hint of mint and cucumber. I pull on black underwear, fluffy, hard-soled slipper socks and soft, grey jogging bottoms. The packet of white cotton bras calls to me as does the yellow, fitted top but they won't get past the cuffs. I clean my face with another wipe, my skin tight from the toilet-water-and-bleach swirly. The final treasure is paracetamol, and I swallow two with the bottle of orange juice from the McDonald's bag.

How could Kai's girlfriend—*ex-girlfriend*—ever think he would cheat? The man is a saint.

I tidy my living space and mirror Kai, my spine to the wall.

"Thank you," I whisper instead of, "Marry me."

"Tell me something real," he says.

Is any part of me real anymore? Safe to share?

"Syn?"

"I'm thinking," I say.

"Don't think."

"Not thinking leads to regrets."

"I'm not asking for dirty secrets."

"Aren't you?"

He snorts, and my mouth quirks, though he can't see.

It feels amazing to be clean. Underwear is my new favourite thing. And being close to Kai makes me happy, though it's just the Lesser connection.

Mostly.

"I cry at romantic movies," I say.

"What woman doesn't?"

"A monster wearing some woman's skin."

He fidgets, and cloth scrapes on stone. "That may have been a bit harsh."

"I like what you carved on my bed."

He clears his throat. "I was angry."

"It made me laugh."

"What else?"

I masturbate to the thought of you.

Nope. Can't tell him that.

"I like your tattoo, and your, um, piercing."

Jeez, Maddy. Too personal.

"Which one?" he says.

My cheeks heat. "The earring."

"Liar."

How can he read me so easily? And from voice alone? No one can read me. They see haughty bitch-face and look no further.

The man is dangerous.

"I was supposed to get married last autumn," I say.

"What happened?"

"He was killed in the initial battle with Julian and Raine and a bunch of Vanatori."

"A Romanov?"

"Dominic." I suck in a breath. It's definitely not safe to say—"I *hated* him."

Oh, man.

A burst of release flows through me, so similar to climax. I feel dizzy.

"Why?" Kai says.

"He was violent and cruel. I was promised to him when I was sixteen. He took advantage."

"He raped you?" Kai growls as if he wants to raise Dominic from the ashes he became just so he can punch him.

"No, he…" I can't admit it, surely? "He bit me. Down there."

Oh, lord. My mouth is running away from me. Why is it cathartic to talk to Kai? I should shut up before I forget myself.

"I've never actually let anyone"—*don't you fucking dare!*—"use their mouth. Down there. Since then."

Kai takes a few minutes to process this in silence while I bang my head against the wall and curse myself.

"Why were you supposed to marry him if you hated him?"

Is his voice different—huskier? Disgusted?

I stop banging my head before I give myself a concussion and join Ailish in the hospital.

"I have to do a lot of things I hate," I say, aiming for cryptic and giving him unvarnished truth.

He fidgets again. Is he looking through the bars? I stare at my hands gripping my knees.

"Do you hurt people so someone doesn't hurt them worse, Syn?" he says.

The heat of his breath brushes my bare arm. His tantalising scent teases my nose and begs me to respond. I grit my teeth.

"Your silence still answers my question," he says.

"No, it doesn't."

"You bit my arm so your sister wouldn't bite off my leg. You patched me up and helped me escape. You stopped me from overdosing."

Dangerous ground. Definitely on dangerous ground.

"You're not as cruel as you want people to believe."

"I am, Kai," I say. "Don't make me prove it."

"I have no doubt you would," he says.

"Your turn for truths."

His chuckle jolts my pulse and shivers into my stomach.

"Goodnight, Syn," he says.

21

Kai appears at my door in the morning and even though I had another interrupted sleep, the delight at his presence brightens my face and curves my mouth in a smile.

Jeez, if I were a dog, my tail would be wagging. No wonder he was pissed off about that part of the Lesser connection.

Caysie stomps into view. I smooth my features to cold and empty. Her expression is as grumpy as mine should be since they kept me awake all night. In the snatches of sleep when they weren't banging on the bars, I burned my cheek on the handcuff chain.

"You look tired," Kai says.

Caysie smirks.

"Bad dreams," I say.

Kai passes a bowl of porridge through the gap in the door. I bet Caysie wanted to sneeze in it. I hold it in one hand and spoon it into my mouth with the other, the handcuff chain clinking on ceramic. Salty and sweet and delicious.

Would he bring coffee?

No. I'll accept everything he gives me but I won't ask for anything. It's too close to manipulation.

"Come on," Caysie huffs. "You have a busy day."

"I need to use the bathroom."

Her lip lifts. "You have a bowl for that."

"Yeah, it's a little full."

Mostly with old wipes to hide the used tampon floating around in there like some exotic pond life.

Kai raises his eyebrow. "Really, Caysie?"

She crosses her arms, her fingers gripping her elbows so hard, her knuckles whiten.

"Oh, how nice for you, Madisyn," she sneers. "You've confused him enough, he wants to protect you. Seriously, show them blonde hair and big tits and men lose all their brain cells."

Considering my hair is a lank, unwashed mess and I'm wearing a sack for a top, I'm not exactly at my most alluring.

"My brain cells are fine, thanks," Kai says. "She should still have fair treatment."

Caysie stabs the key in the lock and twists as if she's trying to snap it.

"When you forget what she is, look at the scar on your arm. Then tell me what's fair."

Kai's eyes meet mine.

"I know what the scar means," he says.

I feign interest in my slipper-snug toes and tell my expression to behave itself. Caysie flings the door open. I ease past her rigid figure with my bowl and bag of goodies. She fumes in silence while I use the bathroom and perform my womanly ablutions. I rinse my stale mouth with a swirl of water from the tap. She tuts, and I ignore her. We join Kai in the cavern after I've left my worldly possessions back in the cell.

My reflection in the mirror was as terrible as I feared—dark smudges under my eyes, blotchy skin, greasy hair. There's a splodge of dried hamburger sauce on my beige top.

Caysie leads us through the cavern, the typical mutters swelling and fading as we pass. She marches ahead up the stairs, nearly disappearing around the twists, her spine stiff, and Kai falls into step beside me.

"I don't think she likes me anymore," he whispers.

I swallow a laugh. "She can hear you."

Caysie shoots us both a glare over her shoulder.

"Whoops," Kai says.

"Dragons have good hearing."

"How good?"

"I can hear your heart beating."

The forenamed organ skips, and he gives me startled eyes. "Can't hide anything from you, huh?"

"You'd be surprised."

Fresh air sears my lungs and I suck it deeper. Gosh, it smells good. Snow dusts the grass and swirls in the air, and I tilt my face to greet it. Flakes land on my eyelids and melt in my lashes. Pines sigh in the wind. Caysie's louder, aggrieved sigh joins them, and I open my eyes to Kai watching me.

I still can't read his damn face.

"What?" I say. "It gets stuffy down there."

We walk around the side of the large house, the windows at the front already replaced. Only a slight scorch on the brickwork remains.

Why are my family taking so long? Julian said he had a plan to delay them. It's obviously worked. Unless they attacked again already and were killed.

No. Caysie would waste no time rubbing my nose in it.

Beyond where Irena crashed onto the back patio, rows of greenhouses replace what I remember of the rear gardens. We follow Caysie into the closest one on the left, the air warmer than outside, though still cool. I glance at the rows of plants, and slam to a stop. Kai walks into my back but doesn't spring away like he did before, when I was leading him to the garage to hide in my car. His fingers curl around my upper arms for a second and, even with my focus elsewhere, the contact tingles to my toes.

Caysie smirks. "I thought you'd like this place."

"I am *not* working in here."

I ease behind Kai until his body is a shield between me and the rows of deadly plants. Thankfully, they're not in flower or breathing the pollen would hurt. The rows and rows of white-veined leaves give me heart palpitations, and Caysie is fucking loving it. How agonising would it be if I fell into them?

"Is this dragon's-bane?" Kai directs a stormy look at Caysie.

"She needs to know what her and her ilk are up against. The old way—*her way*—will be over soon."

It's not my way. I'll be glad if it dies, as long as my family doesn't go with it.

I exit the greenhouse at a brisk pace. Not a run, just brisk. We head for the next structure, our breaths steaming in the air.

"I guess I should have bought you better shoes," Kai says, nodding at my feet.

Dampness soaks into my slipper-socks.

"You bought more than enough." I wiggle my toes. "These are comfy."

Caysie rolls her eyes so hard, I'm surprised she doesn't tip over. She shoves into a greenhouse filled with potted plants on shelves. The back wall contains black-painted jugs, and a small propane heater sits at each end of the long building. Caysie barks instructions. I start to weed and water the plants—peas, broccoli and spinach—and Kai moves to the row opposite so we're facing each other.

"I have to earn my keep, too," he says to my cocked eyebrow. "Do you like it here?"

"It's… interesting. Julian and Raine are cool. I haven't stayed long enough to get to know the others, except for the people who live in the house."

Caysie glowers at us from the far end of the greenhouse. "No talking. Can't you see everything she says, everything she does, is just to use you?"

"Yes, beware—I am the devil," I say, and yank a clump of grass from a pot of carrots.

Caysie mumbles something unladylike but Kai grins. Suddenly, it's hard to breathe. The flash of his dimples short-circuits my nerve endings, and grass and mud slip from numb fingers to patter on my foot. My heart thuds hard against my ribs. Caysie frowns at me, and I duck my head, tugging weeds as if it's the most fascinating thing I've ever done.

We work in comfortable silence, weeding the pots and watering the disturbed soil. Once the rows are finished, we rotate the positions of the containers to control the amount of heat and light the plants get. The small of my back aches but the hours have passed quicker having Kai there, even with Caysie's permanent scowl. He has a smear of dirt on his cheekbone, and my fingers tingle, longing to touch it.

The skinny male Lesser who gobbed in my porridge—it's terrible that I've forgotten his name—slides open the greenhouse door and sticks his head in.

"Caysie and Kai, Julian wants to see you," he says.

Caysie dusts her trousers. "Would you take Madisyn back

to her cell? She can get lunch there."

Oh, goody. More boy spit.

I rinse my hands at the hose near the door, though the mud under my fingernails refuses to budge. The guy spins on his heel, forcing me to hustle to keep up. The greenhouse entrance rumbles shut. I tell myself not to glance at Kai but do it anyway. His dark eyes meet mine, framed by black hair.

Is he worried about me? I suppose people could grab me with their stupid leaves again. Or decide the time has come to kick me to death. It's not like Julian will banish them for turning on their tormentor.

I tear my gaze from Kai, unease churning in my belly. I don't want to go back in the cavern alone. He makes me feel safe. When did that happen?

I pad after the skinny Lesser and wonder if I should apologise for yesterday. It would probably make him angry. He'd think it was a trick. Stick to the programme—act the bad guy, protect my family.

So what the hell am I doing with Kai?

The cluster of heartbeats registers too late. We turn the corner. The boy skips to the side and something cold and wet engulfs my head, splashing on the frozen ground. I blink through dripping hair at the four people sneering at me.

"Now your outside matches your inside," the skinny Lesser says.

I swallow a laugh. Black dye. How cute.

His three compatriots snigger, one swinging the empty bucket. They herd me down into the cavern where the sniggering swells and buoys me to my cell. I give them all a haughty stare while a ball of ice settles in my stomach.

What if it were acid? Why *wasn't* it acid? Or a solution of dragon's-bane.

I sit on the edge of my bed. Food doesn't materialise. The dye itches and my head aches from the chemical smell. Since it doesn't seem I'm going to be allowed to shower, this could get annoying fast.

"Christ, I left you alone for a minute."

Kai opens the door and leans his shoulder on the frame.

"Yeah, clumsy me."

"Was it that skinny kid?"

"I didn't see."

He snorts. "Goth suits you, though you also have a bad case of melanism."

Dye streaks my bare arms and, no doubt, my face. My top is a mess but my jogging bottoms only have a few spots thanks to the sack shape sluicing most of it outward. The slippers are dappled with it.

"Black is the new pink," I say.

"Grab your bag and follow me."

He walks away before I can respond so I do what he says and scurry after him. The whispers in the cavern are different this time—poor Kai, brainwashed by the monster that made him; something should be done; that bitch needs to go. I hold my head high until we're outside then sneak a glance at Kai. He seems to be thinking hard so I keep quiet. He strides for the front door of the mansion.

"Um, I don't think I'm allowed in the house."

"Try not to pee on the furniture and you'll be fine," he says, not slowing.

The door opens into a large, parquet-floored hall. An archway leads off on either side to a dining room and a sitting area, a chandelier still managing to sparkle in the dim winter daylight. Kai hops up the stairs to the second level while I stay close and pray no one sees us. There are heartbeats and voices everywhere, though more muffled than I expect.

Do they have soundproofing between the floors?

Kai unlocks a door three rooms down and ushers me inside, locking it behind us. The room has a four-poster bed so like my own, I have a pang to lie in it. Two cabinets flank the bed with a padded chest at the foot and a cupboard opposite. A red fabric chair faces the bed from a corner, a kettle on a coffee table next to it. Another door heads into what I assume is the en-suite.

It's pretty nice compared to Kai's flat. Less shabby, more furniture. No screaming expletive.

"Shower is in there," he says, nodding at the door.

I blink at him, my plastic bag dangling from my fist.

"To wash the dye off," he says patiently. "Your eyes are red."

I put it down to exhaustion but, now that he's mentioned it, they are stinging a bit.

"You're going to have to cut this top off," I say in my mildest voice.

He watches me for a beat then pulls a slim cylinder from his jeans. A blade snicks free.

More blinking from me. "Do you always carry a knife?"

His mouth quirks. "Only when I'm doing something dangerous."

Oh, man. Why does that shoot a little frisson of excitement to my gut?

He steps close to me and I force myself to stand still when everything inside jumps. The blade slips under the material above my left shoulder. I breathe slow. There's a tug, and stitches part with a whisper.

"Turn around," he says.

I face the bathroom door, my pulse in my mouth. The knife slices the top at my other shoulder. The baggy material pools at my feet with little encouragement, baring me to the waist. Dye stains my chest and circles one somewhat erect nipple.

Half of me wants to face Kai to see how he'll react but I don't dare. I wobble to the bathroom. Just before I close the door, I peek behind me.

It's a compulsion.

Kai hasn't moved, watching me with his stormy, unreadable eyes. The knife dangles at his side.

I shut the door and lean against it, shivery from the heat of his stare.

I may be in trouble.

22

Hot water pounds on my head, and I just stand and savour it for a few minutes, purring low in my throat. Steam soothes my tired eyes, the heat working into aching muscles.

Kai has been here. Naked. Water hissing on his shoulders and slicking his chest, dribbling down the hard lines of his body all the way to—

Okay, enough of that.

I grab the bottle of shower gel hanging from a metal rack and squeeze a dollop into my hand.

Oh, lord. He brought his own and now I'm surrounded by the scent of him.

I massage myself with one hand while the other holds the chain clear of all my exposed skin. My fingers brush sensitive nipples and circle downward over my flat belly. Lower to stiff hairs, my pulse throbbing, eager...

I am *not* touching myself when he's only a thin wall away. This is ridiculous.

I wash quickly. My arms are awkward because of the cuffs and the chain but I scrub the streaks of dye clean. I soap my hair, rinse and shut off the shower, patting myself dry. I pull on clean underwear and the jogging bottoms, stroke the bras with longing, and wrap the towel around my chest, tucking it firmly under my armpit.

Unless Kai has the key to the cuffs, I'm not sure how I'm going to dress my top half.

I ignore the mirror since I'm pretty sure I look silly and no less knackered than this morning. The door opens to Kai sitting in the red chair reading a book, one foot propped on his knee.

1984.

"I've read that," I say, padding out onto the lush carpet in my bare feet. "It was depressing."

He looks up, and his mouth twitches.

I frown. "What? I can read."

The mouth twitching stretches into a smile and my soft little heart goes pitty-pat at those damn dimples.

"It's not that. You really didn't wash your hair very well."

I fist my hands to keep from fluffing the damp mess.

"I am somewhat restricted," I huff.

He places a bookmark between the pages and sets the tome on the arm of the chair. He eases around me into the bathroom, dragging the wicker seat from the wall to the sink.

"Sit," he says.

I cock my eyebrow. "You're going to wash my hair?"

"The tap on the sink extends."

"Oh, well, that's all right then."

I eye him suspiciously and perch on the edge of the chair.

"Lean back," he says.

Ceramic cradles my skull. I roll my eyes to keep Kai in sight. From this angle, his cheekbones are amazing.

The hose rattles as he pulls the tap out. Water hushes on and glugs through the plughole.

Can he see down my cleavage?

I fix my gaze on the ceiling. Water brushes my scalp.

"Is the temperature okay?"

"Fine," I say quickly.

This is weird, right? I could've showered again.

He dampens my hair and squirts shampoo into his palm. Both hands massage my head. My bones turn to liquid, and a noise catches in my throat.

A moan, I suspect.

My eyes flutter closed, Kai's strong fingers kneading me into submission. I slump into the wicker, my muscles following my bones in consistency. My heart rate slows to a lazy thud. Everything goes a little hazy. Water sloshes, magical fingers knead.

Heaven. If I were anymore relaxed, I'd puddle on the floor.

I fall asleep between one breath and the next.

* * *

The scent of cream and mushroom tempts me from sleep. I blink at the gauzy canopy of my four-poster bed.

Wait. My canopy is gold, not white.

I thrust up on one arm, the chain of my cuffs tight across my hip. My elbow tugs on the towel wrapped around my chest and it flops open, exposing my ribs and a goodly bit of side boob. I bend both my arms to hold the rest in place. Kai sets a tray with two steaming plates of pasta on the bedside cabinet. He picks up a fork and slides a knife between the tines, bending one so it sticks out like a broken finger.

"Hold out your hands," he says.

I swing my legs off the edge of the bed, tucking the towel into place, and give him my hands. He eases the bandage off of the lock and inserts the tine. Metal scrapes. He bites his lip in concentration, his gaze focused inward. The cuff snicks and loosens, dropping from my wrist. He does the same to the second cuff while I gape at him.

"Where did you learn to do that?"

He grins. "Juvie, after I got busted for breaking and entering. Wish I'd learned it before. It would've minimised the breaking part."

I have no breath to reply. Is this going to happen every time he smiles? It's hugely inconvenient.

He takes his plate to his chair and chews on a mound of pasta, leaving the cuffs on the floor. I stretch my arms wide, cracking my spine. The towel unravels, and I clamp my hands to my chest. Kai tries and fails to hide his smirk behind his fork. I hook the plastic bag onto the bed and shuffle around on my knees to give him my back. I toss the towel. The bra fits perfectly—how does he know my size?—and I offer a prayer of thanks to the goddess of breast support. The yellow top hugs my ribs.

I wave my freed wrists at Kai, the skin reddened. "Are you sure this is a good idea?"

He shrugs. "They'll have to go back on later."

I sit cross-legged on the bed, and cradle my plate. Happy slurping and munching fill the room.

"Is the juvie thing why your ex-girlfriend's brother thought you weren't good enough?"

"I think it was more the prostitution," Kai says.

I inhale a mushroom. Tears blur my eyes, and I choke. My fist pounds my chest, my throat burning with each cough. Kai slaps me between the shoulder blades and dislodges the offending morsel. I uncurl my fingers from his hip.

When did I grab his hip?

He fills a glass in the bathroom and I gulp water, the cold liquid soothing my throat. I dab my eyes on my sleeves.

"I may need some context," I wheeze.

He reclaims his seat. "So it's my turn to spill dirty secrets?"

"It's only fair."

I still can't believe I told him about my oral sex phobia.

I cough, and drink another mouthful of water. Kai spears a piece of pasta and swipes it through the creamy sauce.

"Answer me one question," he says.

I roll my eyes. "Fine—I hurt people so they don't get hurt worse. Satisfied?"

"Not that."

"Oh."

Whoops. Good job, Maddy.

"Why *do* you act the big bad bitch?"

I sigh. "We have to be brutal or we look weak. If the other families think we're slipping, they'll challenge us. Most of them hate that we're the most powerful even without a matriarch."

"Couldn't your dad have married again?"

"Yes, but he… never got over my mum."

He compromised us but how could I blame him? I'm the only one to blame. I'm the only one who should suffer to fix it.

We sit in silence for a few minutes. I stare at my plate and finish the pasta.

"I'm supposed to marry someone else this autumn," I say without looking up.

"Christ, don't you get a break? Or is this your one true love?"

I bark a laugh. "Hardly. He's less terrifying than Dominic

Romanov but he's basically a caveman." I keep the, "And not as pretty as you," part to myself.

"So your dad can pick who he wants—or not—but you're forced to marry in exchange for what, protection? Coming from a former whore, that's just prostitution without the money."

I wince. "Don't call yourself that."

"It's a little late to worry about my virtue, Syn," he says with a slow smile.

Thank god he can't hear my heartbeat. The stupid thing would give me away.

"On that subject—since you asked me way more than one question—how, why, when? And what? Definitely what."

He licks his fork. The tines scrape against his tongue piercing, and I internalise a shiver.

"The how is fairly self-explanatory. People give you money and you do things—" He chuckles at my scowl. "I was fifteen when my foster parents died. I went back into care but ran away because no one could ever live up to them. I broke into houses and pretended they were mine. A year later, I almost got caught and ended up on the street, nothing but the mementos I'd swiped. I couldn't sell them so I sold myself."

He puts his plate on the tray next to the bed and stacks mine on top.

"What was it like?"

He shrugs, reclaiming his seat. "Probably not as bad as you're imagining. It was a business transaction. I chose my clients. Thankfully, I never got desperate enough to do just anyone. And I wasn't on drugs."

"And the clients were…?"

"Mostly men," he says, and smirks. "Close your mouth, Syn.

It's the twenty-first century."

I close my mouth.

"It stopped when I was seventeen. I got arrested for the B&E and they'd collected my fingerprints in quite a few houses. After juvie, I met Mark in Waterstone's where he worked—where he got me a job."

"And your girlfriend?"

"Was the first woman who didn't pay me for it."

"Did she know?"

"Christ, no."

"But you told her brother?"

He clears his throat. "Well, he and I moved into the flat together. I hadn't met her yet. I was happy to be out of the half-way houses and homeless shelters. I got a bit drunk and thought it would be a good bonding experience."

"He looked like a grumpy basta—person."

"You can say bastard. He *was* a grumpy bastard but beggars can't be choosers." Kai picks up the kettle on the table next to him and gives it a shake. "Do you want tea or coffee?"

I almost slide onto my knees. "Please, god, coffee."

"Getting withdrawals, are we? It'll keep you awake."

I snort. "It won't be what keeps me awake."

"So they *are* torturing you."

He fills the kettle in the bathroom and clicks it on, plonking two mugs on the table.

"I've seen torture," I say. "This isn't torture."

He tosses a peppermint teabag into one cup and fills a mini cafetière with ground coffee. It smells wonderful.

"I could tell Julian," he says.

"Don't. I can handle it."

"You think you deserve it, you mean."

Ooh, Mr Perceptive.

"Milk and one sugar," I say with a sniff.

23

"I have a sensitive, definitely nosy, question." I hug my coffee and inhale the steam, my knees tucked to my chest.

Kai sips his mint tea. "About my real parents, right?"

"It's rude to mind-read," I say.

Can't I hide anything from this guy? It should worry me but it's nice to be myself. She's been withering away behind bitch-Maddy. Dying a little more with each act of cruelty. Kai now knows me better than my own family.

I hope it won't be another thing I regret.

"It's the main topic we haven't talked about," he says. "What's your question?"

"Why are they in prison?"

His eyes go as flat and hard as slate. "Drug possession and child abuse."

"Oh. And you were the child."

"Unfortunately. I don't remember much—they were arrested when I was eight—but they're the reason I have bad dreams and oxycodone."

My fingers clench on my mug and the ceramic protests. I relax my hands.

"I'm sorry, Kai."

One shoulder lifts and drops without jostling his tea. "I

made the mistake of reading articles from the case when I got older. Thought it would give me closure. It just gave me nightmares about things best forgotten."

I gulp a large mouthful of coffee to drown the protective growl and keep drinking until it sloshes in my stomach. Kai circles his finger around the rim of his cup, his gaze dark and far away.

"My real parents often struggled to pay their dealer," he continues as if he didn't pause. "Lucky for them, he liked young boys. Apparently, I didn't speak for two years after I was rescued."

The mug shatters in my hands. I yelp as shards slice my fingers. Blood drips onto the bed covers. Kai's cup slams on the coffee table and sloshes mint tea onto the shiny surface.

"Jesus, Syn."

Before I can move, he scoops me in his arms and carries me to the bathroom. I almost swoon and it's not the blood loss. I have a second of his solid chest against my side, his exotic scent, then he sits my arse on the counter and directs my hands under the tap.

"Fuck," I hiss.

Ceramic clinks on ceramic. Pink water swirls into the plughole. Kai picks a few stubborn shards not dislodged by the flow.

"It's a little off-putting that you can crush a mug with your bare hands," he says.

I grit my teeth. "You probably can, too."

He gives me wide eyes.

"Yeah, you're welcome. Consider this a lesson on how not to be careful."

He pats my hands dry with a towel then uses it to press

against the cuts. I squirm but don't jerk away.

"Sorry," he says, "but I need to stop the bleeding. How long til you heal?"

"By tomorrow night, they'll have scabbed over."

"Nifty."

"It comes in handy."

He pulls a first aid kit from the cupboard under the sink and concentrates on bandaging my fingers with gauze and micropore tape. I hope it distracts him from thinking about why I crushed the mug in the first place. There are only so many, "Why do you care?" volleys I can duck until I tell him the truth.

Because I like you, Kai. I really, *really* like you.

He smooths the last piece of tape and admires his handiwork. I look like I've been juggling a cactus.

"You could tell the people in the cavern I did it," he says with a rueful smile. "That'd shut them up about me being your slave."

I quirk my mouth. "Rankles, does it?"

"I'm no one's slave."

He cups my elbows and helps me slide off the counter, holding me for a heartbeat longer when my feet are on the floor. I shoo the tingles away but they zip to my stomach and bounce around in a swarm. I pull my slipper-shoes on to give them a moment to fizzle out. Kai scoops the handcuffs off the carpet. Blood dots his bed, the shattered mug sprinkled on the covers and floor.

"I should get you back," he says. "If you're not down there for lights out, they'll grab their pitchforks."

"At least let me clean that up."

"It's fine. I'll get it later."

He wraps the cuffs in an extra layer of bandages and twists the micropore around the chain so I finally won't burn myself in my sleep. I hold out my hands.

"Wait." I stretch my arms wide until my spine cracks. "Okay, go."

He smiles and clicks one bracelet closed while watching my face, fastening the other when I don't scream. The second the metal snicks into place, I realise I never thought about escaping the whole time they were off. Not once. I enjoyed sitting on Kai's bed and talking to him.

What the hell am I doing?

Outside, the wind whispers through the trees. Kai shivers and shoves his hands in his jeans pockets. He eyeballs my short-sleeved top rippling in the breeze.

"You really can't feel the cold?" he says.

"Not so much. I mean, leave me in it and I'll get a bit sluggish but that's it. You need a better winter coat."

He cocks an eyebrow. "Not all of us can afford a coat for every day of the week."

"I only have five coats," I sniff.

I drag my feet through the wet grass, unwilling to hurry into the oppressive atmosphere of the cavern and my barren little cell. My hair has dried in a curly mess, and tickles my face.

"Kai?"

He kicks a pine cone and it spirals into the trees. Solar lights mark the path to the underground chamber.

"Why did you…?" I clear my throat. "How could you choose to be a prostitute after you were abused as a kid?"

"My therapist said it's common behaviour."

"To prostitute?"

"Maybe not that but I'm not much of a pole dancer."

To distract myself from imagining him, muscles oiled, tiny briefs stretched across his hips, I blurt, "Your therapist told you, when you were eight years old, you might become a stripper?"

"Eleven. And I think she was using it as an example of destructive behaviour to avoid. Fostering awareness. Anyway, I earned good money."

"No wonder," I mutter.

"What?"

"I hope you were safe," I say louder.

He grins. "Always."

My spine stiffens the deeper we go down the spiral stairs. Angry murmurs swell and sweep me to my prison. Caysie storms towards us before Kai can close the door, her face collapsed in a frown. Her narrowed gaze scans the covered handcuffs and my yellow top, alighting on Kai with accusation.

"You're screwing her now? I thought you'd have a little more dignity instead of becoming her fuck-boy, Kai."

His back is to me so I can't see his expression but his shoulders tense. I smile at Caysie through the bars rather than baring my teeth.

"Like becoming yours, Caysie?" I say, my voice a purr instead of a growl. "You've thought about it. That hard body pressing you against the wall. The tongue piercing. Wondering if he has other, lower piercings. And he does. Imagining when he slides himself inside you. The piercing rubbing over and over. And, yes, Caysie—it feels so. Fucking. *Good.*"

Caysie, whose eyes started at Kai's chest and dropped as I spoke, flinches at the last word. Her cheeks blaze red.

"I hope you die, Madisyn Della Valle," she hisses, and storms away.

I laugh as the outraged thud of her heartbeat fades. "She's definitely going to make me regret that tomorrow."

Kai shuts the door, the lock clunking into the strike plate. He cocks a dark brow.

"Have you seen me naked?" he says.

Only when I shut my eyes.

"Um, half," I say out loud. "Top half."

"So how do you know about the piercing?"

"The...?"

All the blood rushes from my head to throb between my legs. My eyes lower before I can control myself.

Stop looking at his crotch!

I jerk my gaze to his face.

"It's real?" I whisper, and wonder why I'm whispering. "I made that up."

A slow smile curves his mouth, and his dimples taunt me. A flop of emerald-tipped hair hides eyes as mysterious as smoke.

"You're blushing, Syn," he says.

24

Caysie avoids me the next morning, likely planning some spectacular revenge. No one arrives with my breakfast or disturbs me and I'm forced to pee in the stupid bowl. Thankfully, my period is almost done as it only lasts three days. I stick a sanitary towel in my underwear and forget about it.

I wonder where my family are and why I don't miss them as much as I should.

Kai arrives with lunch—pasta salad—and the skinny kid, who sulks when he notices the lack of black dye. We're directed to the final greenhouse furthest from the evil one growing the dragon's-bane and join a group already there, weeding away. Kai finds me gloves to stop my bandages getting dirty.

The afternoon slips towards evening, no one talking to me but Kai. He tells me about his foster parents, their freak accident and the awful few months after their death when he ran away from his temporary care home. He asks me questions but I have to be careful what I say with so many people around us. I'm happier listening to him talk. It's the longest conversation I've ever had.

We separate at dinner, and I scold the little pang in my chest.

I pause on the frost-crisped grass outside the greenhouse, my breath puffing white. The sky is clear and full of stars, no sign of the moon. Kai glances over his shoulder, and I raise my cuffed hands in a wave. A group spills out of the greenhouse at my back, silent but for the rapid thud of their hearts. Kai disappears into the house. The group breathe behind me.

Are they waiting for me?

I start to turn. White explodes in my skull.

Then black.

* * *

I'm lying on something hard. Concrete?

I could have walked to my cell just fine. They didn't have to batter me unconscious.

The back of my head throbs in time to the slow jump of my pulse. The ground is cool but not freezing, the scent of mud strong. Other heartbeats pound beside the steady slap of mine.

"Let's just toss her in," a woman says.

Ailish. I bet it was her who conked me on the skull.

"She needs to be awake," Caysie says. "I want her to feel every goddamn second of it."

Every second of what?

"Someone might come," Ailish says.

My bound hands are pinned under my body, my cheek pressed to the gritty floor. My toes twitch.

I seem to have lost my slippers. And the rest of my clothes. I hope whoever stripped me enjoyed my blood-spotted sanitary towel.

I inhale slow to calm my rising pulse and pray nobody

notices.

"They'll be at dinner a while," Caysie says, "though I almost want Kai to come. He should see this. He'll thank us when he's free."

Disquiet worms into my gut.

Kai will only be free when I'm dead. What are they going to do—chop me into bits? Cut me and watch me bleed?

The scent of fresh, growing things clogs my nostrils. I doubt they're threatening to throw me into the spinach.

My heart skips.

"She's awake!" Caysie yells.

My eyes pop open. Shoes scuffle near my nose—beige Doc Martins and dainty sapphire pumps. I try to shove onto my knees but my arms are numb, and I flop on my side. The whole gang is here—Braelynn, the skinny kid, the tall Lesser female. I hook my foot around Braelynn's ankle and sweep her leg. She collides with the skinny kid and they fall in a tangle of limbs.

"Grab her!" Caysie says, lunging for my arm.

She practically jerks it from its socket. The tall Lesser stabs her hand into my armpit. I scream as loud as I can, but not because it hurts.

"Shut up, you bitch," Caysie snaps.

The tall Lesser clamps her hand over my mouth as I draw breath for more. I twist my head and bite her finger, bone crunching under my teeth. Her turn to scream.

Will anyone come in time? Is the whole house sound-proofed? Will they hear nothing beyond the brick, wandering out, their bellies full of dessert, to find the weeping mess that used to be me?

Or ash.

Ailish appears at the arm abandoned by the tall Lesser, who's collapsed on the concrete path, cradling her hand. I pedal backwards, dragging Caysie, and my spine hits the wall, glass crackling but not shattering completely. The skinny kid lunges for my leg. I kick him in the face. His nose bursts in a spray of red. His cry joins the whimpers of the tall Lesser and he tumbles into the dragon's-bane, crumpling the nearest plants. The white-veined leaves seem to shiver in anticipation.

I suck air and shout, "Kai—"

An elbow catches me right on the cheekbone and paints the starry sky inside my eyelids. Fingers crush my biceps. Arms hoist my legs upwards. I struggle, my shoulders aching, pins and needles prickling my hands. If I weren't half-starved and exhausted, I'd give them a better fight. Plants whisper against trouser legs. Muscles tense. I turn my head to Caysie's glittering hazel eyes.

"I'll make sure he spits on your ashes," she says.

"Caysie, wait—"

They hurl me into the dragon's-bane.

25

My body falls into lava. Or that's what it feels like.

My shriek shatters glass and slams a spike of pain into my ears, though that may be the dragon's-bane. I scrunch my eyes shut and scrabble on hands and knees, my fingers sinking into wet mud, my skin bubbling. The chain of my cuffs tangles in a clump of plants, and I land on my face. My howl sucks a leaf into my mouth and it ulcerates wherever it touches. Copper floods my tongue. I spit out the leaf and stagger to my feet. Tears blur my eyes. I aim for the edge of the cursed greenery. A slap spins me around, and I collapse.

Screaming and thrashing. So much screaming and thrashing.

Somehow, I find myself back on my hands and knees. Still screaming. I can't tell where I am so I shuffle in a straight line on what must be bloody stumps at the end of my arms. No matter what direction I go, legs drive me back, kicking, pushing at my shoulders and rolling me into the unrelenting agony. Breathing is fire. My heart slams against my ribs.

There's nothing but the pain. Shrieking. Yells. Am I yelling?

Hands grab my arms. I try to shake them off but the command to my brain gets lost somewhere, and I twitch and shiver and moan. My body goes limp. The shock is too much.

Cool air. Frozen grass. The wetness should soothe but my flesh has sizzled to the bone.

"Oh, god"—a loud swallow—"her skin came off."

Each exhale is a whimper. Someone retches next to me so I doubt I'm looking my best. I blink my eyes but the blurriness remains. My corneas are scorched. The dragon's-bane has burned my skin deep enough to numb most of my nerve endings but there are plenty left to clamour their pain.

"Jesus-fuck, look at her. Will she heal?"

Is that Kai? It sounds like Kai but the voices are muffled.

"Not without help."

Who is that? How many people are watching my weeping carcass?

"What can we do?"

"She needs to change."

My heart seems to be limping. Weakening.

"How? *Look at her!*" the man (Kai?) shouts.

"There's no one here powerful enough to force her. She has to do it herself."

"Or what?"

"Or she'll die." Julian—I'm pretty sure it's Julian—has the grace to sound sad.

A shape thuds next to me. Something is tugged from my wrists and takes strips of skin with it but all I manage is a whine.

Am I lying on my back or my side? Why can't I tell?

"Syn," Kai says softly. "Syn, you have to change."

Fingers stroke my hair, the only part not burned. I'm just pink and blonde and a red, blistered mess. I close my eyes. Are they already closed? I'm so tired.

"Change, Syn," Kai says, "or I'll make you change."

He can't make me. He's a Lesser, not a Drakul and even if he were a Drakul, he wouldn't be stronger.

I'm going to die because I'm the most powerful here and no one can help me.

I search for the shift, the singing, swollen energy of it, but it dances from my grip like wisps of fog. It's too late. I'm too far gone.

My heart slows. My breathing barely stirs my chest, my skin tight and crispy enough to crackle.

"Last chance, Syn," Kai whispers.

His words fade. I wish I could have told him all my secrets.

My body sinks into the ground and drops towards darkness. Numbness silences my protesting nervous system.

Will I feel myself burn to ash? If Kai is close enough, will I burn him, too?

Move away, Kai. I've hurt you enough. I try to say it but may only think it. Or maybe I say it and he can't understand. Do I still have lips and a tongue?

"Change goddammit!" Kai yells.

His hands grab my shoulders and he shakes me.

He *shakes* me.

The fresh pain zaps my heart into a canter. My scream dissolves to a roar and my tortured skin stretches.

Oh, god, *I can't take it!*

Joints pop and reform. Bones crack and re-knit. If this is how everyone else shifts, I'm surprised they change into their dragon form at all.

Fuck that for a laugh.

The agony barely fades when I'm left panting into the grass, sprawled on my side. The joy of the shift fizzles beneath my exhaustion. My wings shudder with each heaving breath. A cool hand touches my neck. Hesitant and light.

"Syn?"

Kai.

I've let him get too close. Let myself get too close. He makes me want something more. Something different.

Something dangerous.

I roll carefully onto my belly, and gather my haunches. I crack open one eye. Kai kneels beside me, his jeans wet from the frosted grass. He must be freezing.

Stop worrying about Kai.

My gaze meets Julian's where he stands behind him, Raine tucked under his shoulder. The people beyond are a pale-faced blur.

"Maddy," Julian says. "Don't—"

I launch into the sky. My wings flap hard to lift a body that weighs as much as Jupiter. My muscles sing at the freedom but my skin still aches with the ghost of pain. I bank away from the house, flying quickly to put distance between me and the inevitable pursuit, avoiding the orange glow of Peebles. The stars twinkle coldly in their bed of velvet. I fly high enough to claw them but it leaves me winded.

Why am I heavy?

I cock my head. Kai clings to my neck, stark and beautiful and blue with cold.

'What the hell are you doing!?' I shriek.

He flinches, claps his hands to his ears, and drops off my back.

26

Catching a falling human is tricky with my brain babbling at me and my heart in my mouth.

I dive past Kai and roll on my back, spreading my wings against the wind resistance. The move screams in my shoulders but Kai collides with my chest and I wrap my arms around him, my hands clenched to sheath my claws. Another roll points my snout at the ground, and I aim for a block of trees circling a reservoir. Curling around Kai, I crunch through a layer of jaggy spruce and hit the ground on splayed feet, the impact shuddering through my legs.

Kai is limp and cold in my arms.

My tail scrapes branches, needles and cones into a pile around a chunk of deadwood. I suck air and huff a fireball at the pyre, coaxing the stubborn flame when it sputters on damp wood. The fire crackles, and I lay Kai next to it. The tips of his wings stick out below the hem of his leather jacket. He blinks at me, and shivers.

'*Are you okay?*' I say in a tone far less shrill.

He nods and hugs himself. "How are you speaking in my head?"

'*We can choose to project our thoughts to Lessers and other Drakul,*' I say, settling on my haunches and shuffling closer, sandwiching Kai between the fire and the warmth from my flame sacs.

"I feel so special," he says through gritted teeth.

'What the hell were you thinking?'

He shakes his head and shoves up on his bum, his legs pulled to his chest. His teeth chatter and the movement quivers his earring. I inch nearer. He slides me a look, and I stop.

"You were just going to leave?"

'They almost killed me, Kai.'

"And what about me?"

Where is bitch-Maddy when I need her? I should say something harsh. Something like—what about you? You're nothing to me. I saved your life because I pitied you.

The lies curdle on the tip of my tongue.

A shape crashes through the spruce and thumps on all fours, snorting needles. I leap to my feet. Julian scratches behind his horns and tucks his rainbow wings into his flanks. He flares a crest the same colour as his wings, regarding me with his amber and green eyes.

'Don't turn me human, Maddy,' he says. *'I'm not here to drag you back. And it hurts.'*

'Who else is coming?'

'No one else.'

'So why are you here?'

'I came to see what you're planning on doing with Kai.'

We both tilt our heads to look at Kai sitting by the fire. The flame reflects in his eyes, a miniature fire smouldering in ash. The yellow light softens his face, and my wayward heart skips. Julian's gaze shifts to me but I keep my focus on Kai.

"It's rude to talk about someone like they're not there," he says, his shivers slowing.

'Can you hear Julian?' I say.

"No, only you, but it's obvious you're talking about me."

Crap. How can he still hear me? I was directing my thoughts to Julian, not him.

'He can always hear you?' Julian grins. *'So you have to watch what you say.'*

'I don't have anything to hide,' I huff.

'Maddy, you've been hiding your whole life.'

'I don't know what you mean.'

Julian plonks his arse on the ground like an over-sized dog, his tail curled around his feet. *'I tried to hide and it only made me miserable.'*

'I'm not miserable.'

Dragon's don't have eyebrows but I know a cocked brow when I see one.

'You don't have to go back to them,' he says softly.

'They're my family. I love them.'

'What about Kai?'

My pulse betrays me again.

'Take him with you,' I say.

"I'm not going with Julian," Kai says, rubbing his hands then holding his palms out to the fire. "If you want me safe, take me back to Julian's. Otherwise, I'm coming with you."

I bare my teeth at him. His eyes widen a fraction before he scowls.

"Threatening me won't change my mind."

'I can just leave you here,' I growl.

"You won't," he says, smug. "I'll freeze to death."

Julian watches us both with amusement.

'Your family aren't home yet,' he says. *'I called them and said I'd moved you but if they attacked my house again, I'd kill you.'*

168

Another grin. *'A bluff. I knew they'd trace the call but it sent them to a place called Lairg, in the Highlands. My contacts left a trail that's taken them on a nice tour of the Scottish islands. They were on Harris today. If they get bored, they could return tomorrow. If they stick it to the end, the clues lead them right back to Lairg in three days.'*

Kai has managed to control his wings while Julian was speaking, his leather jacket still holding up surprisingly well. Pink returns to his cheeks with the heat of the fire.

"She's not as mean as she pretends, in case you haven't figured that out already," he says.

'Shut up, Kai,' I say.

'I figured it out,' Julian says.

Kai twitches. "Hey, I heard that."

Julian swings his snout to me. *'You were never cruel to me because you weren't cruel, as much as you want the other families to believe it.'*

'You were the only Romanov I liked.'

'Not even Dominic?'

'I hated Dominic.'

"She's not so bad when she finally tells the truth," Kai says.

I bow my head, and sigh. *'Kai, stop helping me.'*

He smirks. "The fire's getting low."

I blow a stream of flame and the burst of orange light chases the shadows from the trees.

'Come back with me, Maddy,' Julian says. *'You and Kai are welcome there.'*

'Caysie would beg to differ. And you know why I can't.'

'Caysie and the rest will be banished.'

'I still can't.'

Julian shoves onto his feet and pads closer. *'Don't wait too*

169

long, Maddy. It's lonely being the odd one out. Seven months ago, I was ready to kill myself and look what I have now.'

'Maybe I'm not as brave as you.'

'All it takes is one step. A terrifying step but you could be happy.'

'I am *happy.*'

"She's lying again," Kai says.

Julian chuffs a laugh but his face sobers. *'Are you sure you can keep him safe from your family?'*

'No, so I'll convince him to go back.'

"No, you won't," Kai says.

I cast my eyes to the stars but the interlocking branches block the view. Julian stretches his wings and settles them at his sides.

'You should tell him how you feel.'

My heart thumps. I glance at Kai but it seems Julian is back to projecting his thoughts only to me.

'I don't know what you mean,' I say.

'You love him.'

'No, I don't.'

'Your heart rate says otherwise.' Julian's tongue lolls in a full-mouthed grin. *'I fell in love with Raine the second she chopped off my brother's head. She fell in love with me after we kissed.'*

'We haven't—'

I shut my mouth and slide a glance at Kai. He watches us intently.

'I saw his face when he pulled you out of the greenhouse, Maddy. You should tell him.'

'It doesn't matter.'

Julian butts his head into my shoulder. *'It's the only thing that matters. Life is too short to spend it alone.'*

'I'm not—' My teeth click together, and I shake my head.

'*You can still be alone surrounded by people.*' His legs bunch. '*Come back to mine and you don't have to pretend anymore. Bye, Kai. Maddy.*'

Julian leaps into the trees and disappears in a rustle of needles. Water droplets splatter the ground. A cone bounces into the fire in a burst of sparks.

Kai pokes a stick into the dying flames. "What did Julian say?"

'*He said I should go back with him.*'

"And are we?"

'*I'm not.*'

Kai narrows his eyes. "Then neither am I."

'*I can't protect you from my family, Kai. Look what happened last time.*'

"Why do you even want to go home?"

I pace on the other side of the fire. '*They're my family—*'

"Yeah, yeah—you love them. But I saw your expression when everyone was describing what you'd done. You were miserable."

'*I'd had a bad day. That's why I was miserable.*'

Kai tosses his stick into the flames. "So, what—you're going to go back to torturing people? Marry some guy you hate?"

'*Yes, if it keeps my family safe.*'

"If your family love you, they should want you to be happy."

'*I'm happy when they're safe.*'

"No, you're not," Kai says quietly.

A growl rumbles in my chest. '*Then what do you suggest I do—abandon them in favour of the Romanovs and watch the other families rip them apart?*'

"You could tell them how you feel."

Goddamn. Why does everyone want me to talk about my

feelings all of a sudden? The stupid things are what got me into this mess.

"Maybe they're sick of being brutal," Kai says while I continue to pace.

I snort. *'You really think Libby pines for a gentler life?'*

"Okay, maybe not your psycho sister but what about your dad? He already shirked convention because of your mum. Wouldn't he do it again for you?"

I stop and gape at Kai. My sarcastic comeback lodges in my brain somewhere, unformed.

Would he? The other families are terrified of Dad. He's swift to assert his dominance and harsh in his retribution, even when he's closed off in grief. But what if he's pretending? What if we've both been pretending this entire time?

A weird pressure expands in my gut. Hope and optimism. I try to quash it but it tingles outward.

I'm tired of being a fake. I never let myself think too far ahead because the thought of what I'll have to do scares me. I often don't have the energy to get out of bed. Being hated— being hateful—is exhausting.

But I'll have to tell Dad the truth about Mum. Then maybe he'll hate me, too.

Or maybe he'll forgive me. Help me. Love me like he used to. Kai seems to have absolved me of my sins against him. If he can do that after I turned his world upside-down, surely my father will also show mercy? He'd want me to be happy, despite everything I've done... wouldn't he?

Kai stands, brushing needles from his jeans. "Let's go talk to him."

'This...' I shake my head. *'This is a bad idea.'*

"But you haven't said no."

'*Would it matter?*'

Kai smirks. "No."

'*I preferred it when you were scared of me,*' I grumble, and paw at the thawed ground. '*I need to eat first, anyway.*'

"Now? And, more importantly, what?" He flashes a full-dimpled grin. "Not me, right?"

'*One bite of you was enough, thank you,*' I sniff. '*Wait here.*'

His face sobers. "I will. So you better come back."

The dwindling flames cast shadows in his cheekbones and smoulder in his eyes. The zip of his jacket has loosened, framing the hollow of his throat. I drag my gaze away and dive through the Julian-shaped hole in the canopy, bursting into crisp air and cold sky.

I admit, abandoning Kai flitted across my mind but it's as much a fantasy as me being forgiven by my father for the death of my mother and getting his blessing to live outside the norms of Drakul society. I mean, dragons are allowed to screw Lessers but they'd never actually mate one.

Not that I'm screwing one. And I doubt the one in question would be so inclined.

What did Julian mean by I didn't see his face? I guess Kai cares enough to dislike the sight of me as a giant, melting flesh-bubble but I'm always going to be the monster who ruined his life. If he doesn't hate me for that anymore, I still do.

I fly as low as I dare, keeping away from the lights of houses and the sweep of headlamps from cars on the roads. A fox chases a rabbit across a field, the prey's heart a constant thrum, and I munch them both, wincing at the fox's stringy muscles.

I usually avoid predators. The meat is lean and tastes funny but a healing change takes a lot of energy and I've not exactly been eating regularly over the past three days.

I sniff out the warren under an embankment of broom, and claw through the sandy soil. Panicked rabbits scatter, two into my mouth, and I scoop another two on the way back to the spruce plantation. A tawny owl disappears down my gullet with a startled, "Twoo."

I drop next to Kai, and he jumps.

"Christ's sake," he says. "You did that on purpose."

'Haven't got the slightest clue what you mean.' I lick blood and feathers from my snout.

"Are we going now?"

'Julian doesn't think my family will be home yet.'

"So we'll wait for them. Crouch down so I can climb on."

I give him a haughty stare. *'I'm carrying you this time. Less chance of an accident.'*

"If you hadn't shrieked in my head, I would've been fine."

'You would've frozen before I got half-way home.'

He opens his mouth to argue then seems to change his mind.

"Fine, but what's to stop me freezing again?"

'Breathing fire makes me warmer.' I sit on my haunches. *'And a winter coat would help.'*

He cocks an eyebrow. "This jacket has sentimental value."

'It can still have sentimental value when I get you a coat with a proper fleece lining. And maybe a hood.'

"You're not buying me a coat."

'Well, I'd give you one of mine but I'm not sure it'll fit.'

"Syn?"

'What?'

"Quit stalling."

I sigh. *'Turn around.'*

He hesitates then shows me his back. His head reaches my shoulder. I step towards him, and he tenses. My heart flops into my stomach. I move slow, corralling him against my body, one arm around his belly, the other diagonal across his chest, talons tucked away.

I look at him upside-down. *'Is this okay?'*

He nods but there's a lot going on in his dark eyes.

"What are the chances of me falling?"

'Nil,' I say.

"How long is the"—he appears to search for a word—"flight?"

'Twenty minutes.'

He takes a deep breath and lets it out. "Do it."

I hop and flap, clawing through the branches in an ungainly scramble instead of leaping and accidentally breaking Kai's neck. My legs shove off the trees, snapping branches. I tear from the canopy and gain height, cradling Kai. His heart beats hard and fast. I keep my flame sacs active but the wind of our flight will be uncomfortable on his face and hands.

What is he thinking? Why would he volunteer to return to the place he was attacked, his life changed forever, to talk to my father, of all things?

Maybe I called his bluff and he was hoping I'd take him back to Julian's. Or maybe he likes me. Really, *really* likes me.

Shut up, Maddy.

I shut up and fly home.

27

My house looms silent and black on the cliff. I circle once and dive off the edge, swooping into the hidden cave entrance. Kai's nails dig in to my arm across his stomach, his body so stiff, he's practically vibrating.

I forgot he can't see in the dark.

'It's okay,' I say. *'I know where I'm going.'*

My soothing tone fails to relax him. I zoom through the gentle curve of tunnels. My wings flap to slow myself and I touch down, claws scraping on stone. I spit fire at the candles on the wall and a soft glow fills the chamber.

It's my favourite one. Quartz and amethyst streak the walls and sparkle everywhere. Stalactites make a ceiling of teeth. Water drips and burbles unseen.

I'm hoping it'll be the least likely to trigger Kai's anxiety.

Reluctantly, I ease away and leave him squinting in the centre of the room. He blinks a few times and looks around. His eyes trace the lines of gems and stop on the bean bag near the far wall. He squats next to the bookshelf and brushes a finger across the spines.

All mine. Mostly romance, some quite erotic. Libby and the twins don't read so I never have to worry about them mocking my choices.

I retreat towards the entrance. *'I'll, um, be right back. Stay here.'*

I skitter out into the corridor before he glances up. If he glances up. Maybe he's engrossed in reading about a woman who trades sex for secrets. Or horny werewolves. Or a million other steamy stories where the female always gets multiple orgasms and definitely doesn't say no to oral.

I dunk my head under the closest waterfall and lap at the chill liquid.

Kai reads books with thematic substance and complex plots. I read books with smut and reverse harems. I bought *1984* when I was in a funk about my own dystopian future. Did not finish. I've never even read the classics.

Why do I care what Kai thinks?

You know why.

Dribbling water, I pad to a narrow chamber and glance both ways down the corridor. My shift is smooth and easy rather than the horror show it was earlier.

That'll definitely be the end of the period since reptiles don't menstruate. I'm not sure why it doesn't return with my human body but it comes in handy. One change and bye-bye bleeding. It's pretty useful for situations where having a period would be inconvenient. Like sex.

Not that that's relevant.

But Kai is in my house. Voluntarily. We could be alone for three days. What are we going to do—watch TV?

Get your mind out of the gutter, Maddy.

Shelves and poles line the narrow chamber, crammed with a multitude of clothes and shoes. I select dark-pink lace underwear—do I think I'm getting lucky or something?—and pull on a pair of jeans that hug my bum and thighs, and flare at the bottom. Low cut. You can see my hip bones. Next, pink wedges so I can almost look Kai in the eye. Good kissing height.

Shut *up*, Maddy.

The top is a dusky floral print with peek-a-boo shoulders and a deep V cut. It looks great with my hair. Okay, and my boobs. I check my reflection in the mirror at the end of the room. Perfect skin and wide, cornflower-blue eyes. I fluff my hair until it falls in messy but artful layers to frame my face and curl on my chest. My outfit highlights my slim figure and the curves where they matter. I apply a slick of gloss—tingly mint—and force myself away.

Putting on makeup would be too much.

I tip-toe to the chamber where I left Kai and scold myself for tip-toeing. But I don't stop. I peek around the arch.

He's sitting in the bean bag, his long legs sprawled out. Spikes of emerald and violet have flopped into his grey eyes, his head bent to read the book in his hands. One of the racier titles. I swallow and nearly duck away. Instead, I raise my chin.

I am Madisyn Della Valle. I eat sexy human boys for breakfast. Or Lesser boys, though that's not technically true. I've slept with humans, never Lessers.

Am I stalling again?

I step into the chamber. Kai glances up and goes very still. His heart beats faster. I peer over my shoulder but there's no one else here. It's me he's looking at like that.

I guess he's not seen me in normal clothes for a while.

He snaps the book shut and places it on top of the bookshelf without taking his gaze off me. Even he can't make getting out of a bean bag graceful—oh god, so cute—but he manages

178

with the minimum of grunts and heaves. He walks towards me in silence. Halts with a couple of inches between us. He smells like coconut and fresh air.

"Expecting someone else?" I say.

It sounded coquettish in my head but it comes out a bit high.

"You should've seen what you were like when I carried you out of the greenhouse. Your eyes were cloudy. You had blisters on the skin you had left, and that wasn't much. I saw your collarbone through an ulcer." He shudders, gripping my chin and tilting my face one way then the other. "Now, there's not a mark on you."

"You shook me," I say with a note of accusation.

"You were dying. I panicked."

"Why—" I clear my throat. Nope. Not asking him that. "Why do you care?"

Okay, I guess I *am* asking him that.

A challenge sparks in his eyes. "That's my question. And the only one you haven't answered."

Oh, crap.

He's still holding my chin. I could easily break loose. Run. Hide. Far enough so I don't have to stare into those intense, lie-detecting eyes.

"Why do you care, Syn?" he says, tugging me closer so I have to crane my neck a little further.

I mash my lips together and glare at him.

"Okay, then," he chuckles. "Just don't bite my face off."

Bite his face off? Why would I...?

His hand slides into my hair. My heart somersaults into my stomach and bounces around like a trapped squirrel. Kai lowers his head and places a light kiss on my mouth. My thighs tremble. My fingers tense on supple leather.

Oh, jeez. I'm unzipping his jacket.

My hands bunch in the thick material covering his firm chest. His heart thrums under my fingers and in my head. It's all I can hear. Or maybe it's mine.

"I knew it," he whispers against my lips.

He kisses me harder. His tongue touches mine with an electric sizzle. We tangle together and he strokes me with the solid ball of his piercing. My knees buckle. His arm loops around the small of my back and catches me, pressing me to him. The reminder of his second piercing does nothing for my motor control.

"Something wrong with your legs, Syn?" Kai says.

I pant in his face. "Shut up and kiss me."

He picks me up. My legs wrap around his waist. He staggers to the bean bag, devouring my mouth all the way, and collapses on top of me. Something pops. Tiny, white balls puff out the side of the bag.

"Whoops," Kai says.

"Ignore it." I fist my hands in his hair. "I'm sturdier."

He groans and claims my mouth. I dissolve into the deflating bean bag.

Romance books talk about the heroine being kissed sense-less. I thought it was just dramatic flare but Kai robs my senses of everything but him. His lips—oh sweet god, I'm doomed. The fresh taste of him and my mint gloss. The scent I drink with every breath. The thunder of his heart. His hips, hard against mine. Everything so hard. I squirm against him, reeling from the overload. He shoves up on his forearms and the bean bag wilts, rolling us together.

"Christ," he says. "Are you still on your period? Though, right now, I couldn't give a fuck."

My lips flap. Nothing of coherence falls out. I manage to shake my head.

Kai smirks. "Madisyn Della Valle stunned speechless. I'm honoured."

I drag his mouth back to mine. His tongue turns my body liquid. Little begging noises catch in my throat, and I rub myself against his rigid parts. The friction is delicious.

"Bedroom," he gasps. "How do we get there?"

I have no idea how we get there in the dark. Sometimes I lead, sometimes Kai leads but we don't stop kissing, and only kissing. I burn for him to touch me everywhere. That tongue... Sucking, licking...

No, I don't mean there.

The pulse between my legs calls me a liar.

Kai pins my hands to a wall and snogs the strength right out of me. I trip on the stairs and end up straddling him. By the time we make it to the bedroom, I'm throbbing so hard, I see stars. The door closes behind us and I sag against it, fumbling for the overhead light. Kai has his back to me. He walks around the bed, trailing his fingers on the covers, to the alcove he squashed himself in. The words carved in wood.

Crap. I forgot.

"We can go in one of the guest rooms…"

My words dry at his dark, hungry eyes.

"Tell me another secret," he says.

I swallow my instinctive, "I don't have any more secrets." He wouldn't believe me. I abandon my support door and manage to make it across the room, grabbing one of the bedposts.

"I've never had sex in my bed," I say.

"What do you do in this big bed, except sleep?"

"I touch your carving"—oh, please, you can't tell him that—

"and myself."

"Show me," he growls.

Oh, man.

I kick off my wedges and shaky-crawl to my pillows. Kai kneels on the end of the bed. My heart slams against my ribs, loud enough for even his human hearing to detect. I can taste my pulse.

"It would help if you got a little naked first," I say, my voice as quivery as the rest of me.

"You getting shy on me, Syn?"

My flushed cheeks betray me. Kai smirks, and shrugs off his jacket. His grey hoodie and t-shirt follow in a oner and I realise my mistake. The sight of his body doesn't settle me. It makes me dizzy. Those broad shoulders, sculpted lines and narrow hips. The raven tattoo I want to explore. His jeans ride low and the obvious bulge in the material gives me heart palpitations. He sits on his heels, knees spread, hands loose on his thighs, and I lose a few minutes staring at the bunch of his abdominal muscles.

"Your turn," he says, and I jump.

I pop the button on my jeans and hesitate at the zip. Nerves churn in my gut. I struggle to take more than quick sips of breath.

This is silly. And hot. Oh, it's fucking hot.

I undo the zip and lift my arse, wiggling out of my jeans, my thighs pressed together. The heat of Kai's gaze flares goosebumps on my skin and tightens my stomach. I gulp when he raises his eyes from my underwear to my face.

"Nervous, Syn?"

"No," I say and it wobbles.

Dammit, Maddy. You're better than this. It's no different to wearing your mask and showing only what you want people to see. Confidence. Allure. Power. He should be the one trembling for it. Begging.

I stroke the lace edge of my panties but can't bring myself to go further, as wet as those panties may be.

"Why haven't you had sex in your bed?" Kai says, his voice steady though his heart pounds nearly as fast as mine.

I'm surprised his wings haven't appeared but then he does have excellent control.

"No privacy," I say. "And it'd be rude to kick them out straight after."

"You going to kick me out?"

I manage a smirk. "We'll see how you do."

That's better. Playful.

"Take off your knickers," he says, and my muscles turn to jelly.

I slide my underwear off, legs still pressed together.

In a society where nakedness doesn't raise an eyebrow, I've never felt more exposed.

It takes all my willpower to part my thighs but I can't watch Kai while I do it. I stare at the covers between my spread legs.

"Look at me, Syn."

The need in his voice drags my gaze up. His hands are clenched on his thighs, the white scar of my teeth visible on his forearm. My arm flops off the side of the bed, my fingers finding the slashed lines. My palm scorches my belly.

"What do you picture when you fuck yourself?" he says, his voice deep enough to vibrate up my legs.

I lick my lips. "You."

"What am I doing?"

"Touching me."

"Show me how."

I squirm at the demand but my hand glides lower. My nails dig in to his carved words, desperate for stability while the rest of me throbs. My finger brushes my clitoris and I clamp my teeth on a moan.

Good lord, this isn't going to take long.

I circle the swollen nub until my breath hitches and my head falls back, my eyes half-lidded. I fight to focus on Kai. The intensity of his gaze tingles where my hand touches, pooling heat and rushing outward. I slide a finger inside and whimper his name.

He launches across the bed with a growl and his mouth feasts on mine. I glimpse a flash of gold before my eyes roll back. I try to move my hand but he pins it in place and his finger enters beside mine, stretching me, filling me up.

"Oh, fuck," I moan into his mouth.

The noise he makes has me tightening around our fingers. His hand grinds my palm on my clit, his finger curled and stroking inside me, slick and gliding against mine. Over and over the soft wall at the front of my body. That sweet, glorious spot. I explode around us both but he shows no mercy, coaxing my orgasm to near-fainting level while his tongue teases mine in time to his finger. The thought of his tongue where his hand is now leaves me boneless.

I think I do faint. Is he calling my name?

"Blink if you're alive, Syn," he says.

My eyelids flutter.

He chuckles. "Close enough."

His finger slips out of me, and I writhe, my muscles still singing from his touch.

"Fucking hell," he groans.

"Hnn…" I manage.

He flops on his side and cuddles me into his chest, his breath hot in my ear.

"I think you need a moment to recover," he purrs. "Let me know when you can say more than consonants."

"Mmm," I say.

Oh, god, sex. His other piercing. If that was foreplay, I may die of pleasure.

I relax in his arms. He's warm and solid and smells heavenly. My body gets heavier. My heart slows to one beat a minute. Gentle darkness sucks me under.

No, I can't. That would be rude. Madisyn Della Valle leaves no man unsatisfied.

But not this time.

28

I swim slowly up from sleep as if I've dived to the depths of the ocean in my dragon form and the darkness clings to me, unwilling to let go. My heart echoes in the weightless void. One breath, I'm floating. The next, I'm lying on something solid and warm.

I don't remember my mattress being so firm. Or my pillow, which seems to have bones. And my bed is breathing.

I snap awake and blink at a pert little nipple in front of my nose. Ribs glide under my hand. The rise and fall rocks me in a gentle motion.

I hold very still. Kai's heart thuds under my ear while mine trips in double time. His breath brushes the top of my head. The zipper of his jeans presses against a sensitive part of me.

Oh, god, Libby would be proud. I got my spectacular orgasm, rolled over and fell asleep. Kai must think I'm a bitch. I just treated him like a whore, without the payment. As if his wants don't matter as long as I get serviced.

Is he sleeping? He can't be sleeping. He must be furious. Maybe he regrets kissing me already. Maybe he got overwhelmed by the Lesser connection. Can it be that strong? Is this all just a lie?

"I know you're awake, Syn," Kai says. "I can feel you

thinking."

I wince and peek through a fringe of hair. Weak daylight filters through the curtains, the main light off. Kai lies pillowed on one arm, propping his head up. It does wonderful things to his muscles underneath me but it also makes his cheekbones and eyes more severe.

"I'm sorry," I say.

"What for?"

"Falling asleep. It was rude."

His mouth twitches. "Rude?"

"I didn't mean to leave you"—what is the best word, unsatisfied? Trembling with lust?—"hanging," I say hopefully.

He coughs. "Hanging?"

"Are you just going to repeat everything I say?"

I sit up and straddle his waist. My dusky-pink top tickles my thighs, protecting my modesty, but I'm very aware of my lack of knickers. Kai is stiffer than the material of his jeans. My hands get distracted by the ridges and lines of his stomach.

Stop petting him, Maddy.

"What did you mean to do?" he says, his deep voice dragging my gaze to his face. To heat and hunger and smouldering grey.

I gulp. "I meant to play with your other piercing."

His slow smile stuns me for a second. Or ten minutes. Those dimples should be illegal.

"You're awake now," he says.

Anticipation fizzes in my gut. It's not the Lesser connection. It's Kai. Just Kai.

Though perhaps the connection is all it is for him. Why else would he care about me? Care if I'm happy? It would explain why he volunteered to come back here. So eager to please me.

Don't think about it.

I ease backwards, my fingers tracing the edge of his jeans. A pulse jumps in his belly. I pop the button and lower the zip. His heart rate picks up.

This is why I love being able to hear heartbeats—every skip and flutter reacting to my touch. It's so fun to tease.

I slip my hand through the slit in his boxers and curl my fingers around solid, scorching flesh that throbs against my palm.

Where is this piercing?

I pop him out through the gap in his boxers.

"Oh, wow," I say.

Kai grins. "You really know how to boost a guy's ego."

Heat blazes in my cheeks and I drop my eyes right back to his penis, which makes heat blaze in lower areas. The silver piercing goes vertically through his shaft just behind the crown and angles backwards. A smooth ball holds each end in place. Muscles clench at the thought of how that must feel, gliding in and out...

"I never knew you blushed so easily, Syn," Kai says, still grinning.

I slide my hand upwards and roll his piercing between my fingers.

"Christ," he says, his breath rushing out.

"Does it hurt?"

He shakes his head, his eyes half-lidded. His heart is really thudding now but I can definitely get it to go faster.

"Will it hurt me?"

I stroke his shaft, trailing my fingers over the piercing and his smooth crown. He moans, and the sound tingles to my gut.

"No," he manages to say.

"What will it feel like?"

I wriggle backwards, continuing to stroke and squeeze. Kai's ribs heave but there's no sign of his wings yet so he's not too far gone.

"Amazing," he gasps, his hands fisted in the covers.

This is better. This is how it should be—me in control, driving him wild, not squirming and breathless after one kiss.

"You seem confident," I say, and suck the head of him into my mouth.

"Oh, god."

His hips flex under my hand, my other hand still wrapped around his shaft. My tongue explores metal and silky flesh. The piercing clicks against my teeth, and I tug gently on it. Kai arches off the bed, the noise in his throat firing an ache between my legs.

Sweet lord, I need him inside me.

I lift my head and get distracted by the sight of him, his spine bowed, eyes shut. He's biting his lip, and I want to climb on top of him and drive him deep. I want him to be the first and only man I have sex with in my bed. I want to banish the memory of his last time here with something good. Something amazing.

And if he later realises he doesn't care about me, I'll have this to remember when I'm alone in my bed with nothing but my fingers and his carving.

I rise onto my knees and shuffle until I'm straddling his waist. He blinks at me. Removing his jeans and boxers seems like too much effort. I need him now.

His heart thunders but beneath it, there's another sound. Faint and unmistakable.

I freeze. "Someone's home."

"Please tell me you're joking," he groans.

I tremble above him. I've never been this horny in my life. The freaking *ache* of it hollows my gut and weakens my legs. I want to lower myself onto him and scream his name to the ceiling.

I huff and swing my leg over, searching for my underwear. "Unfortunately not."

"Goddamn cock-blocking motherfucker," he mutters.

I laugh at his aggrieved expression while he tucks his extremely erect penis back into his boxers and zips up his jeans. I find my clothes, and he freshens up in my en-suite then I use the toilet and fix my hair, my eyes sparkling, cheeks flushed.

"It's not too late to sneak away," I say, leading him into the corridor outside my room.

"Would you come, too?"

"Yes," I say, no hesitation.

His lips curve. "If getting into my pants is all it takes to change your mind, I would've offered earlier."

"Shut up, Kai," I say.

"Anyway, it doesn't matter. If you run away, you put them in danger, right? And you'd just worry about them. So you have to talk to them."

I sigh and start walking towards the front of the house. "I don't know how they'll react. Well, apart from Libby."

Libby will never join Julian and Raine. She revels in the brutality of our society. I love my sister but she really is a cruel bitch.

"Is your dad going to eat me?" Kai says.

"I won't let him."

"That's not exactly comforting."

"Here be dragons," I say grimly.

Kai's stride is somewhat bow-legged and he adjusts his crotch after a couple of steps. Despite the danger I'm leading him into, I can't help a smirk.

"You having trouble, Kai?"

He slides me a narrowed look. His hand snaps out and tangles in my hair. My spine hits the wall. Kai grinds all that hardness into me and reignites the burning ache in my belly.

"If your dad doesn't have me for breakfast, I'll make you pay for that," he whispers against my lips.

His mouth swallows what I suspect is an, "Oh, yes, please." The second his tongue touches mine, my legs turn to slush. I sag against the wall but Kai kisses me until my head reels and I make little begging noises in my throat. He pulls away, and I blink at him for a long, *long* time.

"You fight dirty," I huff when I get my breath back.

He holds his hand out. "I have to, with you."

"What do you mean?"

"You only show the real Syn when you get flustered."

He wiggles his fingers and I reach for his hand. My palm tingles against his. The tingles spread when he twines his fingers in mine.

"Do you know how annoying it is that you can read me so easily? I've spent my whole damn life acting and you see right through it."

His finger strokes my cheek. "You flustered, Syn?"

"No," I grumble.

"Liar."

He steals a kiss. Nothing long enough to weaken my legs, though it shivers in my kneecaps.

"Now, let's go introduce me to your dad," he says.

Oh, *fuck*.

29

"Someone's here," Libby growls.

I sweep Kai behind me and hustle down the corridor to the archway into the kitchen. The granite of the breakfast island sparkles, a glass bowl of apples placed perfectly in the centre. A huge range cooker and American-style fridge hulk between cream cabinets. Recessed lights twinkle on more granite.

"Maddy!" Libby squeals, and throws herself at me. "Did you make those traitors pay? I hope you left enough of Julian and his little slag for me."

"Libby, for goodness' sake," I say, sliding into my familiar role.

Eady and Dory stay perched on stools beside the breakfast island but they babble questions: "How did you escape? What was it like? Did you eat anyone?"

Libby's hair tickles my nose and I inhale the scent of peaches. Dory munches on a shiny, red apple while Eady watches her.

The twins have never been big on affection, except with each other.

"Where's Dad?" I say, caught between joy at being with my sisters and terror for the very same reason.

"He's just coming," Libby says. "He's inviting the Kaskbirches in for breakfast. You wouldn't believe how many places we've searched for you."

Crap. The Kaskbirches are not what I need.

I ease away from Libby, and her gaze snaps over my shoulder. "You found the Lesser."

Her expression freezes my gut—hunger, but not for kissing or tender, intimate things. Hunger for flesh and blood and screaming.

She frowns at me. "What are you doing, Maddy?"

My arm, flung out, bars her from circling around me to reach Kai. His heart is beating fast and the excitement of the sound—the fear, the chase—glitters in the eyes of the twins.

Oh, god, what was I thinking, letting him come here?

I step back to stop Libby squeezing past me on the other side. A cabinet with an orchid in a clay pot blocks her path. Libby cocks her head but stays where she is.

"No one touches Kai but me," I say, calm and slow.

Libby glances towards the French door, probably checking to see if Dad is in earshot. She turns a smirk on me. With her glacier-blue eyes and white-blonde hair, she's ice maiden all the way through.

"Oh, Maddy," she says, "I know he's your first Lesser but I never thought you'd be overwhelmed so easily. Don't get me wrong, it's adorable."

Eady giggles, and swipes the half-finished apple from Dory's hand. Flesh crunches, spilling juice down her chin.

"You'll get bored of shagging him after a week," Libby says, her smile sharp. "The desire doesn't last, not for the master."

She joins the twins at the island, sliding onto a stool and arching her spine, her elbows on the granite edge. Her short skirt barely brushes the tops of her thighs and she treats me—but mostly Kai—to a show of her silky, red underwear.

Her smile sprouts fangs. "Has he twigged that he's basically your sex slave? That he'll always want you, even when he hates you? And most of them grow to. Or is he cute but dumb?"

I ache to look at Kai's face but I don't dare take my eyes off my sisters. Libby and I hardly ever fight over the same thing but when we do, she's a nasty cow.

But is she telling the truth?

My throat closes. I don't want everything Kai feels for me to be a lie.

The French doors swing open and a chill wind licks in, stirring the copper pots hanging from the ceiling. Dad enters ahead of the Kaskbirches, trim and regal next to their blocky statures. Disappointment punches me in the chest at the sight of Irena, bedecked in pearls and glowing with health.

"Daughter, are you well?" Dad says.

His gaze sweeps the room, alighting on the sprawl of my sisters around the breakfast island—though Libby has the decency to cross her legs—then me, tense in front of Kai. The last time they met, Kai was semi-conscious and covered in blood.

"Hi, Dad," I say. "I'm fine."

Irena's mud-brown eyes narrow and zero in on Kai.

"It's lovely to see you home safe, Madisyn dear, but who is your"—her nostrils flare, blanching white—"friend?"

Gerome scowls, his prominent jaw thrust forward. He has a ridiculous silk cravat tied at his chin, desperate to give the semblance of a neck.

"This is Maddy's first Lesser," Dad says.

"My name is Kai," Kai growls.

Anxiety scrapes its claws on the inside of my stomach but my face stays blank and pleasant and as cold as a snowflake.

Irena titters, though her eyes are flat. "If he's just your Lesser, Madisyn dear, I commend your taste—"

"*Mummy*," Gerome whines.

"—but don't forget who you'll be mating in the autumn. Lessers make wonderful playmates. Until the real power arrives, of course."

Irena squeezes Gerome's arm, and he puffs out his chest. My fingers ache to curl into fists.

Her son could be the strongest Drakul in the world and I still wouldn't want him. He looks like some new species you find in the depths of a cave.

"Could I talk to my family alone, please, Irena?" I say, my smile brittle.

"If it's regarding—"

"It has nothing to do with you."

Pink flares in her cheeks, her wide face pinched.

"It seems a few days in the presence of traitors has made you forget your manners. We wouldn't want the Della Valle name to be tainted by association now, would we, dear? Imagine what might—"

"Irena," Dad says.

Her mouth snaps shut. Long nails flutter at the pearls beading her throat.

"Well. We shall take a stroll by the sea. I hope the conversation is more amicable on our return."

With a sniff, she sails out the French doors, Robert and Gerome following in her wake. Their heartbeats fade. The ice machine in the freezer clatters, and I flinch.

A few days in Kai's presence and I've forgotten how to hide.

Dad flicks the kettle on. He must have dismissed the servants while they were away on their island adventure.

"Did they hurt you, Daughter?" he says.

Libby leaps to her feet. "Let's make them regret it. Hit them now."

"Julian and Raine treated me well."

Libby curls her lip but settles onto the stool.

"Did they keep you at the house the entire time?" Dad says. His mouth quirks at my nod. "I should have known."

"Then that gives us an advantage," Libby says, on her feet again. "What defences do they have? How many are there? Did you notice any weaknesses?"

"That is what I wanted to talk about."

Libby claps her hands. "It's finally happening. Finally, they'll get what they deserve."

Dad lines up five yellow mugs on the counter and waves a sixth. "Would you like a drink, Kai?"

"Um, coffee," he says. "Please."

"Madisyn, come in and sit down instead of hovering in the doorway," Dad says.

"We're fine over here."

"When can we attack?" Libby frowns at us. "Tonight?"

I suck in a breath. "We're not going to attack. We're going to leave them alone."

She barks a laugh. "Why would we do that?"

"I'm tired of hurting people. I only did it after Mum—"

"Aww, Maddy's gone all soft. Is it because of your little pet?"

"Libby?"

"What?"

"Shut the fuck up."

Her mouth gapes. Delight glows in Eady and Dory's faces. A spoon clinks on enamel.

"Madisyn Della Valle, we do not use such language in this

house."

"Sorry, Dad," I say.

Steam puffs from the kettle and the switch clicks off. Libby manages to close her mouth.

"They murdered my Lukas. And your fiancé."

"I hated Dominic, about the same as I hated the rest of the Romanovs except Julian and his father."

Dad pauses in the act of scooping coffee into the mugs and turns to look at me. Libby bares her teeth, her eyes glittering.

"Did they brainwash you or something?" she says. "You're not yourself."

"Don't you get it, Libby? This is me. *Finally* me. The other Madisyn is a lie and I hate that bitch more than the goddamn Romanovs. Sorry, Dad."

"Madisyn—"

"What are you talking about?" Libby growls over Dad's admonishment, stalking towards me. Fury twists her face to something ugly.

"I hurt people so someone wouldn't hurt them worse. Mostly *you*, Libby." I poke my finger in her chest. "Take Kai for example."

"Oh, yes. Let's take your little Lesser as an example." She crosses her arms and glares over my shoulder.

"He didn't escape. I helped him escape. When we were running around in North Berwick, I knew where he was. I was just giving him enough time to get on the train."

I raise my gaze to Dad and his furrowed brow.

What is he thinking? Is he shocked? Ashamed? I should tell him the why of everything now. Why I shouldered the responsibility of protecting our family, no matter the cost to myself. Why everything I do is out of guilt. Why I've ached to talk to him sooner, beg his forgiveness, but I was too afraid of losing him more than I already have.

I lost my mother. I can't lose him, too.

"I don't want to be cruel just to stay in power," I say softly, my eyes on Dad's face, praying for him to understand. "I don't want to mate Gerome troll-face Kaskbirch so the other families won't talk. I want friends who are weaker Drakul, and Lessers. I want to be *nice*. Even though it's my fault—"

"Nice?" Libby scoffs. "The Drakul aren't nice. We fight and mate and terrorise the weak. That's the way it's always been."

"It doesn't mean it has to stay that way."

She pokes me right in the boob. "You sound like *them*."

"They're the only ones who make sense."

"Funny how this sudden clarity came after you made your little Lesser. He's screwed you and your priorities." Her grin chills me to my toes. "Well, I know how to fix that."

Bones shift under her face and the space around her shimmers. I'm vaguely aware of Dad yelling, the twins clapping. A mug smashes on the floor, scattering coffee granules.

Stopping the change is like wrestling a bag of hot air, shoving it down into a smaller and smaller size, cramming it back into the body it came from. Libby snarls. I push her hard and she stumbles, colliding with Dad, who was bounding towards us, his expression thunderous. They hit the floor in a tangle, Libby's skirt around her waist, her legs kicking.

"Eady," she spits, "burn the Lesser."

"Eady, don't—"

"Shit," Kai hisses.

Smoke curls from the sleeve of his leather jacket.

"*Eady!*" I scream.

The clay pot is in my hand. The orchid shivers. It flies in an arc, the waxy-green leaves spread like wings. The pot shatters on Eady's face in an explosion of brown shards and soil. The orchid flops onto the breakfast island. The force throws Eady into Dory and they join the rest of my family on the floor. Eady lies still, blood bright on her pale skin.

I grab Kai's arm, and run.

30

"Pull over, Syn!" Kai yells the second time I almost hit a parked car. He releases his white-knuckled grip on his seat and gestures at a giant stone building. "Stop here. You need to eat something."

The Mustang lurches up a short ramp, metal screeching as the car bottoms out. The bare bones of huge trees claw at the grey sky. I brake hard diagonally across a parking bay. The roar of the engine whimpers to silence. My breathing sounds harsh in the small space.

"I can't believe I hurt my sister." I stare at my fingers fused to the wheel.

"Since I saw the guy she turned into a human torch, I'm glad you did."

But the blood. Her pale face. Did I kill her? She's young. Head injuries can be serious for the Drakul.

Mother and sister. What a great protector I am. Another awful thing stacked against me that needs my father's forgiveness.

A sob lodges in my chest like a dragon's-bane arrow. Kai slips out of the car. I force my numb body to follow. Large blue letters spell out 'Macdonald Marine Hotel' on the front of the palatial building. Flags snap in the wind.

Where the hell are we?

After the fight, we ran to my car and I gunned it out of the garage past a startled Irena and Co. returning from their stroll by the sea. The wind carried her, "Madisyn? Madisyn dear…" long after she'd disappeared in my rear-view mirror. I drove without seeing the roads. No idea of direction or destination. Kai was quiet. Both of us lost to our thoughts.

And none of mine were good.

I stumble up the steps into an entrance-way supported by pillars. Kai holds the glass door open and I walk into a maroon-painted reception. Desks circle a compass mural on the floor. A man in a black suit smiles at us from behind a computer.

"Welcome to the Macdonald hotel and spa," he says. "How may I help you?"

Can you fix fractured families and cure my psycho sisters?

His smile wilts around the edges, though the question was in my head. I realise I'm staring.

"Breakfast," Kai says.

The smile flares. "Are you residents of the hotel?" At Kai's head shake the man says, "Not to worry. You can dine with us for fifteen pounds per person."

Kai waves his card at the reader. We're directed into a white conservatory with padded chairs and a view of the turbulent sea. An old couple tuck into bowls of porridge on the opposite side of the room. The waitress simpers at Kai and hands out menus, barely sparing me a glance. He orders two cooked breakfasts and coffee.

Has anyone cleaned up the spilled coffee in the kitchen? Maybe Eady died amid the granules and soil, her skull crushed. Just like Mum's. Or maybe a shard of ceramic lanced through her brain.

I clamp my hands in my lap and frown at my fingers, willing the tears away. Kai sits and breathes and says nothing, staring out the window, his eyes as cloudy as the day. My stomach shrivels.

How can I possibly eat?

The food arrives, wafting delicious scents, and my belly rumbles. My fork squeaks on china. The old woman glowers at me. I dip a hunk of sausage in egg yolk. Slice, dip, chew, repeat. My plate empties to blobs of yellow and orange floating in grease. The first sip of coffee flows soothing heat all the way to my toes.

"Is it true?"

I jerk at Kai's voice. His gaze is on his food, the bacon the only item missing. He herds his mushrooms from one side of the plate to the other. He looks up when I don't respond.

"Am I a slave?" he says as if the word tastes bad. "Will you get bored?"

How could I get bored? Even now, worried about my sister and sick at myself, I want to climb into his lap. I want him to hold me, comfort me, tell me everything will be all right. This is not the gentle longing I felt at the start. It's intense. *Burning.* I've never seen anyone act this way around their Lessers.

But what if Kai is a slave? What if he only wants to please me because I bit him?

"I don't know," I mumble. "I've never made a Lesser."

"I'm not lesser."

"That's not what it means. Just… lesser than a Drakul."

"That's everyone else to you people."

He balls his napkin on his plate and directs his stormy focus at the sea. The food congeals to a greasy lump in my stomach. The simpering waitress clears our plates but her flirty sparkle fizzles at our silence. She bids the departing old couple farewell in an overly cheery voice and disappears into the kitchen, the door swinging shut behind her.

Kai sighs, his eyes hooded. His shoulders slump.

"I can't do this, Syn," he says softly. "I can't."

Chair legs scrape on the parquet floor. It takes an age to raise my head. Already, he's turned away from me. My throat closes to nothing.

"Wait," I choke. "Kai—"

He strides for the door and doesn't look back.

I struggle to breathe. A circle of moisture appears on the tablecloth. Another. And another. It takes all my years of faking to firm my wobbling lip and banish the tears. I stand up, clamping a hand on the back of the seat when the room sways. I raise my chin. Place one foot in front of the other.

I am Madisyn Della—

Oh, god, *am I* a Della Valle? Have I been disowned?

Now I'm hated by everybody, even the people I love.

I find myself in a restaurant perfectly laid for dinner. Or lunch. Do they serve lunch? Heavy brocade curtains dim the light through the windows. The room has the same compass mural and circular layout as reception.

"Ma'am, we're not serving in here yet," the waitress from the conservatory says. "Can I get you something else?"

I slap my credit card on the bar. "The Fireball whisky."

She hesitates but slips behind the shiny wood. It's after 10am so it's not illegal but it's definitely a little early for the hard liquor.

She selects a cut crystal glass. "Has your friend left—"

"The bottle," I say.

Her hand jitters. "Ma'am?"

"I want the bottle."

"Of course, ma'am."

I wrap my fingers around the neck and carry the whisky into reception. The thud of my heart pulses nausea between my temples. I smile at the man behind the desk, and his eyes widen.

"A room, please," I say. "One I can use now. With late check out."

His head bobs. Fingers tap-tap-tap on the keyboard.

"Have you stayed with us—"

I wave my hand. "Just the key. Not the spiel."

"Of course, ma'am," he says, his gaze flicking between my face and his computer. "Your room is on the second floor. Accessed via the lift."

I snatch the keycard and scuttle towards the metal doors, my body shaking with effort. I jab the button. Again. *Again.* The doors ping then slide shut behind me. Classical music drifts from unseen speakers. The mirrored walls reveal my polite smile to be a grimace, my eyes shiny and mad with tears. A sob bubbles up but I crush it and it hurts.

Not yet. *Not yet.*

I lurch into a carpeted corridor, nearly colliding with a room service trolley. The hum of a vacuum drifts from an open doorway. I march on stiff legs in the opposite direction. It takes three tries to insert my card in the slot. I snarl at the blurry green light. Everything is blurry.

"Fucking man up, *Syn*," I spit, and gulp another sob.

A turquoise tartan bedspread drapes the foot of the king-size bed, matching the pillows embroidered with a thistle. The curtains are grey and turquoise. Heavy, like the ones in the restaurant. Two grey fabric chairs with turquoise thread are angled between a small table in the bay window, looking out at a view of the sea and waves crashing on rocky islands—Lamb island, flanked by North and South Dog islands.

So I'm in North Berwick. The place I took Kai to set him free.

I crawl onto the bed and bury my face in the crevice between the mound of pillows.

Then I sob my stupid little heart out.

31

Between sobs, I swallow cinnamon whisky and enjoy the heat unfurling in my stomach. I drink until I can't feel Kai getting further and further away. Drink until the bed spins. Drink until the pain fades.

But it doesn't.

Tears dampen the pillows, my hair, my cheeks. I curse myself for being weak. For letting a Lesser boy break my heart. Who knew it could be broken so easily?

I use the bathroom. Weep at my blotchy skin and red eyes. Drink some more. Sloppy fingers jab at my phone. The ringing stops. Soft breaths whisper into my ear, my own heavy and wet.

"Is she dead?" I croak.

Silence. The ground yaws beneath me. I take a desperate swallow of whisky to drown the rising panic.

"Eadrea is fine," Dad says, "but—"

"I need to tell you something—"

"—I think it best you don't come home—"

Rustling obscures the words.

"—can't talk now," he says.

"Dad—"

The phone bleeps the end of the call. It slips from numb

fingers and bounces on the carpet. The rim of the bottle clinks on my teeth and I suck another burning mouthful. My stomach rolls, slopping and full. I wrestle the urge to vomit.

Sometimes I doze. I cry when I'm awake. Drink and cry, sad and alone in my hotel room.

Pathetic.

What a wonderful idea it was to tell my family I want to be a nice dragon. A *good* dragon, like Julian. Look at the uproar.

And I never even got to the really bad part.

I snort and the blast of air hoots in the neck of the whisky bottle. Liquid sloshes. Half gone.

I may drink myself into a coma. Like Kai but more successful.

The bottle clunks on the bedside cabinet and I blubber into my pillow, stirring the snotty tissues scattered on the lovely bedspread. My head throbs.

The last time I cried this hard, my mother had just died.

Someone bangs. Maybe on the door, maybe on the wall. It's hard to tell with the room spinning so much.

Am I sobbing loud enough to annoy even weak, human hearing? Well, screw them. My life is falling apart.

The banging continues.

I launch out of bed, bottle in hand. My shoulder hits a wall I'm pretty sure wasn't that close a second ago. I slide along it, dragging myself past the door of the bathroom, the light still on from whenever I used it last.

Whoops. How wasteful. I'm killing the planet as well as my brain cells.

More banging. A growl rumbles in my raw throat.

Wait til I give the knocker a glimpse of my monster. They'll piss their pants.

I stutter past the corner and into space, ping-ponging down the short corridor to the door. I fumble at the handle. It shoogles in my fingers.

Am I shoogling it? What way is it supposed to shoogle?

That's a funny word, shoogle.

The door swings towards me and I almost face-plant into the hall, though there's a figure in the way. Dark and tall. Grey. I seem to be having trouble focusing and can't pick out much else.

"Jesus, Syn," the knocker says.

Words tumble in my mouth—don't call me Syn, my name is Madisyn to you—but nothing falls out except a belch. I stumble backwards, forward a little then back again.

Man, I'm dizzy.

A hand touches my upper arm. I jerk and sit hard on the edge of the bed, whisky slopping onto the pretty turquoise. I stare at the stain, and a tear wibbles and falls to join it.

"Syn—"

"Fuck off," I say. "Fuck off and do what you can't somewhere else."

I wriggle onto the bed and kick with my heels until my spine sinks into damp pillows. Tissues puff onto the floor. The mouth of the bottle bruises my lip but I drink deep. The bed bucks and turns a full circle. I go to take another swallow and the bottle disappears from my hand. I clench and unclench my fingers but it doesn't materialise.

"You've had enough," Kai says, capping the whisky and plonking it on top of the wardrobe. Like I did to him.

"Give it back," I whine. "I'm awake, ergo, not had enough."

Did I just say 'ergo'? It's the first time I've used it in a sentence. And people say drunks are stupid.

"Regretting your decision to leave me already? Well, no back-takes." I sway onto my knees. "Take-backs. But look what you'll be missing, you dumb—you dumb fucking *human*."

I grip the hem of my top. The dusky-pink material is wet with tears, probably snot and definitely a lot of booze. I yank it over my head and swing it around. Sexy, like a stripper. I fling my top off the side of the bed but somehow go with it, thudding onto the carpet beside the chairs in the bay window.

It's dim outside. Getting dark? What freaking time is it?

Why am I on the floor? Oh, yeah.

I crawl towards Kai. In my mind, I'm a seductive, stalking tigress but in reality, I'm probably more one-armed gorilla.

I run my hands up Kai's long legs and hook my fingers in his waistband, pulling myself to my knees, my face at crotch level. I forget I'm meant to be rubbing his nose in what he can't have. I try to undo his jeans but the intricacies of button mechanics escape me.

I want to feel anything but this awful sadness. Kai ramming his magical piercing inside me will do just fine.

I nuzzle his crotch. He grabs my wrists and tugs me to my feet. Instead of crushing me to him, his mouth on mine, frantic with lust, he holds my sagging body at arm's length.

"Christ, Syn," he says. "I don't want—"

I flop onto the bed, the rest of his words lost in a buzz of drunken humiliation.

He hates me again already. And I never even got to sleep with him. I pass out while bemoaning the injustice.

Or just moaning.

32

Sunlight burns my eyes through my closed lids. I squint awake to a blazing headache as bright as the unholy fireball shining through the bay window.

My first hangover. Can't say I'm enjoying it.

The covers of the bed trail on the floor. My top hangs off one of the chairs. I cautiously roll onto my back and my brain somersaults long after the move is complete.

No Kai. Did I dream him?

Nope. If he were a dream, we would've had hot, amazing sex. I wouldn't have humiliated myself and been rebuffed.

He must have fled pretty soon after I passed out but my body aches too much to focus on the Lesser connection. And I'd rather not know just how far he ran from my pitiful display.

I groan and cover my eyes with my arm, willing myself not to cry. My head will explode.

A whiff of cinnamon whisky, no doubt soaked into the bedspread, invades my nostrils and clenches my stomach. My ribs heave.

Oh, crap.

I stagger from the bed, trip on the covers and crawl in my bra and jeans to the bathroom. A stinging rush of liquid sears my throat and splashes into the toilet bowl. My brain attempts to escape by hammering through my forehead. I gag and choke and vomit until tears stream down my cheeks and there's nothing left in my gut.

No wonder Kai hated me after I stuck my finger down his throat.

I jab the flush and flop on the floor, my skull pressed to wonderful, cold tile. My mouth tastes like a slimy plughole, and my stomach gives a weak protest. I drag myself up by the edge of the sink and guzzle water straight from the tap, most of it running down my chin. My legs wobble but I manage to stand, stripping off my clothes and half-falling into the shower. The Elemis products replace the sharpness of vomit with lime and lotus flower.

Naked and dripping, I fling the bedspread on the floor and collapse onto the mattress, wrapped in a single sheet. A pillow over my head blocks the searing sunlight, and I drift.

Doors open and close. Voices pass.

Did I leave the shower on? I don't care, I'm not moving.

The headache fades to a manageable throb. My stomach settles. I tunnel deeper under the pillow and the sheet slips, exposing my lower back to cooler air. The radiators are on low so it's not unpleasant.

A scent teases me from my doze. Coffee and coconut.

Man, I would kill for a coconut latte from Costa right about now. Hot, sweet and exotic. It won't solve any of my problems but it's more reliable than a man and it won't torture anyone for fun.

I crack open one eye. Folds of a pillow greet me in my dim crevice, the mattress against my cheek since I'm sprawled on my belly. I raise my head and the pillow on top flops onto my back. A silver coffeepot sits on the bedside cabinet, steaming gently.

Thank you, oh lord of hangovers.

I reach for the pot and it's whisked away to be replaced by a banana.

"Eat that first," a voice says.

I peek over my shoulder through a mess of damp hair. Kai holds the coffee hostage, standing far enough that I can't get it without sliding out of bed.

Suddenly, I'm very aware I'm naked. The sheet barely covers my arse, the pillow flopped across my back hiding a little more.

I shouldn't care. I *don't* care. He's seen me naked. Lots of people have seen me naked. I should sit up and whip the cover off. Embarrass him with his silly, human sensibilities.

My arm clamps the pillow to my chest. I grab the sheet and shuffle backwards to lean on the headboard. Then I pull the cover to my chin. Kai smirks.

My body wars with itself, my soft heart fluttering while fury churns in my stomach at the effect he has. I wish it *was* just the Lesser connection.

"Screw you and your banana," I say, my voice husky.

"Potassium is good for hangovers."

The sleeve of his leather jacket is singed. My heart does the fluttery thing again and I tell it to fucking *quit it*.

I lobbed a freaking plant pot at my sister's face and Kai still thinks I'll get *bored*. Hello, big goddamn clue right there. Does he need me to spell it out?

"You're an arsehole," I hiss.

"So you don't want the coffee?"

"Of course I want the coffee. What I don't want is…" The last word gets stuck.

I frown at the offensive piece of fruit on the bedside cabinet.

I can't even lie to him. How pathetic that a Lesser has more power over me than Evelyn Romanov herself when the scary bitch was alive.

"Eat the banana," Kai says, "then you get coffee."

I bare my teeth but he turns and pours a stream of heavenly liquid into two mugs. My taste buds salivate. He dumps a spoonful of sugar in one cup followed by a healthy swirl of milk. The other, he leaves black. He cocks an eyebrow at me. I scowl at him, my fingers gripping the sheet so tight my hands shake.

"I'm done being humiliated by you," I sniff. A sniff of outrage, not a sniffle. "Leave the coffee, and go."

"I'm sorry I walked away," he says quietly, not looking at me.

"You *left* me. After what happened with my family. All I wanted—" I snatch the banana and take a huge bite, forcing the glob past the lump in my throat.

All I wanted was a hug.

A tear leaks onto my cheek and I swipe at it, furious. Kai takes a step closer, his expression not helping my fragile state.

"Don't," I bark. "Don't touch me. Just go."

"You hate people seeing you fall apart."

"That's just it, Kai—*no one* sees me fall apart. I don't get drunk for *anyone*. I don't hurt my sister for *anyone*. I don't—"

My breath hitches and I throw the banana at him. It bounces off his shoulder and splats on the bathroom door. I curl into a ball and hide my face in the sheet tucked over my knees.

Arms come around me. I stay rigid for a second—don't yield, *don't yield*—then I melt against him and burrow into his neck, his feather piercing tickling my nose. I manage to cry softly rather than wail in his ear. He perches on the edge of the bed and holds me while I tremble. The sheet has slipped to my waist and my breasts press into the soft material of his jacket, warm from his body.

"I guess I'm an idiot and an arsehole," he says into my hair.

I burble my agreement, and he chuckles. The sound vibrates in his chest and tightens my nipples, pressed so close.

"I couldn't take another loss so I left you first"—he clears his throat—"which sounds pretty stupid when you say it like that."

"It wasn't the slave thing?" I sniffle.

Damn. Definitely a sniffle.

He tries to pull away, probably to look at me, but my swollen, blotchy face is the last thing I want him to see right now. I tighten my grip, and he relaxes.

"I'm not worried about the slave thing."

"I am," I say in a small voice.

Freaking hell, Maddy, have some dignity.

His palm glides up and down my back. My bare back. Tingles zip everywhere, and I shiver. Now that I think about it, his other hand sits very low, fingers spread just above the curve of my bum. My *bare* bum.

More shivering.

"Are you cold?"

"Nope," I say, cuddling nearer.

"You know I'm not going anywhere, right? You don't have to crush me."

"Shut up, Kai."

Another chuckle.

"Why aren't you worried about the slave thing?" I say when he just hugs me and breathes.

"Because if I only did things to please you, I wouldn't have made you eat the banana."

I snort a laugh. "And I have yet to receive my coffee so consider me thoroughly displeased."

He eases me away, his fingers on my shoulders, and I forget to fight him. He grins and his dimples turn my already pickled brain to mush. His gaze drops, darkens. His fingers clench. My heart thumps.

"Goddamn, why did you have to be naked?" he groans.

He leaps to his feet and paces the carpet, avoiding my eyes.

"I didn't take advantage of you when you were drunk," he mutters. "I'm not taking advantage when you're sad and vulnerable."

"That's why you stopped me last night?"

He pauses, his back to me. "Why else?"

"I thought… I thought you didn't want to touch me anymore."

"Now who's the idiot?" He turns with a smirk but his eyes immediately fall to my breasts and he lunges desperately for a mug. "Fuck's sake, drink your coffee and cheer up."

I clear my throat to mask a giggle and pull the sheet to my chest in one, clenched fist.

"Sorry," I say but my voice wobbles.

"Something funny, Syn?"

"Nope."

I accept the cup and take a demure sip. My eyes roll back at the taste. Heat soothes my prickly stomach and massages invisible fingers into my muscles.

"Oh, that's so good," I purr.

Ceramic clunks, and I open my eyes to Kai slumped on the edge of the table. A slop of coffee pools at the base of his mug.

"Syn, for the love of god…"

I sip again, peeking at him through my lashes. "You know,

I'm feeling much more cheerful."

"Thank fuck," he growls, and stalks towards me.

33

My mug barely touches the bedside cabinet before Kai launches himself on the bed and claims my mouth, swallowing my yelp. He buries his fingers in my hair, controlling my head, his lips hard, insistent, opening for his tongue and I meet it and *damn*, that piercing.

My bones start to liquefy.

My hands slip inside his leather jacket, aching for skin. I shove at the material until Kai gets the hint and releases me long enough to shrug the jacket off. I pull his hoodie and t-shirt over his head then he goes right back to kissing me boneless. My fingers devour his skin—the spread of his ribs, smooth chest and the firm ripple of his belly. I grip his shoulder blades and the thought of his wings—his beautiful wings—arched above me tingles into my belly.

God, I can't catch my breath and he hasn't done anything yet. Though his kisses should come with a warning.

The sheet bunches at my waist and my breasts press against his solid chest, my nipples so pebbled he must be able to feel them. I have no problem undoing his button today but he still grabs my hands and pins them to the pillows. I whine into his mouth. He shoves himself up, all cheekbones and dark, hungry eyes.

"Not yet, Syn," he says.

"I thought you were desperate."

His wicked grin stuns all motor function.

"Oh, I am desperate."

He rolls his hips, rubbing himself between my legs, the sheet so thin, it doesn't mask the bulge through his jeans. I bite my lip on a moan, and grind against him.

"I'm going to make the sheet wet," I gasp.

"Fuck me," he sighs, and nibbles my neck, my pulse frantic against his lips.

"I'm *trying*."

He chuckles, and his teeth scrape my throat. He kisses lower, nuzzling the curve of my breast and sucking a nipple into his scorching mouth. My breath hitches. He teases one taut little bud with his tongue piercing, then the other, and everything below my waist throbs. I squirm underneath him. It takes a long time to realise he's stopped moving to watch me. I manage to blink at him and he gives me a tender smile.

"Do you trust me?" he says.

"Mm…" I say.

"Close enough."

He kisses the quivering muscles of my belly. Lower, to my bellybutton. And lower…

"What are you doing?" I squeak.

"I'm not going to hurt you, Syn. I promise."

My legs want to close but his body is in the way. My heart slams against my ribs. Kai places a soft kiss on my hipbone. The sheet barely covers my crotch and inches down with each move he makes.

"Do you believe me?"

I manage a rapid nod, though tension vibrates in every

muscle. His hands are light on my waist. I'm trying very hard not to crush him between my thighs.

"Do you want me to stop?"

"Hmm," I say.

"You're going to have to speak the word, Syn," he says gently.

I gulp. I open my mouth but nothing comes out. I clear my throat. Twice. Thrice. Foice?

Four fucking times.

Kai watches me patiently, not moving, though each exhale blazes heat on a sensitive, throbbing area so very close to his face.

"No," I whisper.

"No, you don't want me to stop?"

I nod again.

I can't concentrate with him down there. Can't breathe. Can't speak. How do women do this? Let someone so close to such a vulnerable place?

"Say it," Kai says.

I bite my lip. His fingers tighten on my waist.

"I don't want you to stop," I say in a rush and immediately feel woozy, as if all my blood has rushed out with it.

His smile starts slow, the barest hint of dimple, then widens to a grin. But not cruel, like Dominic's. Hot and horny and confident I'll enjoy what he's about to do with his mouth.

A shudder runs from the top of my head to my toes.

Kai wriggles backwards on his elbows, taking the sheet with him and exposing me completely. He eases my legs wider, his thumbs brushing my inner thighs, and I can't help a whimper. Anticipation, fear? Both. Kai stuns me with another smirk.

"I'd like you to remember this moment," he says, "since it'll be the only time you don't beg me for it."

I herd my expression into a haughty stare. "Excuse me, a Della Valle does not—oooooohhhh *god…*"

He props himself up. "I'm sorry. I didn't hear that over your moaning."

My eyelids flutter. His thumbs massage my thighs but he doesn't touch me anywhere else. My hips twitch, aching for another glide of his lips. It wasn't even his tongue.

Oh, man, I'm in trouble.

"Please," I pant.

I'm pretty sure I meant to say something else but I can't recall what it was.

Kai treats me to another pantie-melting grin. "Christ, Syn. You make me so damn hard."

He lowers his head and sucks on my clit. A noise spills from my mouth. A guttural, animal noise I've never made before. I struggle to focus. Kai watches me while his mouth works between my legs and the sight of him bows my spine, my cry echoing from the ceiling.

Sweet lord, I hope the walls aren't thin because there's no way I can be quiet.

The tip of his tongue laps at my labia, circles my throbbing clitoris. My hips writhe, the effort quivering through my abdominal muscles and heightening everything. The ball of his tongue piercing teases my opening and, yup, I'm sobbing his name. He strokes me with it, over and over. Pressure builds. Heat, weight, *aching*, oh, fuck.

The orgasm erupts from his glorious mouth and blasts outward. I must look like I'm having a seizure. His tongue plunges inside me and I lose my grip on reality for a while, reduced to howling, swollen sensation.

I come slowly back to myself. The first thing I recognise is a heartbeat, galloping and wild, and a second, steadier heartbeat. My ribs heave. Are my eyes open or closed?

Definitely closed.

I blink until the world resolves to a white ceiling, sunlight through glass and my body purring like a tamed lioness. Or was I a tigress?

Jeez, who am I?

My chin hits my chest and I blink some more at the figure kneeling between my legs.

Kai wipes his mouth and grins at me. "I don't think anyone's screamed my name quite that loud before."

"Hnng," I say.

He crawls up my body and nibbles my ear.

"No rest this time, Syn," he whispers. "Can't have you falling asleep."

I scrabble at his jeans and unzip them after two attempts, sliding my hand into his boxers. I squeeze rigid, pulsing flesh, and Kai pants in my ear.

"Fuck me while I'm still wet from your mouth," I say.

Take that, unintelligible consonants.

"Christ," Kai groans.

He rolls off me and wriggles out of his jeans. I prop myself on my side to watch the show. Silky muscles, carved lines and his penis, hard and flat on his belly, the silver piercing winking in the light and sending a shiver between my legs. His tattoo is on his other side so I can't see it from this position but the rest is just lovely. He tugs a square packet from his jeans before tossing them on the floor. His fingers start to twist one ball of his piercing.

"What are you doing?"

He slides me a glance. "I have to take it off or it might tear the condom."

"Did you wear condoms before?"

"I only got it when I was with my ex so didn't have to. But yes, always condoms before. And I got tested."

I put my hand over his and squeeze the crown of him. A moan catches in his throat.

"No condoms," I say. "You can't dangle how amazing it feels in front of me then take it out."

"Well, it seemed a bit rude to assume… Unless you have other birth control?"

"I have an IUD."

He Frisbees the packet across the room.

"No condoms," he says, and rolls on top of me.

My laugh dissolves in the heat of his mouth, my taste still on his lips. The glide of his tongue sends a pulse of remembrance between my legs. It bows my spine and rubs Kai through all the slickness he left behind.

We groan together.

He shoves up on his arms. The head of him slides inside me, the balls of his piercing stretching me, stroking me. He goes no deeper than the tip, easing in and out and teasing my sensitive opening. My fingers grip his arms, his skin rougher over the scar.

God, he wasn't lying. It *is* amazing.

I whisper his name. Plead. Effort shudders up his arms. His wings unfurl and catch the light in a halo of gold.

I picture him, new wings covered in blood. Scared, hurt and furious.

But there's no violence here. No pain. No hate. His wings arch above his shoulders, curling gently with each thrust of his hips and—

"Syn?"

I blink a blurriness away and focus on Kai's face.

"Are you crying?"

"No," I say, though my voice seems a tad wobbly.

He touches my cheek and a tear quivers on his fingertip.

Great, Maddy, because a girl weeping during sex is what every guy wants.

"I'm not sad," I say quickly, scrubbing my face. "It's just... I know you hate them. But I think they're beautiful."

He glances over his shoulder, the rest of him very still. He stretches his wings to their full extent and gives an experimental flap. The move eases him deeper and I bite my lip, trying not to squirm.

"I guess they're not so bad."

"You're beautiful, Kai," I say and it sounds suspiciously like a sob.

He lowers himself in a push up, still barely inside me, and kisses me lightly.

"Are you going to cry the whole time?"

"I'll try not to," I sniff. "But this is happy crying, not sad and vulnerable."

"Well, thank fuck," he says, and slides himself deep.

I sob his name but it's different—throatier. Frantic. He circles his hips and I gasp, "God, yes, please keep doing that." Thankfully, he shuts my mouth with his and stoppers whatever ridiculous begging thing I was going to say next.

Then he really starts to move.

Every part of him is hard but the piercing is just *extra*. Unrelenting. Stroking with every thrust of his body. His wings pulse on each long glide. I whimper and arch to meet him. My hands curl around his sides to grip the shafts of his wings, squeezing in time to his rhythm. He groans in my mouth. Maybe my name. His heart thunders. Vessels throb beneath my fingers and the throbbing arrows between my legs. Pleasure builds, aches, spills and drags my mouth from his to shout at the ceiling. He manages another glorious thrust and collapses on top of me, panting into my neck.

I listen to his heart slow while mine skips along. His weight presses me to the covers, the heaviness comforting. My body feels liquid enough that he may just melt straight through.

"Kai?" I say when I get my breath back.

"Huh?"

Ooh, look at him with his fancy vowel.

I stroke the shafts of his wings as if they're something else, though that part of his anatomy is a bit difficult to reach at the minute. He shivers and I clench around him, sending us both writhing.

"I'm not going to get bored," I say.

34

Kai rolls onto his back and gouges the headboard with the spike on his wing.

"Goddamn," he sighs. "I need to get corks for these fucking things."

I prop myself up on one hand. His wings lie flat on the bed on either side of him. My fingertips trace the thin bones and delicate scales. Kai shivers.

"That may not be the only damage we do to this room," I say.

His brow quirks. "How rough do you think I am?"

I cuddle into his side. His arm comes around me and his wing curls, folding me in a warm, coconut-scented cocoon. Safe and snug. No one else in the whole world can hold me this way.

"Not rough," I whisper, "but the day is young."

His pulse flutters against my cheek, a microsecond behind his heartbeat. The soothing thud weighs my eyelids and slows my breathing.

"You know, I don't think my ex would've touched me if she found out about the prostitution," he says.

I yawn and snuggle closer. "Then she never loved you."

His heart kicks, teasing me from my post-orgasm haze.

What is he excited about? Wait. What did I say?

"Deserved you," I splutter. "I mean, she never *deserved* you."

Freaking Christ, Maddy. Distract him!

I climb on top, careful not to kneel on his wings.

"You trying to tell me something, Syn?" he says.

"Shut up, Kai."

I fist both hands in his hair and kiss him until neither of us has the breath to continue. I rub myself against his growing erection, gasping at the hard bead of his piercing. It feels amazing even on the outside of my body. He's definitely ruined all other penises for me.

I knew he was dangerous.

He grips my waist and I raise myself, letting go of his hair long enough to guide him inside me. I rock my hips, and kiss him.

Lord, that tongue. Give me strength.

I shove myself up and the angle slides him deeper. I get distracted by the sight of him underneath me, wings spread, a flush pinking his cheeks. Smouldering eyes. His magpie-wing hair mussed by my fingers. The raven peeking around his ribs.

So. Freaking. Hot.

"Lean back," he pants.

I arch my spine and rest on my hands, the position tightening my stomach muscles. He thrusts his hips and bumps all that wonderful hardness against the front of my body.

"Oh, *god.*"

There's that guttural noise again.

He licks his thumb and rubs my clit and it's the most erotic thing I've ever seen. I moan, head thrown back, my body stretched and full. He massages with his thumb, his other

226

hand gripping my hip and driving me onto him, merciless while he thrusts deep.

Fuck, so deep.

I match his pace and can no longer deny it—I'm grunting. Loudly. On every thrust. My hair sways. My arms shake. My heart is playing the xylophone on my ribs. The pressure builds, throbbing and heavy.

Then I'm screaming, bucking on top of Kai while he rams the head of his cock, his glorious piercing, over and over the spot inside me that makes my bones dissolve.

My arms collapse. I sprawl on my back between his legs and whimper at the ceiling, my feet somewhere around his ears. I rest my blazing cheek on his shinbone. Lips brush my ankle.

"Never would have guessed you were a screamer, Syn."

It soothes my pride no end that his voice sounds as breathless and strangled as mine no doubt will. I raise a finger without moving the rest of me.

"I don't scream for just *anybody*," I groan.

He chuckles. I wave a hand in his direction and he pulls me the right way up. I slide onto my side and he copies me. A feather spirals into the air and slowly settles on his cheekbone. He huffs and it loops away.

"I destroyed a pillow, didn't I?"

"And me," I say.

He grins and kisses my palm. My hand tingles under his lips. I stroke it down his ribs and finally pet the raven tattoo. I wriggle lower, tracing inky feathers with lips and fingers. Kai shudders, and goosebumps flare on his skin.

Cute.

I kiss the raven right on its wicked beak.

"You really like the tattoo," Kai says.

I walk my fingers up his chest, and lie down.

"I really like everything, Kai."

He wiggles until his lips brush mine. Each gentle kiss tugs at my belly, flaring longing that climbs to ache in my chest and throat. Kai kisses me, just lips, tender and undemanding, and a feeling like sadness films my eyes with tears.

But it's not sadness.

"Are you going to cry again, Syn?"

I clear my throat. "Nope."

He tucks me into his shoulder and I breathe onto his collarbone. The longing steadies to a dull ache. Joy flutters butterfly wings against my heart.

So this is what it's like to be happy.

"I have one more secret," I say, my voice as languid as the rest of me.

"Uh-oh," Kai says.

"It's nothing bad. Well, not bad for you. It's about my mum."

"She died in a car accident."

I nod against his shoulder. His fingers stroke my back, dipping into the cleft of my spine and drawing swirly patterns. I manage not to purr but it's a near thing.

"It was my fault," I say.

35

A log cracks in the wood-burning stove, and sparks patter on the glass. Yellow flames twine with the smoke sucked into the flue. Footsteps tap on parquet. I drag my gaze from the fire and jump to my feet, clenching my hands when I want to wring them in my lap.

Kai walks through the archway from reception, the lounge at the front of the building. I meet him before he's half-way to the leather couches in front of the fireplace and slide my restless fingers inside his jacket. His arms come around me.

"Missed me or you're nervous about your dad?" he says.

I snuggle my cheek on Kai's warm chest. "Both."

"You know, you're quite cuddly, for a psychopath."

"Shut up, Kai," I say, and pinch his ribs.

He wriggles in my hold and guides us back to the sofa, tripping over our feet. I slump into the soft material and he thumps next to me, his shoulder pressed to mine.

"The hotel will charge your card for the damage to the room," he says, taking my hand and putting it on his thigh.

"Did they ask what happened?"

Kai quirks his mouth. "I offered no explanation."

What will the housekeeping staff think—gouged headboard, slashed pillow, the stink of alcohol and sex? Maybe they see it all the time.

I play with Kai's fingers. My gaze shifts to the archway with each new noise. Another heartbeat. The squeak of the front door. No one enters the lounge.

"He's not going to blame you."

My eyes flick to Kai. "You don't know that."

"You're his daughter. And he didn't seem so scary. He was the only one in your kitchen who didn't want to eat me."

"He was being polite."

Kai kisses my knuckles. "Long may that continue."

A footstep scrapes on concrete outside. I sit up straighter. The powerful, steady heartbeat is as familiar as a voice. I leap upright. Kai stands at a more sedate pace.

My father pauses on the threshold. His pale-blue eyes drop to our linked hands. He's wearing a matching shirt tucked into grey trousers. His stern face offers nothing, though the lines seem more pronounced.

"Daughter, are you well?"

"How's Eady?" I say at the same time.

"Healed."

"And Libby?"

His gaze rests on Kai for a second then returns to me.

"She is taking your change of behaviour quite hard."

I take a slow breath. "What about you?"

"I admit I am... surprised."

Better than angry. Or disappointed.

Those will come later.

I lower myself onto the couch, smoothing my palms over my jeans. Dad crosses the plush rug.

Kai stays on his feet and holds out his hand. "I'm Kai."

"I remember."

Dad takes Kai's hand. Fingers clench and squeeze.

Dad could crush all his bones with only a small flex, though Kai is slightly sturdier as a Lesser compared to a human.

Kai's face remains bland and pleasant, and Dad smiles.

"I like him," he says to me.

I let out a breath and grab Kai's hand, tugging him down onto the sofa. No signs of pain.

"Your heart is racing, Daughter," Dad says. "I'm not used to seeing you so... emotional."

"Yeah, me neither," I mutter, and Kai slides me a smile.

"You truly do not want to mate with Gerome Kaskbirch?" Dad perches on the couch catty-corner with ours.

I blink at the change in topic but really it's because the possessive heat in Kai's eyes has me a bit dazzled.

"Not even a little," I say.

"You could have talked to me. I would never have forced you into a match."

"I wanted to keep us safe."

"It is not your job," Dad says softly. "And that is my fault. I let you stand for us, for me. You took charge of your sisters. I see now what I should have years ago—you sacrificed your happiness to protect us. You have not been happy for a very long time."

My heart skips. I struggle not to glance at Kai.

Who knew the men in my life could be so perceptive? Or maybe I've never been good at pretending.

Sadness clouds Dad's face and pales his eyes to the blue of a winter sky.

"You remind me of your mother," he says.

A sob lodges in my throat. My words croak when I say, "Don't. Don't look at me like that when I'm the reason she's gone."

His turn for a slow blink.

"Explain, Daughter," he says in a careful voice.

Kai's thumb skims my knuckles, back and forth. I swallow hard but keep my gaze on my father.

No more secrets between us. I can't bear it.

"We were arguing," I wheeze. "In the car. That day."

"About what?"

"Dominic Romanov."

Dad snaps the perfectly pressed leg of his trousers over his knee. "Another suitor I have so recently learned you hated."

"He scared me. I told Mum that. Told her I didn't want to mate him. She said I should be *grateful*. Grateful for everything that crazy bit—" I gulp air until my pulse calms instead of throbbing in my temples. "Grateful for everything Evelyn Romanov did for us. I accused Mum of not caring. She took her eyes off the road for a second..."

I stare at my lap, hiding behind a curtain of blonde and pink. A tear trails down my cheek and plops in a dark circle on my thigh.

"She was scared, too," Dad whispers.

It makes me raise my eyes to his face and the anguish there.

"What do you mean?"

"Adira always said our lives would be easier if we were a weaker family, though she knew it wasn't entirely true."

I hold my breath.

It's the first time I've heard Dad speak my mother's name since her funeral, as if the very syllables were too painful for him to utter.

"Once you've reached a certain status, there's no going back." Dad sighs and scrubs his cheeks, stubble rasping against his fingers. "Before the twins were born, when you were a baby and Libelle was five, there was a family who showed us the horror of that lesson. They gave birth to a daughter but she was like Julian Romanov—a non-colour. I believe it was only Julian's father who stopped Evelyn from drowning Julian like the runt of a litter but he paid for it. And he was forced to watch Julian pay for it every day of his life. I wonder if it would have been more merciful not to have stayed Evelyn's hand."

I find I'm shaking my head. "Julian wouldn't see it that way. He's stronger because of what she did to him."

"You admire him."

I open my mouth. Close it.

"Julian and Raine are good people."

Dad nods. "Evelyn was not nearly as forgiving for a female born from a powerful family to have such a deformity. She demanded the child be culled. They could always have another and pray this was a fluke. The family tried to run."

"What was their name?"

"Contrera."

"I've never heard of them."

"They were American." Dad picks an imaginary piece of lint off his knee. "And there is no one alive who carries their blood. Not even a trace."

I shiver.

Thank god there's nothing left of Evelyn Romanov but ash.

"Jesus," Kai says into the quiet, "are you always that brutal?"

Dad gives him a tight-lipped smile. "When we have to be."

"That's why Mum acted like she did around Evelyn Romanov—it wasn't respect, it was fear."

"Yes." Dad shifts in the seat and the leather creaks. "Everything she did was to keep us safe."

I give a bitter laugh. "And she's dead because of me. But I'm not as good at continuing her legacy."

"Madisyn Della Valle."

The crack of the words drags my gaze upwards.

"You did not kill her. You were a child. A teenager. Even if Adira had had her eyes on the road, I suspect the outcome would have been the same." Dad's sad smile slices across my heart. "You know your mother always drove too fast."

The sob spills out of my mouth instead of lodging in my throat this time. Dad slides onto his knees. I'm enveloped by the scent of lavender and wood. Tears dampen the shoulder of his crisp shirt.

"I'm sorry," I whisper.

"I am, too," he says. "For not paying attention when you needed me most. For neglecting you—all of you—in my grief."

The clink of crockery drives us apart, plus the tantalising smell of fresh coffee. Dad reclaims his seat while Kai pours three cups.

"Thought we could do with a pick-me-up," he says.

I huddle around the warmth and Kai sits next to me, touching from shoulder to hip.

He sips from his mug. "I'm guessing there are other families who want to continue with the status quo, even though Evelyn Romanov is dead?"

I meet Dad's eyes.

"The Kaskbirches," I say.

He gives a terse nod. "Libelle has been getting cosy with Irena since your abrupt exit. She says she will mate with Gerome and solidify our power base since you've taken leave of your senses."

"I'm sure she didn't phrase it quite like that."

Dad quirks his mouth. "No, she was disparaging of your choice of mate."

My whole body aches to turn towards Kai but I stare at Dad, not blinking.

"What about you?" I say, and it barely wobbles.

"He is quite fascinating"—Dad grins, giving a flash of his younger self—"for a Lesser."

Kai salutes with his cup. "And you're not bad, for a dragon."

They share some kind of manly understanding while I slurp my coffee to hide my shaking hands.

"What are we going to do about Libby? And the Kaskbirches?"

Dad places his cup on the table and clasps his hands. "I will have a talk with Libelle. I should have been stricter with her, controlled her influence on the twins. As for the Kaskbirches, that solution may be a little messier."

"Irena is still terrified of you."

"Yes, but that gives her all the more reason to want me dead. Let me think on it for a few days. Will you stay here until then?"

I peek at Kai.

"We're going to Julian's," he says before I can open my mouth.

Dad slaps his thighs, and stands. "Then perhaps I will see you there."

"Shit, this is really happening," I blurt.

"Madisyn—"

"Sorry, Dad, but this is unprecedented. No one is going to believe that the Della Valles are... nice."

"Yes, we may have been too skilled in our pretence and our rigid commitment to the rules of our society."

"It's not pretend for Libby, Eady or Dory."

"Leave your sisters to me."

If only I could. I love my dad but even his power may not be enough to tame my feral siblings.

What the hell is Libby planning?

36

My Mustang purrs up the winding driveway beneath the trees. The sun sets behind the needled branches of pine, casting clawed shadows on the ground. Kai watches the flicker of trunks pass through the window.

The entry gate opened, to my surprise, after my somewhat hesitant, "It's Madisyn," into the speaker box.

The colonial mansion appears between one blink and the next, set back from the edge of the trees on a short, rolling lawn. Bright green cherry laurel is a splash of colour from the maze to the right of the house, the entrance to the underground chamber on the left. Bare rose bushes rattle their thorns in the sharp bursts of wind.

I park in the semi-circular drive and switch off the engine. Silence settles in the car, buffeted by the occasional gust from outside.

Kai has been quiet on the drive over from the hotel after saying goodbye to my father. Maybe he's regretting his decision to stay with me. The Kaskbirches won't go down without a battle. And my sisters will not be so easily cowed.

What kind of life have I forced him into?

The front door of the mansion swings, and Julian and Raine walk down the steps towards us. A black hoodie with red zips frames the hollow of his throat. Raine is bundled in a fitted jacket the colour of autumn leaves.

I was hoping to hide in the car a little longer but they must want me here or they wouldn't have let me in. Or they'd like another chance to toss me into the dragon's-bane.

I shiver and step out of the car, my boots crunching on gravel. I walk around the front of the Mustang to stand next to Kai.

Julian grins at me. "So you told him?"

I follow his gaze to my hand in Kai's and fight the blush threatening to pink my cheeks.

Seems I can't be anywhere near Kai without touching him, even unconsciously.

"Something like that," I say.

Kai cocks an eyebrow at me. "Told me what?"

"Nothing," I say, and glare at Julian. "Is the offer to stay here still open?"

"Taking Kai home not work out?"

"Not so much."

Raine pinches Julian's ribs and he wriggles away, giving her a tender smile.

"You two may not feel the cold but the rest of us do," she says. "It's not a day to stand out and chat."

Wind howls around the eaves of the house. She and Kai share a shudder, though her jacket looks cosier than Kai's leather one.

I really need to buy him something more appropriate.

"What my lovely wife is trying to say is, yes, of course you're welcome to stay." Julian cuddles her into his side. "Kai's room is still free if you don't mind sharing a bed."

I don't need to look at Kai to feel his smirk.

"That won't be a problem," he says.

I open the boot of my car. Kai's scent lingers on the interior. I remember him folded into the small space, eyes narrowed and distrustful. Now those grey eyes watch me with a possessive heat, like he's the predator and I'm the quivering creature waiting to be eaten.

It's not something I ever thought I'd feel. This weakness. But I've lost control of everything. My family, bitch-Maddy. My heart.

It's freeing yet utterly petrifying.

I grab a powder-blue backpack and slam the lid, the suspension of the car squeaking in protest.

Dad brought me the bag from home, which was either a very bad sign or just good planning.

I sling the strap over my shoulder and follow Julian and Raine into the house. Three people stand in the grand, parquet-floored hallway, one the tall Vanatori who told Caysie she wouldn't be allowed to torture me when I was first captured. The other two stand arm in arm, the woman stunning and dark, the guy swamped by baggy clothes.

"So this is the wicked bitch from the west," the woman drawls, her accent making the words exotic.

"From the east, actually," I say.

The woman grins and flips her glossy black hair over her shoulder, revealing a hoop earring large enough to wear as a garter.

"As long as you are the bitch on our side, who cares where you are from."

"That's if she's actually on our side," the American says, "and not just a spy."

Serious eyes sweep me from top to toe.

"I will let her actions speak for themselves. And we all know we can trust Raine's instincts, do we not, honey?"

A look passes between the quartet of Vanatori. I feel like I've missed something but the American relaxes his broad shoulders a fraction.

"Madisyn Della Valle, this is Sofia, Dustan and Nate, the last remnants of the Titan Group and part instigators of this little coup we're having," Raine says, sweeping her hand out to cover the woman, the skinny guy and the American.

Dustan, who needs to get clothes that fit him better, holds out a hand. "I saw you around before but most people described you as Evelyn Romanov's protege so I didn't exactly want to introduce myself."

My lip curls before I can stop it, and Dustan's eyes widen.

"Wow, it's true. You really do hate her."

I shake his long-fingered hand, careful with his delicate bones. Humans are so easy to hurt.

"Maddy was better than me at hiding what she truly is," Julian says, Raine tucked back into his side.

Dustan tilts his head. "And what is that?"

"A friend."

"It seems I'm not great at hiding anymore," I say and it sounds grumpy.

"Some things just make us tired of hiding."

Julian's different-coloured gaze drops to my hand in Kai's. Something close to panic tightens my chest.

I should let him go. Step away. Get some distance, not cling to him. But if I do that now, it'll be obvious, especially to Julian, the perceptive little bastard.

Does everyone know? Are my emotions plastered across my face for all to see? I struggle for nonchalance but have forgotten what the fuck it even means.

I draw a measured breath to slow my heart rate. At least Julian is the only one who can hear it ping-ponging between my ribs.

"It's terrifying, isn't it?" he says.

"Not hiding? Yeah. Can't say I'm enjoying it."

Julian gives me a gentle smile but doesn't correct me.

Damn him.

"I never would have believed a Della Valle could be an ally," Nate says, giving me another searching look. "The brutality of your family is legendary."

"Well, I wouldn't get too cosy with my sisters."

"You telling me the great Jackson Della Valle is a closet softie?"

"Just don't say that to his face," Kai says with a laugh. "He'll still eat you."

Nate cocks a dark brow. "It seems we have a lot to talk about."

"The last few days have been a little… unpredictable," I say.

Kai's thumb tickles across my palm, and my heart does a slow roll in my chest.

He's the only solid thing left but also the reason all my foundations have crumbled. The ground is sinking beneath my feet. What am I supposed to do, stay at Julian's forever like a stray puppy? Conspire with my enemies? I fantasised about joining Julian and Raine but now that I'm here, I don't know what the hell I'm doing. What if I have to make a choice—Kai or my family? I've always chosen family. Always.

Or has that choice already been made?

"You look pale, Madisyn," Raine says softly. "Maybe you should go lie down."

"I'm fine," I say but my voice is hollow.

Kai tugs on my hand. "Come on. I could do with a nap."

He leads me upstairs, and I don't protest. I float along behind him like a balloon on a string. I blink and we're in his room, the door closed.

Is this what shock is?

The backpack slips from my fingers onto the padded chest at the foot of the four-poster bed. A pang flares behind my sternum.

Will I ever sleep in my own bed again?

I walk to the window overlooking the rear grounds but back away at the sight of the greenhouses. The wind swirls a storm of leaves into the glass of the one containing the dragon's-bane.

"You hungry?"

I jump at Kai's voice. His proximity breathes along my skin. The room seems smaller—too cosy, too intimate—even though it's bigger than the hotel room.

"I don't think I can eat."

I pace around the bed but Kai stands on the other side between me and the door.

Trapped.

I'm not trapped.

I suck air in and out, my chest tight.

"You want to lie down?"

I shake my head a little too hard. "I'm not sleepy."

Tiredness grits my eyes. The remnants of my hangover plus the emotional turmoil of hurting Eady and the confession to my father. My restless energy clenches my stomach and shivers through my heartbeat. Exhausted but too wired to relax.

"Talk to me, Syn."

"How can I stay here?" I huff on an explosive sigh. "It's too strange."

"You sent *me* here."

"I know. But I've never lived anywhere without my family." I frown at the kettle on the coffee table next to the red chair. "I've never lived with a boy."

"We've just spent the day together in the hotel. And I stayed overnight in your bed."

"I was practically comatose. That doesn't count. We could be here for weeks while we figure out how to stop Libby and the Kaskbirches."

Kai grins. "I can show you the benefits of living with a boy."

"I don't think that's a good idea."

"What am I going to do to you that I haven't already done at the hotel?" He stalks towards me. "Though I can think of one thing I'd like to do."

Heat starts at my toes and sweeps all the way up into my face. The backs of my knees hit the padded chest but Kai catches me before I topple. He presses me against him, and I swallow hard.

"Nervous, Syn?" he says.

I raise my chin. "Why would I be nervous?"

"That is the question, isn't it?" he says, and kisses me softly.

The glide of his tongue piercing turns my bones to jelly. He peels me from my dusky-pink peek-a-boo top, washed at the hotel so it's no longer saturated in whisky and snot. My bra disappears before I can think about anything but the taste of Kai. He spins me around, my butt in his crotch, and nibbles on the sensitive skin beneath my ear. My legs quiver more than the rest of me. Kai guides me to kneel on the soft lid of the chest.

His fingers curl in the waistband of my jeans. "Give me a nod if you're all right with this, Syn."

I nod and manage a, "Mmm hmm," for good measure.

He chuckles and spoons against my back, the leather of his jacket cool, the zipper a chill line. His warm hands palm my breasts and pull me upright. I crane my neck to meet his lips. He kisses me until I flop bonelessly onto my hands when he lets go. He unfastens my jeans and yanks them to mid-thigh, underwear and all, exposing my arse to the room.

"Um, Kai..."

His finger slides inside me, his thumb massaging where no man has ever touched. My words evaporate in a blast of heat and spill from my mouth in a moan.

"Hell, Syn," Kai groans, "you make me want to be wicked."

A zip lowers. All that hardness brushes my opening but he eases only the tip inside to tease me with his piercing. My heart hammers into my throat to stopper my gasp, my fingers tangled in the sheets. Kai grips my hip with one hand, the other fisting in my hair to pull my head back and arch my spine. He slams the full length of himself inside me and I cry out, the noise strained with the angle of my neck.

"I fantasised about doing this to you," Kai gasps, sheathed as deep as he'll go, "right when I both hated and wanted you. As if it would be a punishment."

He draws himself back until he's almost out, caressing his piercing on that part of me just inside, around and around as he circles his hips. Pleasure builds in a tingling rush, glowing beneath my skin and pulling more sounds from my throat.

"But you will be screaming by the end," Kai says, his voice strained.

He thrusts into me, hard and fast, driving himself deep with his hand on my hip and in my hair. I sob his name. The position stretches the muscles of my throat and tightens my stomach, heightening the sensation of each stroke, each slap of skin on skin as his body meets mine. The orgasm catches me between one breath and the next, and I manage a strangled scream. Kai shudders, his rhythm faltering, and buries himself to the hilt until I can feel him twitching as he spills himself inside me.

We end up sprawled on the bed, my trousers around my ankles, Kai fully dressed except for his unbuttoned jeans. He cuddles me into his chest and I listen to the thunder of his heart slow to a trot. My pulse throbs in my ears.

"You can punish me anytime," I mumble, and fall asleep.

37

Soft breathing slithers into my ear from the phone pressed to my head. The silence solidifies in my stomach and drops it towards my toes.

"Eady," I say quietly, my throat tight, "I'm sorry. I didn't want to hurt you but I couldn't let you hurt Kai, either."

The breathing stops. I strain to hear something, anything, curled in the pillows of Kai's bed, wishing I hadn't asked him to give me some privacy.

"You really are a traitorous little bitch, aren't you, Maddy?" Libby says.

I yank the phone from my ear and stare at it as if my sister might crawl through the screen and claw out my eyeballs. Her laughter tinkles as sharp as glass.

"Where's Eady?" I say with only a little wobble.

This is ridiculous. I'm not afraid of Libby. She's my sister. I've dealt with her brand of insanity my whole life.

"Eady doesn't want to talk to you."

"Let her tell me that."

Libby laughs again. "Yes, well, it would go against the whole not wanting to talk to you part."

More silence. Heavy, hissing breaths.

I try again. "Is Eady there?"

"No, darling sister, she is not and she will continue to be absent until you remember where your loyalties lie." A whoop of air. *"And it's not with the fucking abomination and a worthless Lesser!"*

The roar of her voice batters my eardrum, and I wince. Libby's pants return to soft sibilance.

"Has Dad spoken to you?" I say in a quiet voice at odds with the rage seething through the speaker.

"Do you know how hard I've worked to be his favourite?" she says, her words cold and precise. "Mated Lukas, the eldest Romanov. Behaved as a Della Valle should. As you did, until you lost your fucking mind. It helped that you reminded him too much of Mum. But, no, as soon as you crook your finger, he comes running."

"We're worried about you."

She snorts. "You're worried I'll do what any powerful Drakul would. What has to be done and what you would have done only a few weeks ago. I'm just trying to help you, sister dear. You've let your little heart cloud your judgement."

The 'dear' sends a shiver down my spine, so reminiscent of Irena with her plump, sneering face.

"I told you—who I was a few weeks ago wasn't the real me. It was an act, a good one, and it made me miserable."

"Well, excuse me if I'm not too fond of the 'new you'."

"I'm still me, Libby. Still your sister."

"I don't know who you are," she says. "We used to have so much fun together. How can you throw that away?"

"It's time to stop abusing people. Stop pandering to the threat of the other families."

"Oh, Maddy," she says. "The strong have always ruled the weak. That is our right."

"I don't want to rule anybody. I just want to be happy."

"I *was* happy." Her voice crackles across the line. "Julian and his whore took that from me."

"They were protecting themselves."

"They can't protect themselves from vengeance."

I ease a breath in and out until I feel calmer, settling more firmly into the pillows.

"What would it take for you to leave them alone? To leave Kai alone?"

"Nothing," she snaps.

"Kai hasn't done anything to you."

"He has befuddled my sister and turned her into a bleeding heart who weeps for the less fortunate. He's turned you into a *joke*."

"All he's done is let me be myself. The real me."

"Oh, yes, the real Maddy. Well, fantastic, she's a snivelling cow—*I don't want to hurt anyone, don't harm my little Lesser, boohoo-hoo.*" Her falsetto drills into my ear.

I grip the phone hard and it creaks in my hand.

"At least I'm not an evil, crazy bitch," I snap back.

Libby laughs. "Don't you get it, Maddy? You were. And I liked her."

I pinch the bridge of my nose, my eyes closed, and will my heartbeat to slow. My anger fades to leave me tired and hollow.

"You've changed, too," I finally say. "I thought you didn't want to mate with Gerome."

"Well one of us has to placate his mother."

"Since when have you cared about Irena? Why are you getting so cosy with her? She's part of the problem."

"Nothing to worry your pretty pink head over," Libby says.

I can picture her, stretched out on her bed, one leg crossed over the other, bare foot bobbing in the air while she examines her nails.

"You hate Irena," I say, ignoring a pang of homesickness. "And Gerome."

"They're not so bad. We want the same thing."

"And what is that?"

"You'll find out."

I feel her smile through the phone like a lick of frost. The weight in my stomach increases.

"It doesn't have to be this way, Libby."

"You're right, Maddy," she says, from cold and calculating to reasonable. "Just bring me the head of your little Lesser boyfriend and I'll call it quits. I'll even leave Julian and his slut alone."

"You know I can't do that."

A sigh eases through the speaker.

"Then you leave me no choice," she says, and hangs up.

Funny, she doesn't sound too upset about it.

38

"How can we stop them?"

Raine's voice is serious, though she's cuddled next to Julian on the chaise longue in a living room as opulent as my own. Silver leaf decorates the sleigh-like sofa, which was handcrafted by Boca do Lobo in Portugal. Sofia, Dustan and Nate lounge on pieces by Bentley. The chandelier is by Anna Casa.

"My dad will try to keep them in line from his threat alone," I say, snuggled into Kai on the Chesterfield, "but I think it may be too late if Libby is plotting with the Kaskbirches."

It's a day after my ominous call. My stomach has been churning ever since.

"They'll attack again," Julian says, no doubt in his words.

His fingers twine in Raine's, their hands in his lap. Their wedding rings glint, at odds with the grey, wet day. Bursts of wind pummel a torrent against the windows.

I nod. "They'll get more families this time."

"So we can't stop them," Raine says grimly.

"Let them come," Nate growls, his crossbow resting on the side of the couch. "We've fought through worse odds."

"If we defeat them, it could signal the end of their reign in Scotland," Dustan says, his eyes glowing. "No more owning a

Scottish estate as a second-home tax dodge."

Sofia slaps him on the shoulder. "What do you mean 'if'?"

He grins and captures her hand, kissing her knuckles.

"Sorry, my love. We have the great Madisyn Della Valle on our side. How can we lose?"

"Not so great going by what happened during our first attack," I mutter.

"You underestimated our defences." Julian smiles but it fades to a frown. "They won't this time."

"And what side will Jackson Della Valle fight on?" Nate says, giving me an intense stare from eyes as black as my sister's heart.

"I'll talk to him," I say. "But he's spent most of his life doing whatever it took to protect my family. Fighting alongside Libby maintains that charade. Fighting with me threatens everything he's built."

"And can you fight against your sisters? Your family?" Nate says.

I drop my gaze to the carpet. Kai runs a soothing hand up and down my arm.

"I don't want to hurt them," I say quietly, but raise my eyes to cover everyone in the room. "I want to capture them like you captured me. I want you to promise you won't kill them unless lives are at risk."

"Libelle isn't exactly stable, Maddy," Julian says. "You really think you can talk sense into her?"

"She's my sister. I have to try." I quirk my mouth. "And look how I turned out after a few days of imprisonment."

Julian's grin flashes. "I'm not sure we have another Kai to tempt her from the dark side."

My cheeks flush but I stare at Julian instead of looking away.

Kai gives a soft chuckle.

Definitely not looking at him, either.

"Promise me you'll spare my sisters. And my dad if need be."

Julian glances at Raine, and she does the whole silent eyeball communication with her hunters.

"We'll try," she says. "But Libelle is still getting a punch in the mouth."

I laugh. "That's fair."

"What about the Kaskbirches?" Julian says.

"To hell with them and anyone else they bring."

The Vanatori whoop. Nate seems primed to storm the battlements already with his wicked crossbow and assassin clothes.

"How long do you think we have?" Raine says, a glint turning her eyes to steel.

She appears so fragile, so tiny, yet here is the glimpse of the warrior who lopped off Lukas Romanov's thick head and spitted his mother on her sword.

"Libby isn't known for being patient so I don't imagine it'll be long. A day, maybe—"

"Sorry to interrupt," whispers a voice from the doorway.

The girl ducks her head at our attention, hiding behind her silky hair. A Lesser servant, though I've forgotten her name. She can morph fangs that are terrifying in her delicate face.

"Yes, Delilah?" Julian says gently.

"Libelle, Eadrea and Doria Della Valle are at the front gate requesting an audience," she says, still examining her toes.

"What the fuck?" I gasp.

Julian's lips twitch into a half smile. "Not long at all, then. Did they say what it was regarding?"

"They wish to discuss a truce."

"Bullshit." Nate leaps to his feet, his crossbow already in his hands.

"Delilah, please tell our guests we'll join them at the gate."

Delilah bobs a curtsy at Julian and slips from the room.

I close my mouth, take a deep breath then say, "This is a trap."

"Probably," Julian says, "but we'll meet them anyway."

We climb to our feet and head for the hall, Sofia and Dustan peeling off to arm themselves and warn the other residents. Nate and Raine already have their weapons of choice.

"Kai, you should wait here," I say.

"The hell I should."

I slide him a glare. "Eady has already tried to set you on fire and Libby wants your head."

"I'm not letting you face them alone."

"I won't be alone. You're the most vulnerable. I don't want you anywhere near my sisters."

"Raine and her hunters are human. I'm sturdier than them now."

"But they're all trained at fighting."

Kai gives me stormy eyes. "I'm coming down, Syn."

Nate watches our argument with his usual intensity, Julian and Raine standing off to one side in the grand hallway.

My fists clench but I force my fingers to uncurl. "If you come down, I'll be distracted trying to protect you. Just wait up here until we know what they want."

"I can protect myself, Syn."

"No, you can't!" My voice rises and I struggle to control it. "You can't. Especially if they've brought other families with them. I don't want you hurt—"

"Why are you so worried about me?"

"What the hell kind of question is that?"

"One you need to answer."

A spike of violet-tipped hair flops into his eyes and I ache to brush it away, even when I'm furious enough to toss him over my shoulder and lock him in our bedroom.

Air whistles in my nose. "This is hardly the time—"

"Just answer the question, Syn," he growls.

Heat bubbles in my chest and rushes up my throat.

"Because I love you!" I shout. "*Obviously.*"

The words echo in the high ceiling. My heart swoops into my stomach and mortification blazes in my cheeks.

Kai takes one stride and his body collides with mine—lips, chest and hips, his strong fingers on my chin. His kiss bruises my mouth but I try to climb inside him, tongue first. My hands slip into the warmth of his leather jacket. His piercing works its magic and turns my kneecaps to water. His arm around my waist keeps me on my feet.

"There, was that so hard?" he says while I pant and blink at him. "I love you, too."

"So you'll stay here?" I manage.

He smirks. "Hell, no. I'm still coming to the gate."

"You really are a bastard," I sigh.

39

The wind and rain whip my hair into a pink and blonde mess by the time we reach the gate, Kai and the other humans shivering in their jackets. Dad's silver Mercedes purrs beyond the barrier of spiked metal. Water drums on the roof and slashes through the headlight beams that shine on the wet road. Two security cameras point, unmoving, at the car. Three doors open then thunk closed. Libby approaches the gate, looking like a Nordic princess with her ice-blue eyes and fur-lined coat. She'll settle in well on the Kaskbirch's turf in Scandinavia. Eady and Dory trail in her wake, wearing matching cropped tops and jeans that are quickly soaked.

"I'd appreciate it if you wouldn't point that thing at me," Libby says with a gentle sneer, "since we're being peaceful and all."

Nate frowns at her down the length of his crossbow, droplets beaded on the wicked point of the bolt. Raine touches his arm and shakes her head. He lowers the weapon after a pause.

Libby's gaze shifts to Raine. "So you're the bitch that murdered my husband."

"And you're the bitch who tormented mine," Raine says without missing a beat. She holds a hand out to Julian and he wraps his fingers in hers.

Julian nods. "Libelle."

Libby's face stays smooth and beautiful but I've had years to study my sister's expression. Whatever she's thinking has nothing to do with peace and everything to do with Julian broken and bleeding in the dirt.

"Why are you here, Libby?" I say.

Her cold eyes fasten on mine. Wind howls between the bars of the gate and ruffles the fur of her hood. Her heartbeat, faint over the roar of pine trees, is as steady as her gaze.

"Ah, my dear sister and her little concubine. We're here for a truce, of course."

"Then you might want to try some diplomacy."

Libby laughs and tosses her head. I glance over her shoulder at Eady but Eady and Dory seem to be focused on Nate, probably since he's the only one with an obvious weapon. The guns Sofia and Dustan brought into the hall have vanished into their jackets, along with enough blades to open a butcher shop.

"Oh, I can be very diplomatic," Libby says, pouting at me. "Come home, Maddy. I miss you."

"What about Kai?"

She bares her teeth in a smile. "I'd love to get to know him better. Eady is sorry for trying to set him on fire, aren't you Eady?"

Eady's pale-blue eyes flick to us for a second then back to Nate. Her white-blonde hair is plastered to her cheeks in dark strands.

"Sorry, Maddy," she says, watching Nate the way an alligator would watch a steak that happened to plop down in front of it.

"Stop staring at me," Nate growls, his crossbow twitching at his side.

"But you're such a sexy hunk of man flesh," Eady says, cocking her hip. "What's your name?"

Dory titters. "I bet you taste as good as you look, Vanatori."

"And the Kaskbirches?" I say to Libby, ignoring Nate's grumble of discontent.

"They're not family." A capricious gust blows her hood back and dances her hair around her face. "They need to learn their place."

"Did Dad speak to you?"

"We had a very enlightening talk."

I squint at her through a burst of rain. "Your sudden change of heart is difficult to believe, Libby."

"Dad explained how much you'd both sacrificed."

"Where is Dad? I'd find this easier to swallow if he were here to verify."

"He wanted to come but he had an emergency at work. You know how it is." She blinks at me, perfectly serene.

But I'm not buying it.

"So, to clarify—you're going to leave Julian and Raine alone when slaughtering them is all you've wanted to do since Lukas died?"

Her lips twitch. "It was the grief but now I've finally reached the acceptance stage."

"Cut the shit, Libby."

She grins at me. "Madisyn Della Valle, such language! What would Dad say?"

Eady and Dory giggle, their jeans moulded to their long legs. They haven't taken their eyes off Nate, and vice versa, though I suspect in his case it's because he doesn't trust them not to leap the gate and bury their snouts in his abdomen. You never know with the twins—could be sex, could be dinner time.

"Can we at least keep the tall, dark and handsome?" Eady licks her lips, and Dory blows Nate a kiss.

Before he can respond, a rumble shudders through the trees behind us.

"Was that an explosion?" Dustan says.

Libby bats her eyelashes. "Sounded like thunder to me."

"The bloody witch has been a distraction," Sofia says, her gun materialising in her hands, hoop earrings quivering in fury.

Julian's phone peals. He utters a few tense words before snapping it shut.

"Some kind of rocket hit the eastern fence. A group has just passed through. The Barreras, the Gants and their Lessers."

The next two powerful families after the Kaskbirches. The Barreras hail from the Serra da Estrela Natural Park in Portugal, the Gants from Iceland, though they fled there from Germany back in the World War years.

Libby has been busy. But where are the Kaskbirches?

Nate raises his crossbow and points the bolt at Libby's chest. My heart leaps into my mouth to stopper my protest. He glances at me and I realise I've taken a step to put myself between him and my sister.

"Nate," Raine says to his glower, "take Dustan and gather the rest from the underground. We'll stay on the gate."

"Aww," Eady pouts.

Dory wriggles her fingers at Nate. "We'll see you again soon, sexy."

Nate and Dustan sprint up the slick road, quickly lost from sight through the trees. Sofia aims her gun at my sisters, which isn't an improvement on Nate's crossbow.

"It's not too late to stop this, Libby," I say quickly. "No one has to get hurt."

"Oh, it's way too late for your little friends," she says, her face smug.

Five figures slink from the trees on either side of the Mercedes. The family of trolls I expected but not the other two.

Julian frowns. "Caysie, Cameron, what are you doing?"

Caysie and Cameron Vanderbelt stand on the opposite side of the car to the Kaskbirches. Cameron huddles around himself, refusing to look at anyone, but Caysie raises her chin and glares at me, her hazel eyes sparking.

"The enemy of my enemy is my friend, bitch," she spits as if I asked the question instead of Julian.

"What about Julian and Raine?" I say mildly.

"They chose you—*you!*—over me. I should've been congratulated for throwing you in the dragon's-bane, not banished."

"You really are a bitter little cow, aren't you, Caysie?" I say.

Her whole forehead wrinkles into a scowl. "I don't care as long as you finally get what you deserve."

She joins her brother in frowning at the ground, both of them a picture of misery in the battering rain. Seems she does care, just a little.

"I am disappointed in you, Madisyn dear," Irena says, a mustard-yellow cagoule not flattering her squat frame. "Your mother would be so ashamed."

"Your son is a snivelling mummy's boy who looks like he lives under a rock. *You* should be ashamed for ever thinking a Della Valle would touch him." I turn to Libby and talk over Irena's indignant splutter. "Where the hell is Dad?"

"Sleeping," she says.

"Libby, what have you done?"

"He's *sleeping*. Unlike you, I'm not big on parenticide."

I flinch at her sneer. Kai touches my shoulder blade, and I straighten my back, meeting Libby's accusing glare.

"I didn't—"

"Your dear father has suffered without the strong hand of a matriarch." Irena's voice starts as a growl but calms to her insufferable condescension. "It's time for him to step down."

"Irena?"

"Yes, Madisyn dear?"

"It's time for you to shut the fuck up," I say sweetly.

Her broad cheeks, shiny with rain, flare a lovely puce. Gerome puffs to the size of a boulder and takes a step closer, his hands in fists at his sides. Irena catches his sleeve and tugs him back, her gaze flicking to Sofia's gun.

"Today, many abominations will be silenced," Irena says, drawing herself to her full height, "including you, Madisyn dear."

As one, the Kaskbirches, the Vanderbelts and my sisters duck behind the Mercedes, moving in what is likely a blur to human eyes. Sofia strafes the car bonnet, and the holes steam like dragon's breath. The engine rattles and dies. Raine has her Celtic leaf-bladed sword ready, Julian unarmed beside her, his face grim and wary. The boot of the Mercedes pops open.

What the hell are they doing?

An object flies through the air, trailing fire. Sofia dives into a smooth roll. Julian grabs Raine around the waist and hoists her clear, her sword bobbing over his shoulder. The object shatters on the road in a waft of cheap whisky, the ball of flame quickly smothered by the wind and rain. A second Molotov cocktail arcs towards me and Kai. A shoulder slams into my stomach. My wet hair blinds me as the world spins. I land on my back on the bare ground at the edge of the trees, a weight driving the breath from my lungs, a pine cone burrowing into my ribs. Glass smashes with a blast of heat then sizzling fire.

I scrape my hair off my face and blink at Kai. "You know I'm flame retardant and you're not, right?"

He pushes himself up. The coloured tips of his hair stick to his cheekbones, his eyes as grey as the storm. A golden shadow rears behind him. I shove hard, bowling Kai over and swapping our positions. Agony slices up my back, and I scream. I'm jerked from Kai like a fish on a hook. The wet ground whips past beneath me. The talons slip from my flesh, and I skid to a stop on my face, tasting mud.

'That was your fault, Maddy,' Libby says, lumbering up the road, encouraged by a burst from Sofia's rifle. *'I obviously wasn't aiming for you.'*

"Fuck off, Libby," I groan.

She roars and lunges for a streak of rainbow, chasing Julian in his smaller dragon form. They disappear up the driveway towards the house, followed by a parade of gold and black dragons. Cameron, a sapphire like his sister, plucks the gun from Sofia's grip and tosses it into the trees. He harries Sofia and Raine with snaps of his teeth but seems unwilling to touch them, retreating on skittering claws as they advance with axe and sword. Kai scrambles closer but Caysie lands between us, her blue wings arched wide. Her tail sweeps Kai off his feet and tumbles him into the woods.

"Kai!" I shout, and wince.

Pain flares in my back, burning lines running from hip to shoulder. Warmth spreads in a wave.

If I shift, I'll heal. Kai wouldn't have been so lucky.

Caysie bares her impressive teeth. *'He's still going to thank me once you're gone.'*

"Oh, get over yourself," I huff. "If you kill me, Libby won't let you live. Neither will Kai."

Caysie snorts. *'We'll be gone before your idiot sister knows what happened. And Kai will be free.'*

I shift onto all fours, and her eyes widen. Scraps of bloodied cloth swirl to the ground. My talons sink into the mud. I leap over Caysie's head in a flurry of wings and land on her back, her scales slick beneath me. My teeth close on the stem of her wing. Bone snaps. Caysie shrieks. I jerk my head and tear her wing off, spitting the flop of sapphire onto the road. Blood patters, hot in comparison to the rain. Caysie collapses in a thrashing heap, and my feet slide on the tarmac as I jump clear.

'Why do I always have to hurt you for your own good, Caysie?' I say.

'I hate you, Madisyn Della Valle,' she manages to hiss at me, glaring from one baleful eye, her claws furrowing the carpet of pine needles.

'Well, I don't hate you, though maybe I should.'

Kai stutters to a halt on the edge of the trees, his knife clasped in his fist.

"Are you all right, Syn?"

I stretch my wings to show him my back, golden and untouched.

'All healed,' I say.

'You two deserve each other,' Caysie moans.

'Finally, something we agree on.'

Kai cocks his head, only getting my side of the conversation it seems. Cameron howls and his wings beat the air, Sofia's axe buried in the muscle of his chest. In one bound, I straddle Cameron's back, trapping his wings.

'Change to human or I'll rip them both off,' I growl.

He whimpers. Bones shift and crack. His scales shudder and dissolve into fragile skin. I step carefully away as his body shrinks. The axe clunks to the road. A naked Cameron cowers on his knees. Caysie finally stops her flailing, her chest heaving.

I imagine she'll change to human once she has enough control. It'll help with the pain. She's no longer a threat since she's too weak a Drakul to shift a second time and rejoin the fray.

"We will watch them," Sofia says but looks to Raine, "if you are okay with that, honey?"

Raine nods, her eyes huge and dark in her delicate face, though her sword is steady in her hand.

"Protect Julian," she says, her gaze on me. "Don't let them hurt him. Please."

'Tell her they won't ever get to hurt him again,' I say to Kai since I can't project my voice to humans.

"I'm coming with you," Kai says.

'Then you'll have to catch up.'

I bunch my legs.

A tentative hand touches my long neck. "Syn, wait."

I turn slowly, and the hand trails upward to cup my jaw. Kai leans his forehead on mine.

"Be careful," he whispers, "you monster wearing my woman's skin."

I grin at him, and he tenses but doesn't jerk away.

'I love you,' I say.

The words are so new, they still sound weird whether they're in my head or out loud.

Before he can reply, I take a couple of hopping steps and launch towards the clouds.

40

Gunfire and screams fill the forest containing the Romanov mansion, the surrounding wooded hills barely visible in the low clouds and sheeting rain. Mist cloaks the pine trees. Drakul swoop through the air, high enough to skim the clouds. Golds, blacks and a smattering of bronze and silver dragons maul the rubies and sapphires and emeralds. Groups of Vanatori track them from the ground, their faces pinched with frustration.

Seems they've not had enough practise on avoiding friendly fire in the chaos of battle. I imagine things were much easier when they could just shoot any monster they saw.

I zoom up the ribbon of tarmac, level with the tree canopy, avoiding the hunters and their dragon's-bane bullets. Lessers grapple among the trunks and wrestle in clumps of ferns. Julian twists to avoid Libby's snapping teeth and disappears behind the bulk of the house. I flap harder, kicking off the roof to propel me up and over.

A black dragon crouches in the grass in front of the green-houses, his snout buried in the abdomen of a violet Drakul who struggles weakly, her wings twitching. He raises his head, crimson dripping from his jaw. Intestines bulge from a ragged hole.

'If it isn't little miss perfect,' sneers Anton Barrera. *'How far the mighty have fallen, eh, Madisyn?'*

'Eaten any dogs lately?' I say, stooping towards him.

He puffs a fireball at me, ducking his head to avoid my slashing claws. Flames lick my scales dry with tongues of orange and yellow. The violet dragon shudders as Anton resumes his exploration of her abdominal cavity. I tuck my wings for another pass but the violet crumbles to ash.

I never knew her name.

Anton sneezes, shaking his head and swiping at me as I blast by in a billow of dust. He bounds in pursuit, as ungainly on land as a seal. We join the convoy chasing Julian. My sisters and the Kaskbirches try to cut him off, herd him towards their jaws and talons, but Julian twists clear.

'You all right?' I say to him only.

He dives into the pine forest in a puff of needles. *'A break would be nice.'*

'I'll see what I can do.'

'I knew I'd like having you around.'

Libby's wings stroke the trees, her lumbering shape too large to fly between. Eady and Dory crunch through the canopy while Libby and the Kaskbirches circle the woods. They turn their heads as one, probably alerted by Anton on my tail.

'Dad wouldn't want this, Libby,' I say, flying closer. *'It's not too late to stop.'*

Gerome and his father attack me from either side, mouths snarling wide. I duck, their scales near enough to brush me, and their bodies smack together. My wings power me into a loop, and I rake a claw through Gerome's wing. He shrieks, spiralling towards the ground, torn flesh flapping. His father shouts his name, and follows.

'*That will be the last time you dishonour my family, you Lesser-slumming slut,*' Irena growls. '*You will rue the day you thought yourself better than us.*'

'*Really Libby? You're siding with her and her family of cave-people?*' I dodge Irena's tail, swooping up under my sister.

'*The dozy boot thinks I'm going to marry Gerome and let her rule,*' Libby says to me only since Irena offers no squawk of protest. '*Join me, Maddy. We can be more powerful than Evelyn Romanov. You're my sister—I don't want to risk you dying with the traitors.*'

Kai reaches the fight. I've been aware of him getting nearer, slower on foot up the winding driveway. He wades in to help a group preventing a mob of Lessers from overwhelming the Vanatori. His fist catches a Gant's Lesser in the mouth, and the man collapses.

Irena and Anton hound me closer to the ground, dragging my gaze from Kai.

Why couldn't he have stayed with Raine and Sofia at the gate in relative safety? How am I supposed to protect him and Julian?

Julian bursts from the trees and leaps into the air, flying at my side. Libby utters a barking cough and banks for him, her eyes slitted.

'*I'm going to tear your legs off, runt,*' she snarls, '*then I'm going to eat your little murdering wife in pieces.*'

She sounds like Evelyn Romanov already.

Julian and I evade her slashing limbs, rolling away from Irena and Anton. Below us, Gerome and his father have been surrounded by a protective circle of their Lessers. Gerome licks at his torn wing. His father huffs fire at a Lesser I've seen around the greenhouses and the man is engulfed before he can scream. A blackened lump flops into the dirt.

Julian's long throat bobs as he swallows, his different-coloured eyes on the scene below. *'Where's Raine?'*

'She's still at the gate watching Caysie and Cameron with Sofia. I told her I'd help you. What happened to Eady and Dory?'

'They got distracted by Nate. He's holding them off in the woods.'

We soar together, keeping ahead of Libby, Irena and Anton, occasionally joined by some of the Gants. Anton's parents distract the hunters with barrages of flame, their constant forays setting the pines alight despite the rain.

'We're losing, Maddy,' Julian says quietly.

I glance at the battle below us and confirm Kai is unhurt. The Vanatori shoot controlled bursts into the air when they're not being hassled by Lessers or the Barreras. But their bullets aren't enough to kill a dragon on the wing unless they manage to obliterate the brain or heart.

'I thought after your attack we could actually do this. Defeat the other families. Live without fear.' Julian shakes his head. *'That down there shows me how wrong I am.'*

Bodies lie scattered in the ferns and on the road, casualties from both sides but dominated by Julian's people. Patches of damp ash show where his dragons have fallen.

'It's not over yet,' I say.

'There are too many of them. They—'

Kai's scream cuts through Julian's words in my head.

41

'*Look what I've caught,*' Libby says, her fangs bared in a grin.

Kai dangles from her foot, her talons sunk through his leather jacket and into his shoulder. His hands are wrapped around her ankle to try and relieve the pressure as she flaps harder, lifting him higher.

High enough to kill.

His eyes, dark with pain, meet mine. My heart drops to the unyielding ground.

'*Let him go, Libby,*' I say and, even in my head, my voice wobbles.

'*Are you sure you want me to do that, dear sister?*' She shakes her leg, and Kai grits his teeth, his face pale. '*Do you think he'll still look as pretty once he hits the dirt?*'

'*Libby, please...*'

I can't seem to breathe. My chest heaves but there's a blockage in my throat. My eyes blur with rain and tears. My smooth soar has become the disjointed flight of a bumblebee.

Julian slaps me with his wing. '*Force her to change.*'

'*I can't,*' I say, barely enough control left to project just to him. '*It takes too much concentration to do when I'm flying. I won't be there to catch...*'

My throat closes.

'*I'll catch him.*'

I shake my head, unable to speak. Irena is taunting me, circling around Libby as they aim for the clouds, but I struggle to focus on the bloated cow's words. Some drivel about her son.

'*I'll catch him, Maddy,*' Julian says. '*I promise.*'

Libby gives Kai another shake, and he cries out. His jacket has bunched up, exposing a line of flat stomach. A trickle of red stains the waistband of his jeans.

'*Julian surrenders right now or I drop your precious little Lesser,*' Libby barks.

I stare into Julian's green eye.

'*Catch him,*' I whisper. '*Please.*'

Julian banks for Libby and Kai. Irena roars in triumph and dives for him. I land on the roof of the Romanov mansion, my claws skittering on the tile.

'*Libby! Don't make me do this.*'

'*You can't stop all of us.*' Libby smirks, continuing to climb. '*You wouldn't hurt your own sister, would you, Maddy? Not after you've spent your life protecting me.*'

Julian dodges Irena's clumsy tackle and spirals towards the ground. She dogs him but he darts upwards, and her heavier bulk is slower to respond. Gerome and Robert shout encouragements from the road. Anton rolls in the sky, tucks his wings and arrows for me.

'*I'm going to bury myself inside you, Madisyn,*' he says. '*And not in the fun way.*'

'*Get her, Daddy,*' Gerome squeals.

His father bounds two steps and leaps into the air. Wind whistles over Anton's scales. Julian's people shriek and die. The bullets of the Vanatori falter.

I focus on the Drakul. The heat of their energy in the sky. I can fold all that warmth away until scales run to delicate skin.

But I've only ever done it one at a time.

I shut my eyes against the sight of the two black dragons slicing towards me, the carnage strewn across the compound, Kai dragged into the heavens, dripping blood, his gaze on me. I shove at that heat, all but Julian's, crushing it down like fire cupped in my hands until the flames wink out.

Screams. So many screams.

My eyes snap open.

A naked Anton Barrera pinwheels his arms but his momentum slams him head first into the pitched tiles. Bone snaps. His limp body catches on a chimney. A startled Robert Kaskbirch grabs for the edge of the roof, leaving nothing but his blanched fingers clutching the gutter. The metal sluice wrenches from the wall, and Robert yells as he falls.

I wobble on the roof, dropping to all fours, my vision feathered with grey and white. My brain buzzes, pulsing stronger with each heartbeat. I struggle to raise my head, struggle to focus.

Where is Kai? Where is Julian?

The sky swirls. My side hits slick, cold tile and my breath huffs out, sprinkling water droplets from my snout. My wings tangle my legs. I start to slide. I try to push up onto my arms, to slow my momentum, but my claws screech on slate and refuse to catch. Dizziness rolls from my head to my stomach. My shoulder hits the edge of the roof. Someone shouts my name but the word escapes me.

Was it Syn or Maddy? Syn or Maddy?

Wind greets me in a rush, and I drop into nothing.

42

White films my eyes, my lids heavy and unwilling to flutter open. My shoulders sink into softness. Something constricts my chest with every shallow breath. Heartbeats echo in my skull, one fast.

Is it mine?

I force my eyes open. More white. A gauzy canopy on a four-poster bed, so like my own but for the colour.

Kai's bed.

I sit up. Or try to. I get no further than tensing my stomach and chest before I groan and flop into the pillows, a wave of dizziness bucking the mattress beneath me.

"Easy, Syn. You're still healing."

A figure stands over the bed, haloed by daylight. Broad shoulders, narrow waist. The flash of a feather in his ear. Shadows hide his face, framed by the blackness of his hair and the green and violet tips. Two people cluster on the opposite side of the bed beside a drip that snakes into my arm.

A tear trickles down my cheek. "You caught him."

"I promised I would," Julian says.

Kai leans over and places a soft kiss on my lips. I stroke his jaw, the warmth of his neck and the curve of his shoulder. My fingertips brush rough material. I try to sit up again, to ease him away to get a better look, but dull aches chase from my ribs to my hips.

Kai straightens and turns slightly, the light from the window bright on a sling around his left arm. Dressings stretch his t-shirt at his shoulder.

"How bad?" I manage.

"Muscle damage," he says and adds, "I'll be fine, Syn," when I start hyperventilating.

He takes my hand and I grip it as tight as I dare.

"I'd like to say it gets easier but it doesn't." Julian loops an arm around Raine, who cuddles into her usual position at his side.

"What doesn't?" I say.

Julian gives me a gentle smile. "Loving someone more fragile."

My gaze darts to Kai. He shrugs then winces. A sob catches in my throat, more tears spilling to tickle down my neck.

"He's not the fragile one," I say, bubbling like an idiot and hiding my face in the hand not clutching at Kai.

His thumb rubs back and forth across my knuckles. I want to throw myself at him, bury myself against his chest and have his arms wrap around me. But he only has one uninjured arm and I feel like an elephant has been rolling around on top of me.

I take a few shaky breaths and scrub at my tears, lowering my hand to stare at the canopy of the bed instead of the three faces around me.

"What happened?" I say, my voice steadier. "The last thing I remember is watching Robert Kaskbirch and Anton Barrera fall."

"You landed on top of Robert Kaskbirch," Kai says.

I glance at him but his tender expression makes my chest hitch and I return to studying the ceiling.

"He cushioned your fall but you still broke some ribs and your hip," Kai continues. "That was two days ago."

I force the next words out. "And my sisters?"

"Eady and Dory were already on the ground so they're fine," Kai says. "Though it hasn't stopped them from pestering Nate for some tender loving care. I believe they want a sponge bath and a healing massage. Julian did some impressive juggling with me and Libby."

Julian grins. "She is not happy I saved her life."

I reach out and he shuffles closer to the bed with Raine so I can squeeze his hand.

"Thank you." I clear my throat. "She tormented you for years. I can't imagine how tempting it was to let her drop."

He chuckles. "I only managed to grab her hair with my foot since my arms were full of Kai. She got some bruises and scrapes since it wasn't exactly a gentle landing. Oh, and some bald spots. Raine was more than happy to show her a mirror."

Raine smirks. "You should have heard her screech."

"And she owes me a new jacket," Kai says.

I shudder, though anger fizzes in my stomach. "I'm going to punch her for that."

"Get in line," Raine says with an evil little smile.

* * *

Two days later, I'm able to walk, if somewhat gingerly, my bones re-knitted but liable to ache. Kai is happy to act as my crutch and ferries me from our bedroom to the dining room and anywhere else I need to be.

Except here. Not for the first visit.

My passage through the underground chamber still causes a stir but no icy daggers stab into my back from numerous glares and the swell of whispers lacks the hissed insults. My wrists are free, no collar chafing my neck, no stupid ball and chain. Nothing like turning the tide of battle to make them accept me. Some of them might even like me.

"Well, look who it is," Libby sneers as soon as I get close enough to the cell, "my dear, traitorous sister."

Her pale face glowers at me through the bars of the door, a wrapped collar and cuffs keeping her from shifting or using her hypnotism. Blonde fuzz already covers the bald spots on her scalp. My beautiful sister is dishevelled and currently wearing a hideous pair of neon-yellow capri pants and a strapless top the colour of snot.

I hide a smirk, and cross my arms. "I could say the same about you."

"I'm not the one who joined the abomination's army."

"You threatened to kill the man I love," I say through my teeth.

Eady and Dory are perched on the edge of the fold-down bed attached to the wall, swinging their coltish legs, dressed in baggy, faded t-shirts and over-large shorts. Dragon's-bane cuffs bracelet their wrists, all the metal covered by cream bandages. They watch the exchange between Libby and me through identical eyes.

"Love," Libby scoffs. "How can you love a Lesser? They're only good for screwing and slavery."

"That's going to change. Amongst many things."

Libby rolls her eyes. "You really have become such a bore, Maddy. Is your little Lesser so good in bed, you've forgotten who you are?"

"This is who I've always been, I'm just not hiding it anymore."

"So you're going to leave us here to be tortured by your new friends? How very noble of you."

Eady and Dory crowd around Libby, straining to see through the bars without touching them.

"Speaking of new friends," Eady says. "Where is tall, dark and American?"

Dory giggles. "We'd like to be tortured by him."

"Yeah," Eady says, joining her giggling twin, "we need a firm spanking."

"No one's going to be tortured. Or spanked." I lean my shoulder on the rough-hewn stone of the doorway and meet Libby's accusing stare. "But you are all going to change."

"I like who I am just fine," she says.

"The world's evolving, Libby. Drakul ally with Vanatori. Hell, maybe one day we won't even need hunters anymore."

"I will *never* bow down to that runt and his murdering whore."

"He saved your life."

Her lip curls in a snarl. "I wish he'd let me die."

"Well, I don't," I say. "But you will bow down to someone." She snorts. "Oh, yeah? Who?"

"Me," I say.

43

My knuckles thunder on ornate oak as thick as my leg. Brass rings, inlaid in the centre, shiver under the onslaught. A bright security light bathes the stone steps and a cluster of bushes hiding the entrance from the rest of East Preston Street. A car rumbles up the road behind me.

"Open up, Gerome," I yell, "or I use my key and seek you out."

My mum loved the townhouse, though it's a lot cosier than our home in East Lothian. She loved being surrounded by the bustle of Edinburgh. The thud of hundreds of heartbeats. It's a disservice to her memory to allow it to remain as the refuge of a family of trolls.

I pummel the door again. "You have ten seconds, Gerome."

My hip and ribs have started to ache from being on my feet all day but this is thankfully our last stop. And the most satisfying.

I step off the stairs and stand in a cramped line on the narrow path, Kai on one side, Julian and Raine on the other, all bleached white in the glare of the light. Kai's arm is still in a sling since he hasn't inherited super healing with his super strength and speed. I told him to stay in our room and he, as usual, ignored me.

Why do I find that sexy *and* frustrating?

"Sofia and Dustan confirm there's no movement at the back," Nate says from behind us, no doubt listening to their report in his earpiece.

Behind Nate and sitting in cars up and down the whole street is our show of force. Lots and lots of heartbeats.

Julian and Raine were having trouble uniting the Vanatori to their new way of thinking, most of them squabbling and achieving nothing. Fighting in the power vacuum created by the death of their Principal. Then word of our battle reached them. If a Della Valle can be turned to the good side, even the heads of the main groups couldn't ignore the truth.

Not all Drakul are monsters.

Rapid footsteps and a rapider heartbeat approach from the other side of the solid oak door. Bolts clunk free. A tiny gap reveals the slab face of Gerome Kaskbirch.

"What?" he barks.

He definitely wants to call me a name but the press and pulse of my welcoming committee stills his tongue.

He's always been a coward.

"Good evening, Gerome," I say, cheerily. "How is your father?"

Gerome's jaw bulges. "You broke every bone in his body."

"It was nice of him to cushion my fall," I say in the same sweet, so-friendly-it-makes-your-teeth-hurt voice. This voice I like. "Of course, I won't ask after your mother."

Turns out, Irena's thick skull was not so thick after all.

Gerome's mud-brown eyes narrow. "You damn bit—"

"I'd watch what you're about to say," Kai growls.

Gerome swallows his insult, his mouth puckering as if he's tasted something rotten.

278

"What do you *want?*" he whines. "I already agreed to your terms over the phone."

"We're here to serve you notice of eviction," I say.

He goggles. "Huh?"

"You have outstayed your welcome in Della Valle property, and this country. Don't feel too bad, though. The Gants and all the other brutal families who made the same choice as you will no longer be allowed to return to their second homes. Just be thankful we're letting you live."

"You can't force us to leave."

"The Barreras thought so, too. In fact, they laughed when I confronted them in their holiday estate on Skye."

We visited them first in the hours before dawn, reaching them on the wing since the isle is a six-hour drive away. It was an odd sight—a flight of Drakul carrying Vanatori riders.

I reach into my jacket and pull out a jar. The screw-top lid scrapes as I twist it, the glass cold in my fingers. Ash patters onto the bottom step and puffs into the still air.

"Losing family can force you to do stupid things," I say. "Don't make their mistake."

Neither the Barreras nor the Gants had fled to their territories after the battle. The arrogant bastards thought we'd leave them alone to lick their wounds and regroup. The Drakul who weren't involved but who still believe it's their right to terrorise humans also received a phone call from me yesterday. I racked up quite the bill with the number of countries I had to contact. I told them they had two choices—swear their allegiance to Julian and Raine Romanov and embrace vegetarianism or have their identities and addresses shared with the Vanatori.

Being a Della Valle gave me unfettered access to the highest, and most twisted, levels of our society. I have details the Vanatori would have sacrificed limbs for before. Details Julian wasn't privy to as the reviled Romanov runt.

But all our secrets are out.

Gerome gulps. "How long do we have?"

"A day," I say, glancing at my watch, "which gives you until 5pm tomorrow."

Gerome's jaw thrusts into a pout. "Daddy is not fit to travel."

"Daddy will have to suck it up." I close the jar and shake the remaining contents. "Tick-tock, Gerome."

It was a fifty-fifty split between the swearers and the scoffers. Of course, I'm not just going to let the brutal families rein from their fiefdoms unchecked. This Madisyn Della Valle is no longer that callous. Those who chose a gentler life will be policed very closely over the next few months. Or years.

Monsters can never be trusted. Their brutality will no doubt end in blood and ash.

I turn to leave, Kai, Julian and Raine following suit. Nate talks to his warriors beyond the night-shrouded shrubs, speaking quickly into the microphone in his sleeve.

"Oh, and one more thing." I hold up a finger, and face Gerome's mulish expression. "In case you're harbouring a fantasy of pretending to leave, a group of Vanatori will remain behind to watch the house. If you're not gone by 5pm, they'll kill you. Otherwise, they'll escort you to the airport. Safe travels back to your cave, Gerome."

I walk away to the sound of Gerome's teeth grinding together.

44

Raine kept her promise and punched my sister in the mouth. I've never seen Libby so surprised as she tumbled arse over tit, blood a red slash on her lips.

Yes, I say arse and tit now. Out loud. Societal conventions have changed.

It may take Libby a little longer to accept the new normal after that dignity-destroying punch but I have high hopes for my sister. She wasn't a total monster before Lukas Romanov. She can be that woman again. I've hired a grief counsellor and a behavioural therapist to help her through the transition. She's still sulking and throwing tantrums but she'll wear herself out soon enough. The therapist is a hottie, and a silver dragon. I picked him deliberately.

I know my sister.

Caysie and Cameron are under house arrest with their parents, who were ashamed at their behaviour. Apparently, they've always admired Julian and were the ones who encouraged their children to offer their support after the evil was removed from his family.

Dad is also being extremely supportive. He and Libby have long talks into the night, after she tries pleading, bargaining and, finally, yelling at him to remove her dragon's-bane collar.

None of which works.

His clout helped some of the families who were pretending, like us, to step into the light and apologise to the people they'd abused. Mostly Julian since treating him like dirt guaranteed Evelyn Romanov's approval. May that bitch never rest in peace. Dad protected us further by contacting the families even I didn't know about, lurking in the world's remotest islands. Well, I say contacted but he returned a day later, reeking of soot.

We're finally safe.

It's what Mum would have wanted.

* * *

I unlock the side entrance and tip-toe into the servant's pantry. Kai bangs the door a little too hard, and I wince.

"Dammit, Kai, we're trying to be sneaky."

His grin is unabashed. "We have a perfectly good bed back at Julian's."

"I told you why I want it to be mine."

"Tell me again," he says, and my cheeks flush.

"Because I've never slept with anyone in my bed," I mutter.

"I've slept in your bed," he says. "As I recall, we did a little more than just sleep."

Kai watching me touch myself. Launching across the bed, his mouth hot, his hand on mine between my legs…

My blush flares brighter. Going by Kai's chuckle, even his human eyes can see it in the dim light.

"But we didn't have sex," I say despite my blazing face. "I want to make love until we pass out and wake up, all cuddled together."

"You're getting soft, Syn."

I go to slap his shoulder but stop myself, his sling glowing white. The claw marks and muscle damage from Libby's attack are healing well but he's still got a few days before he can start his physical therapy.

I volunteered to go on top for the love-making, on account of his injury.

"While all that sounds great to me, I'm a little concerned your father will hear us," Kai says, capturing the hand I was going to hit him with and kissing the knuckles. "He might still eat me."

"That's why we're sneaking," I say.

I keep a hold of his fingers and tug him through the kitchen and into the hall, remembering when he first kissed me and we'd barely made it up the stairs, still kissing.

Speaking of kissing…

Half-way up the stairs, I push Kai against the wall and thoroughly explore his mouth until both our knees are weak. The slide of his tongue piercing starts the flutters in my stomach, especially at the thought of another, lower piercing and where that might glide—

"Madisyn?"

I jerk back with a gasp. "Dad!"

Dad appears at the top of the stairs. I jump away from Kai, too distracted by his magical piercings to have noticed the approach of Dad's heartbeat.

"Um, hello Mr Della Valle," Kai says.

His shirt is rumpled from where I slipped my hands underneath to caress along the taut muscles of his belly. His new leather jacket was bought using Libby's money and makes him look even more gorgeous and dangerous. His lips are half-parted, soft and plump and begging—

Oh, crap.

"Where's Libby?" I say in a rush, unable to mask the thrum of my heartbeat. Not from Dad, anyway.

Dad glances down the opposite corridor towards Libby's room. "She had a difficult session today so she's sleeping. She's really trying, though. I'm proud of her. Are Eadrea and Doria with you?"

"They're still at Julian's," I say.

I don't tell him they're hounding poor Nate who doesn't seem to know what to do with them mooning over him. Two Drakul teenagers, all legs and pert little breasts.

I'm sure he'll figure it out.

"Did you need anything?" Dad says, his eyes darting between Kai and me.

"I, ah, was going to take Kai to my room... for a bit."

Why am I embarrassed? Dad had no problem with Libby dragging Gerome off to her room to 'listen to music'. Though Dad always had higher standards for me.

"In that case, Madisyn, I might go for a walk. A *long* walk." Dad clears his throat. "Phone me when you're... Phone me when it's safe to return."

Then he runs out the front door as if the ghost of Evelyn Romanov is on his heels.

I pull Kai into my bedroom and shut the door.

Sometimes, I really love my family.

Let Me Know What You Think!

Thank you for reading my book! I love hearing from my readers so please leave me a review.
Can't wait to hear from you!

To get a free character sheet for everyone in the Vanatori's Titan Group, join my mailing list at http://nadinelittle.com/character-sheet by scanning the QR code below:

Have you read *Who The Monsters Are*, book 1 in the *Hunters & Dragons* series?
Raine Waller hunts dragon shapeshifters for the Vanatori. Jay could be the key to finding the monsters that murdered her parents. Or he could be leading her into a trap.

About the Author

Nadine Little lives in Scotland and is an ecologist, though her specialism is botany, not dragons (unfortunately). She loves dragons so much, she has a tattoo of Julian in his dragon form on her back, rainbow wings and all. She thinks this is perfectly normal. When she's not writing steamy science fiction and paranormal romance, she can be found falling over in bogs and into the occasional pond.

One day she hopes to be a famous writer who lives in the woods.

For more on her books and a peek behind the scenes, sign up to her mailing list and follow her on social media.

You can connect with me on:
- https://nadinelittle.com
- https://twitter.com/Nadine_Little_
- https://www.facebook.com/nadinelittleauthor

Subscribe to my newsletter:
- https://nadinelittle.com/character-sheet

www.ingramcontent.com/pod-product-compliance
Lightning Source LLC
Chambersburg PA
CBHW051134190726
48290CB00006B/1837